Praise for James Owens's

"That none of the Chronicles of the Imaginarium Geographica have yet won a Caldecott or other such award is an egregious error that should be corrected as quickly as possible."
—*The Trades*

"This astonishing book is just what a literary pastiche ought to be, and one hopes there are more adventures to be chronicled in this universe."
—*KLIATT*

"Owen's amazingly detailed pen-and-ink illustrations, dark and atmospheric, lend a real storybook flavor."
—*Booklist*

"Owen's magnificent story, which he also beautifully illustrated, will appeal to all fantasy fans."
—*VOYA*

"Is there anyone who wouldn't enjoy reading *Here, There Be Dragons*? If there is such a person, I haven't met him, and I doubt that I would like him if I did. I am only disappointed that, because this book is so new, I'll have to wait too long to read the sequels."
—Orson Scott Card, author of *Ender's Game*

FOR ALEX —

BEST WISHES!

HERE, THERE BE DRAGONS

2.0.1.0

Written and illustrated by

James A. Owen

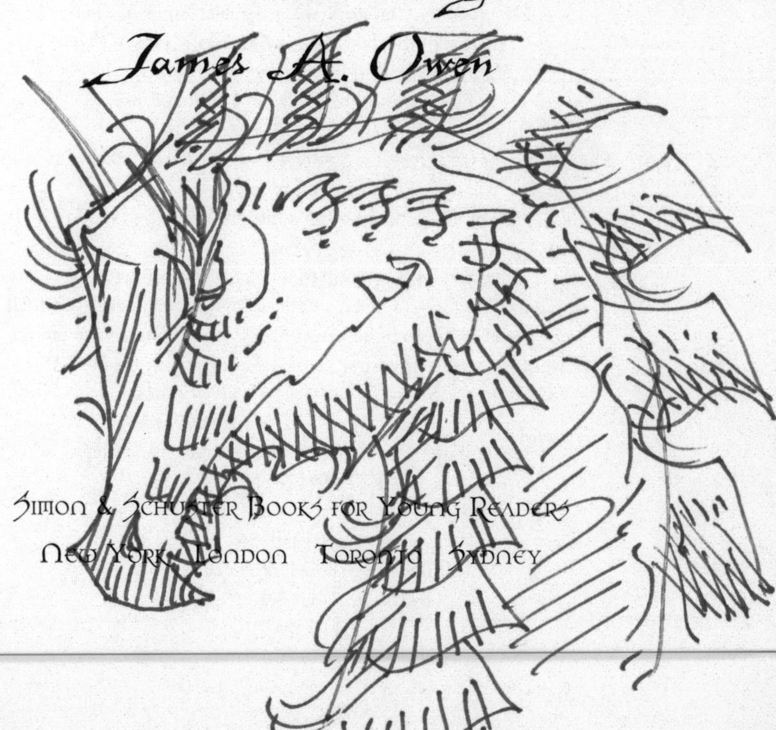

Simon & Schuster Books for Young Readers

New York London Toronto Sydney

SIMON & SCHUSTER BOOKS FOR YOUNG READERS
An imprint of Simon & Schuster Children's Publishing Division
1230 Avenue of the Americas, New York, NY 10020

Also available in a Simon & Schuster Books for Young Readers
hardcover edition.
Designed by Christopher Grassi and James A. Owen
The text of this book was set in Adobe Jansen Pro.
Manufactured in the United States of America
First Simon Pulse edition October 2007
8 10 9 7
The Library of Congress has cataloged the hardcover edition as follows:
Owen, James A.
Here, there be dragons/ James A. Owen.—1st ed.
p. cm.
Summary: Three young men are entrusted with the
Imaginarium Geographica, an atlas of fantastical places to which
they travel in hopes of defeating the Winter King whose bid for
power is related to the First World War raging in the Real World.
ISBN-13: 978-1-4169-1227-9 (hc)
ISBN-10: 1-4169-1227-4 (hc)
[1. Time Travel—Fiction. 2. Fantasy.] I. Title.
PZ7.o97124He2006
[Fic]—dc22
2005030486
ISBN-13: 978-1-4169-1228-6 (pbk)
ISBN-10: 1-4169-1228-2 (pbk)
0110 MTN

For Nathaniel

Contents

List of Illustrations

Acknowledgments

Here, There Be Dragons began its life as an uncompleted ten-page outline, which was my last presentation to the last producer I met on an interminably long trip to Hollywood. It was that producer who worked with me to shape the story over the next few months, and who, in November of 2004, suggested that we begin approaching publishers. The book you are holding would not exist if it were not for the interest, advice, and encouragement of Marc Rosen, and the support of David Heyman.

My home team at the Coppervale Studio, Jeremy, Lon, and Mary, were invaluable in assisting me with layouts, backgrounds, commentary, and various forms of moral and medicinal support as I worked on the illustrations. They're all better at their jobs than they know they are.

Craig Emanuel, my rock of an attorney, gave me to Ellen, Julie, and Lindsay, my managers at the Gotham Group, who took all of a second to "get" the story, not much longer to sell it, and a great deal much longer holding me up while I finished writing it.

My editors at Simon & Schuster, David and Alexandra, taught me what editors are for, and made me look good, and smarter than I am. My art director, Lizzy, reminded me how fun collaborating can be and made the book look wonderful. And my publisher, Rick, made a publishing deal feel more like an invitation to a family reunion.

Kai Meyer, who as a fan of my comics work was the first to ask if I'd like to write something in prose, along with his colleagues Frank, Hannes, and Sara, are the reasons I had the experience and confidence to write this book. My mother Sharon and wife Cindy are the ones who offered understanding, support, and sympathy when I decided to illustrate it, too.

And finally, in the most unlikely pairing I can think of, I want to thank my daughter Sophie and my friend Dave Sim, the former with drawings and the latter with twenty-year-old essays, for reminding me that I love what I do.

You all have my gratitude and sincere thanks.

Prologue

It was a very distinct sound, the quiet scraping of steel on stone, that first told him that his visitors had arrived, followed by a strange sort of tapping and the shuffling of feet.

The tapping outside in the alleyway became more pronounced, and he suddenly realized it was less the sound of tapping than it was a soft cacophony of claws, snapping together in anticipation. He set aside his pen and notebook and settled back in his chair. There was no denying it. It was time.

The strained amber light of an English afternoon streamed through the greasy windows of the door as it slowly opened into the study.

He refilled his pipe with his special cinnamon tobacco mix and noted with passing interest that clouds were beginning to gather on the far horizon.

A storm was coming.

It didn't matter, he thought to himself with some satisfaction. He had said the things he needed to say to the person who needed to hear them. He had protected that precious stewardship that needed protecting, and passed it to those who would use it wisely and well.

There was, he concluded, not much more that could be asked of an old scholar, in this world, in this lifetime.

The silhouette in the doorway gestured to him, and he caught a glimpse of wickedly sharp steel, which curved to a point, as the visitor's arm rose and fell. The clicking noises in the alley grew louder.

"Greetings, Professor," the shadowy figure said. "Might I have a word with you?"

"It's not here," the professor said, lighting his pipe and drawing deeply on it. "You're too late."

His visitor appraised him for a moment before concluding that the professor was speaking the truth. "I'm very sorry to hear that," he said. "That does not bode well for you."

The professor shrugged. "What happens to me is no longer important. You may claim my life, but I've put an empire forever out of your reach—and when all is said and done, which of the two matters more?"

The visitor gestured again, and the tapping noises outside gave way to snarls and animal howling.

There was a rush of bodies, and in seconds the small study was filled with ancient steel, and pain, and blood.

When the noises again faded to silence, the visitors left the study as they had found it, with one exception.

It would be several hours before the first raindrops from the approaching storm would begin to freckle the paving stones in the street, but the professor would not see them fall.

Part One

The Imaginarium Geographica

"There's a very strange man outside," said Jack.

Chapter One

The Adventure Begins

The slim, cream-colored note may just as well have been inserted into a bottle and tossed into the ocean rather than sent by post, for by the time John received it, the professor was already dead.

For perhaps the hundredth time, John took the note out of his pocket.

> *My Dear John,*
>
> *Please make all haste to London. There is much, too much I'm afraid, that should have been explained to you well before now. I only pray that this letter finds you well enough to travel, and that you will bear me no ill will for what is to come. I do not know if you are ready, and that is my own burden to bear. But I believe you are able, and mayhap that is enough. I hope it is.*
>
> *Professor Sigurdsson*

The letter had been dated a week earlier, the ninth of March, 1917, and had reached him at the hospital in Great Haywood the day before. John cabled a reply to his mentor, requested a temporary leave, dispatched a note to his wife of less than a year at their home in Oxford, explaining that he would be absent for perhaps several days, and immediately arranged passage to London.

It was the messenger who delivered the cable who found that a murder had occurred and notified the police. John knew without asking that the officer waiting at the platform in London was there to speak with him, and why.

The train from Staffordshire had run late, but this was not unexpected, nor was it any longer even an inconvenience. It was simply one of the erosions of normality that came with a constant state of war.

John had been on leave from the Second Battalion for several months now, since before the holidays. To the doctors, he had pyrexia; it was "trench fever" to the enlisted men. In simpler parlance, his body had grown weary of the war and manifested its protest with a general weakness of the limbs and a constant fever.

On the train John fell immediately asleep, and his fever coalesced into a dream of a mountain of fire, spewing hot ash and lava into the trenches of the French countryside, consuming his comrades as they held fast against the German offensive. John watched in horror as those who fled the trenches were cut down by gunfire. Those who remained, crouched in fear, were swallowed up, the sons of England become children of Pompeii as they died in flame and smoke. . . .

He awoke to the shrill whistle of the train, signaling their arrival at the station in London. He was flushed and sweating and looked for all the world to the awaiting constable as if he was complicit in the murder of the man he had come to see. John wiped his brow with a kerchief, shouldered his backpack out of the luggage racks, and stepped off the train.

His arrival, and his subsequent departure with the policeman, were noted by no less than four individuals, mingling invisibly within the crowds exchanging places between the platform and the trains. Three of them were cloaked and walked a bit awkwardly, due to the inverted joint in their lower legs that made them walk as if they were dogs, striding upright on two legs.

Exactly as if they were dogs.

The strange figures disappeared into the throng to report what they had seen to their master. The fourth, which had been sitting alongside John on the train, slipped out of the station and turned down the street taken minutes before by the constable and the young soldier from Staffordshire.

"I'm just saying that there are a number of uses for an English night far superior to investigating a murder," said the inspector in charge of the murder scene, a stout, affable fellow called Clowes. "You can bet the killer, whoever he may be, isn't out traipsing about in this muck. No, he's home by now, having done his business for the day, warming his toes by the hearth and sipping a nice mulled brandy, while I have to be out here on the verge of catching my death. . . ."

Clowes caught himself mid-complaint and gestured in apology. "Not that talking with you lot is all that bad, mind you. Circumstances."

It took John a few moments to realize that he was not the only one being interviewed that evening about the professor's murder. For the first time, he noticed the other two cuckoos, shivering, nodding at the questioning police, wondering how they'd come to be in this particular dreadful nest.

Shaking hands, they introduced themselves. The younger one, called Jack, was straw-haired and fidgety; the older, Charles, was bespectacled and efficient. He was answering the constable's queries as if he were tallying an account at Barclays. "Yes. I arrived in London promptly at four forty. No, I did not vary from my planned agenda. Yes, I realized he was dead right away."

"And your reason for the visit?" asked Clowes.

"Delivery of a manuscript," said Charles. "I'm employed as an editor at the Oxford University Press, and Professor Sigurdsson was to add annotations to one of our publications."

"Really?" said Jack. "I've just been accepted there."

"Well done, Jack," said Charles.

"Thanks," said Jack.

"So, boy," said Clowes. "Your name is Jack, is it?"

"Yes sir," Jack said, nodding.

"Ah. Not the Jack from up Whitechapel way, are you?" asked Clowes.

"No," Jack replied before he had time to realize that the inspector was making a joke. "Oxford."

"Two of you at Oxford, eh?" said Clowes. "That's an interesting coincidence."

"Not coincidence," said Charles. "Selective association is a privilege, not a right."

"I'm a Cambridge man myself," said Clowes.

"Oh, uh, sorry," stammered Charles.

"Never actually did go to university myself, mind you," Clowes said to John behind his hand. "But he looked like I'd seen him in the Queen's knickers, didn't he? By the way—where are you from, ah, John, is it?"

"Birmingham, although I'm billeted at the hospital in Great Hayward at present."

This was not entirely correct, but John thought that pointing out that all three of them were actually from Oxford might not make his evening any easier, nor theirs, for that matter.

There was a certain kind of brotherhood that arose from the shared experiences of warfare, particularly among young men who had shared a trench for a fortnight. It was a different kind of fraternal experience to have been brought together as strangers, who otherwise had very little in common, united only by a murder.

"Never met him," Jack said of his affiliation to the corpse. "In fact, I had just arrived here in London for the evening, to deliver papers for a solicitor in Kent."

The inspector blinked, then blinked again and turned to Charles.

"My story is not much different from his, I'm afraid," Charles said, adjusting his glasses. "I was only here on university business."

"That leaves you, John," said Clowes. "I suppose you didn't know him either."

"No," said John. "I knew him quite well. He was my tutor."

"Really?" said Clowes. "In what studies?"

"Ancient languages, primarily," said John. "That was the bulk of it, with additional coursework in mythology, etymology, history, and prehistoric cultures. Although," he added, "in point of fact, I was a rather less than diligent student."

"Aha," murmured Clowes. "And why is that? Was he not a good teacher?"

"An excellent one, to be precise," said John. "But the priest who helped to raise me when my father passed, who paid for the bulk of my schooling, in fact, believes that this kind of study is, ah . . . not practical."

"I see," said Clowes as he scribbled on his notepad with a stubby piece of graphite. "And just what is 'practical'?"

"Banking," replied John. "Commerce. That sort of thing."

"Humph," snorted Clowes. "And you disagree?"

John didn't reply, but merely shrugged as if to say, *What can one do?*

"Well," said Clowes, "I'm just about done here. But as you seem to be the closest thing Sigurdsson had to family, would you mind taking a look at the scene of the murder? It may be that you can spot whether something is amiss, where another could not."

"Certainly," said John.

Jack and Charles waited with the constable in the foyer while John and the inspector proceeded to the library. The smell hit John first—burned leather, accented by the cinnamon-tinged tobacco that only the professor smoked—but the room itself was a disaster.

Books were strewn about everywhere, and the backs of the shelves had been hacked to pieces. There was not a single piece of furniture unbroken. A number of books had been placed in the hearth to burn, with limited success.

"It was the bindings what done it," said Clowes. "Leather, with metal clasps. Thick, holds moisture. Made a stench like the devil, and smoke black as his beard. That's what drew the attention of the messenger when he got no reply at the door."

John glanced around the room, settling his gaze on a dark, crescent-shaped stain on the rug near the partners desk where the professor worked.

"Yes," said Clowes. "That's where he was found. Bled out quick—he didn't suffer, lad."

John thought this was a lie, but he appreciated the gesture nevertheless. "I couldn't tell you if anything's missing, inspector. It seems that everything that isn't chopped to bits or burned is . . . well, nothing worth noting. The books have some value, but only to persons like myself—and there's nothing here worth killing for."

Clowes sighed. "That's what we were afraid of. Well," he concluded, snapping his notebook closed, "I appreciate your time and cooperation. And I'm sorry for your loss."

"Thank you," said John. He turned to leave, then stopped. "Inspector? If I might ask, just how was the professor killed?"

"That's the other thing," said Clowes. "He was stabbed, of that there's no doubt. But the point of the weapon broke off against a rib, and so we got a good look.

"As far as we can tell, he was killed with a Roman spear. A Roman spear of a make and composition that hasn't been forged in over a thousand years."

◆ ◆ ◆

The gray drizzle of the evening had become a truly miserable English night, and the business of the murder investigation had kept the three newfound companions out past the last scheduled trains.

"I know a club just a few streets over," Charles offered. "Shall we repair there and remove ourselves from this dismal, damp night? We can catch our trains in the morning, after we've had a bit of warmth and a nip of something to settle our nerves."

Jack and John concurred, and they let Charles lead the way through the labyrinth of streets.

"Funny that he was a book collector," Jack said after they had gone a few blocks. "A Shakespeare scholar, even."

"Funny? In what way?" asked John.

Jack shrugged. "Because—he was killed yesterday, on the fifteenth."

Slowly it dawned on John, then Charles. "Julius Caesar," John said.

"Yes," said Jack. "It may not have meant much in Caesar's time, or even in Shakespeare's, but it would've been a warning well heeded last night, if anyone had been around to sound it.

"Beware the Ides of March."

As it turned out, the club to which Charles led them had literary allusions of its own. It had been a privately rented flat not two decades earlier, and had since been transformed into a club accessible to a private group from Oxford, of which Charles was a member.

"221B Baker Street?" John said with a hint of incredulity. "Are you quite serious, Charles?"

"Completely," Charles replied. "Oxford paid for its conversion, and it's very useful to have such a retreat when on business in London."

He opened the door and ushered his two companions into the entry hall. The main establishment consisted of a couple of private meeting rooms and a single large, airy sitting room, with adjacent entryways to what John assumed were the neighboring flats, converted to a similar use. The large room was cheerfully furnished, and illuminated by two broad windows that looked out onto a solitary gas lamp and the worsening gloom of night and storm. The fireplace, attended to by an inconspicuous manservant, was at full roar and brightened their spirits considerably as they moved toward it, their clothes exchanging dampness for a light draping of steam.

"Much better," said Jack.

Jack took up residence in an immense Edwardian wingback chair and made himself quite at home. John preferred to lean on the hearth, the better to warm himself and dry his clothes, while Charles, with an ease born of familiarity, opened the liquor cabinet at the far side of the room and began pouring drinks.

"I've let the manservant go for the night," said Charles. "I don't expect any other members will be turning out on a night such as this, and to be candid, after our adventure with inspector Clowes, I rather appreciate the privacy."

"I'm looking forward to doing as you have, John, and joining the war effort," said Jack. "I was hoping to get in a term or two at school, but it seems the chancellor has other plans."

"You're young," said Charles. "You may find time and experience curb your taste for adventure."

"That was a bit of an adventure tonight, wasn't it?" Jack continued. "Imagine getting mistaken for the student of a dead professor. . ."

Charles's scowl wasn't quick enough to cut off the younger man before a pained look crossed John's features.

"Oh, dear—Look, John, I'm sorry," said Jack. "I wasn't thinking."

"It's all right," John said, staring into the fire. "If the professor had been here, he'd have thought it was funny."

"You must mind your decorum," Charles admonished Jack. "Especially once you've begun your courses at . . . Jack—I say, are you listening to me?"

The younger man shook his head, stood, and crossed the room.

"There's a very strange man outside," said Jack. "He was standing across the street under the lamp for several minutes, and then he crossed to the corner, where he stood for several minutes more, and he is now standing outside with his face pressed to the window. . . ."

As one the three companions swung around to meet the surprised gaze of a strange apparition: a smallish man, seemingly cloaked in rags and wearing an outlandishly tall pointed hat. He was indeed pressed to the window, his nose pushed flat and his handlebar mustache askew with dampness.

The tatterdemalion at the window abruptly disappeared. Almost immediately came a solid rapping on the door.

". . . and now he's at the door," finished Jack.

"Bother," said Charles. "This is a members-only club. We can't simply be catering to every vagrant who hasn't the sense to be home on such a night."

"Oh, come now, Charles," said John, rising to answer the door. "If it wasn't for you, Jack and I would be in the same boat, and we've only just met."

"That's different," Charles sniffed. "You're Oxford men."

"I haven't actually begun yet," admitted Jack.

"A technicality," said Charles.

John opened the door and the strangest little man any of them had ever seen stepped inside and shook himself like a mongrel, spraying water all throughout the entry hall.

His appearance was what might result if you shredded an illustrated edition of the works of Jacob and Wilhelm Grimm, then pasted the pieces back together in random order. His coat and trousers were equal parts *Old Sultan, Rumpelstiltskin,* and *Hans-My-Hedgehog*; his shoes, the unfulfilled aspiration of a hundred cobbler tales. And his hat was some ruthless combination of *The King of the Golden Mountain* and *The Shroud*. His eyes twinkled, but his hair and mustache were sopping, and he looked as if he'd been beaten about the head and shoulders with some sort of shedding forest mammal. The only organized aspect of his appearance was a large parcel wrapped in oilskin, which he clutched tightly under one arm.

"Dreadful night," said the man, still dripping. "Dreadful. Twenty pounds of misery in a ten-pound sack. If I'd ever known such a night was going to come about, I'd have told my own grandmother not to bother having my father, just to avoid the trouble."

"Well, once you've dried off a bit, you'll have to leave," said Charles, covertly hiding the good bottle of brandy behind the inferior brands. "This is a private club. What were you doing watching us?"

"Is this a question for a question?" asked the man. "I answer yours, then you answer mine?"

"Can't say that isn't fair, Charles," said Jack.

"All right," said Charles.

"Good," said the strange visitor. "I was watching to make sure no one else was."

"What kind of answer is that?" sputtered Charles. "That's not a proper answer."

"Oh, come on," said John. "Be a sport." He turned to the little man. "Your turn. So what's your question?"

"I thank the gentleman," the man said with a slight bow. "And now my question:

"Which one of you is John? And do you know that Professor Sigurdsson is dead?"

Chapter Two

An Unusual Tale

After a brief, stunned silence, John regained his composure. "That would be me," John said, standing and proffering his hand.

The apparition grasped his hand in return, pumping it frenetically. "At last, at last!" he exclaimed. "So happy to make your acquaintance, John, my dear, dear boy. And what better place than here at Sir Arthur's home-away-from, eh? So grand, so grand. Yes . . ."

Jack and Charles exchanged skeptical glances, and Jack twirled a finger at his temple.

The little man continued undeterred. "I trust you can take it from here, correct?" he said, thrusting the oilskin-wrapped parcel in John's direction. "You know what must be done. The professor would not have left you unprepared for this."

John waved the parcel away. "I haven't the slightest idea what you are talking about. We've only just ourselves come from the professor's house, and I haven't known of his death for but the last day."

"I see. Well then, if your apprentices might help me unwrap the *Geographica*, we can get down to business."

"Assistants?" said Charles. "I'm not—we're not—sorry, Jack—

"I trust you can take it from here, correct?"

his assistants—apprentices," he sputtered. "I'm an editor for the—"

"Yes, I'm sure you are, and a fine one at that," the little man interrupted. "But that can only mean . . . John, tell me, are you—were you—the professor's only student? Were there others?"

John shook his head. "Not with the war going on. We had to prepare well in advance just to meet. I don't think he had the time for much correspondence and private tutoring with anyone else."

"Interesting," said Charles. "How did you come to such an unusual arrangement?"

"Hard to say, really," said John. "He came upon a few stories I'd written—trifles, really—and took a liking to them. He found I'd been billeted in Great Haywood after my return from France and came to see me with a proposal that he tutor me."

The little man did not respond to this but simply nodded, watching.

"It is a terrible loss for you, I'm sure," said Charles. "I now regret even more the lost opportunity to meet him. He sounds like an extraordinary man."

"He was," said the strange visitor.

"We only came here tonight because of Charles's membership in the club," said Jack, "but you came specifically seeking John. How is that?"

"Happenstance. Turned the wrong way and saw you enter. I can't keep these streets in order any more. Always lose my way. But even that is providence, for if I'd found the harbor earlier, when I was supposed to, I'd never have found *you*."

"What's at the harbor?" asked Charles.

"My ship is anchored there. Now, we must—"

"One moment," John said. "For all we know, this could be the murderer. He knew of Professor Sigurdsson well enough to know of me, but we know nothing of him."

In response, the little man rooted around inside his threadbare cloak for a moment before locating a crumpled note, which he proffered to John. It was, save for the person to whom it was addressed, identical to the one John had received from the professor.

"I trust that will suffice as evidence?" he asked. "I arrived from my travels abroad just yesterday and removed the *Geographica* from the house for safekeeping. The professor insisted on remaining there to wait for you. We were to reconvene in his library, this evening."

"This is the *Geographica*, then?" asked Jack, gesturing at the parcel.

"It is."

"What is it?" John asked.

The little man blinked and arched an eyebrow. "It is the world, my boy," he said. "All the world, in ink and blood, vellum and parchment, leather and hide. It is the world, and it is yours to save or lose."

Without waiting for a further response, the man carefully hefted the large parcel onto a table and began to unwrap the layers of oilcloth.

"It looks like a book," said Jack.

"I can see you're the smart one of the group," said the little man.

"Thanks," said Jack, beaming. "I'm Jack."

"Pleased to meet you, Jack," said the little man. "Call me Bert."

"Okay, Bert," Jack said, stepping forward to help uncover the parcel.

Under the oilcloth lay a largish leatherbound volume, worn smooth with use—or great age. It was tied at the open edge with cloth straps, and debossed on the front, its letters still bearing glittering traces of golden embellishments, were the words *Imaginarium Geographica*.

"Hmm. 'Geography of the Imagination,' is it?" said Charles. "Interesting."

"Close," said Bert. "A better translation would be less literal: 'Imaginary Geography.'"

"Imaginary?" said John, peering at the large book. "Of what use is an atlas of imaginary geographies?"

The quick smile almost hid the shadow that passed over Bert's features before he answered. "Why, you are of course having a game at our expense, young John. It serves exactly the use one would think: to guide one to, from, and across imaginary lands.

"All the lands that have ever existed in myth and legend, fable and fairy tale, can be found within," continued Bert. "Ouroboros, Schlaraffenland and Poictesme, Lilliput and Mongo and Islandia and Thule, Pellucidar and Prydain; they are all there.

"Collectively, the place where these lands exist is called the Archipelago of Dreams—and it was for this book, this guide to the Archipelago, that the professor was killed."

"This looks like Greek," said Jack, his nose an inch from the open spread of the first map.

"Smart lad, Jack," said Bert. "There are a number of such maps at the beginning, but as you can see, several have been annotated in other languages, including English—although most of them are still untranslated," he finished, elbowing John. "Lucky we have you here, eh, my lad?"

"Wait a moment, just wait," said John, backing away. "I don't understand what this has to do with me, or how you even knew who I was, for that matter."

"I knew who you were, John, because I was the one who read your writings first. I was the one who sought you out and advised the professor that you were the ideal man to become his successor. I was the one who saw within you the potential to become the greatest Caretaker of them all.

"I had assumed that your companions were in turn *your* apprentices—no offense, Charles—but only because there have always been three."

"Three? Three what?" asked Jack.

"Caretakers of the *Geographica*," said Bert. "Now, we don't have time to dawdle," he continued. "The race has already begun."

"What race?" asked Charles.

"The race," said Bert, "to avoid catastrophe, my boy—with the whole of human history as the stakes. We can only hope the education you have had thus far has been enough."

"My *education*?" John said, incredulous. "But why is—"

Before he could continue, the night air was split with the long howl of a hound. It rang deeply and loud, finally fading into profound silence. Then the howl came again, joined by another, and another.

And another.

But this time, it was closer. Much closer.

Behind the horrible harmonies of the howling was a faint staccato—the shouts of men, angry, seeking. The sounds of a mob.

For the first time since he had entered 221B Baker Street, Bert's face became drawn and somber, and tinged with fear.

"That's it then, lads. We have to go."

"We?" sputtered Charles. "I'm not going out in this! Especially with some kind of . . . of *beasts* running amok in the streets!"

"You have no choice, I'm afraid," said Bert. "They're coming for John and me, so we *must* leave—but if they come here to find we've gone, you would fare the worse for it."

"Coming for me?" said John. "Why?"

"Did you think they would stop with the professor?" asked Bert. "They can't—won't. They haven't gotten what they're seeking—this," he said, slapping his hand on the *Imaginarium Geographica*. "And as it is now yours, I'm sure they'll have no problem cutting you down as easily as they did him."

Bert began to wrap the atlas in the oilcloth, and Jack stepped in to help him. "Quickly, now," he said to the three young men. "We must fly!"

"Fly where?" said Charles.

"To the harbor, of course," said Bert. "To my ship. My crew is waiting for us now, and they are beginning to worry, no doubt."

Charles began to protest, but Bert cut him short.

"These are not rioters coming for us. They are not soldiers. They are not even, in point of fact, *men* as you know them. But whether or not you believe my warnings, or that I have a ship awaiting us in the harbor, or that anything I have told you tonight is true, believe this: If we stay here a minute longer, we shall all be dead."

If Bert's appeal was not convincing enough, the shadows that appeared on the opposite street corner pushed the companions' motivation to the fore.

The band hunting them brandished swords and spears of an unusual make. But stranger still was the fact that they appeared to walk on all fours, claws clicking on the cobblestones, only occasionally standing upright to sniff at the air before rending the night with more earsplitting howls.

"Wendigo," Bert murmured to himself. "He's pulling out all the stops—and it can only get worse. Charles," he asked, turning quickly, "did Sir Arthur have a back exit to this place?"

"Yes," said Charles. "This way. Hurry."

Bert, Jack, and John followed Charles through a warren of small rooms to a door at the end of the apartment. "Here," said Charles. "They expanded into the adjacent flat, and it has a door that opens onto an alleyway."

As they entered the hallway, there was a crash and a splintering of wood from the foyer behind them.

"Hurry, lads!" said Bert. "Hurry!"

Finding the exit, the four companions moved quickly but cautiously into the alley, which was empty. Heading for the intersecting street, their steps became more and more hurried, realizing that it would only be a matter of time. . . .

When they were a block distant, the angry howls of their pursuers told them their path away from the club had been discovered. The hunt had ended. It was now a race.

In moments the companions were running at full speed toward the harbor.

Chapter Three

Flight to the Harbor

By daylight the streets and alleyways of London were a conundrum; at night, in the middle of a rainstorm, the maze became an impossible labyrinth to the four men running for their lives from a pack of hunters that could, apparently, pursue them by smell.

"What are they?" said Jack. "You called them 'Wendigo.'"

"Our enemy's huntsmen," puffed Bert. "They are his bloodhounds, and if not the worst abominations under the sight of Heaven, they are easily contenders for the crown."

"Are they men, or beasts?" asked Jack.

"Both, I'm afraid. When it's required, they may comport themselves as men—but they become more lupine with every kill. Their bodies have been misshapen by the evil they do, and thus they have gained the senses of hounds, as well as their agility and speed."

"How do they become this way?" asked John.

"By terrible means," said Bert. "To begin with, they must be black-hearted men. But to become Wendigo, they must eat the flesh of another man."

"Cannibals," breathed John.

"The Indigo Dragon," *Bert said proudly.* "My ship."

"Yes," said Bert, "but not just. It is rumored that to truly become Wendigo, the first flesh they taste must be that of their best friend or a loved one. After that, it doesn't really matter."

A horrified expression crossed John's features as the implications of this settled in. "Do you think they . . . the professor's body?"

"No," said Bert. "I believe he was killed while they interrogated him as to the whereabouts of the *Geographica*. Killed, but not eaten. Wendigo . . . Wendigo like their meals *alive*."

"Do you really think there's a boat?" Jack said some minutes later, panting.

"I doubt it," Charles replied, "but I'm not of a mind to stand around and debate it."

"Shilling that there is," said Jack.

"Done."

The cobblestones were slick, and the companions had to measure their steps so as not to fall and risk twisting an ankle. Bert led the way. His admitted memory lapses of the geography of London streets seemed not to affect his pace—he moved from corner to corner under the gaslight with a speed and agility that belied his appearance.

"Almost there, lads," Bert said. "You can smell it, can't you?"

"Ew," said Jack. "That's really rank. What is it?"

"Fish and offal, offal and fish," said Charles. "Commerce. You know—like the kind of work John doesn't know if he wants to get into."

"Clever," said John as Bert disappeared around the corner ahead, whooping in triumph.

Turning the corner himself an instant later, John stopped in his tracks, which caused Charles and Jack to crash into him in turn.

Bert had spoken the truth. There was indeed a ship moored and floating in the harbor. A ship unlike any they had ever seen.

Jack held out his hand. "Shilling."

"Drat," said Charles, dropping a coin into Jack's hand.

"The *Indigo Dragon,*" Bert said proudly. "My ship."

"Is it a galleon?" asked Charles. "It seems Spanish, but—old."

"Sixteenth century," said Bert. "At least, the newer parts. I believe the oldest parts of the hull are Greek, but I can't really be sure. There's a little of everything in her, I think. But she gets the job done and always takes me safely to home port."

"And where is home port, exactly?" asked Jack.

"Later, later," said Bert, eyeing the shadows of their pursuers stretched tall in the gaslight behind them. "Let's to safety first—there will be time to talk later."

None of the companions paused to ask what Bert meant by "later," or the broader insinuation that the dialogue was meant to continue after the danger had passed.

Bert broke into a trot and moved swiftly across the dock to the gangplank that connected to the ship. Standing at the fore of the gangplank was a young woman—tall, dressed like a pirate out of Stevenson, and displaying a commanding appearance that belied her obvious youth.

"Father, you're late," the woman scolded. "We were preparing a landing party to go in and retrieve you."

"Not necessary, Aven," said Bert. "As you can see, my young friends and I have everything running well according to plan."

From the dock, a sleek Egyptian spear flew through the night air and pinned Bert's cloak to the prow, narrowly missing his shoulder. "Oh, ah—well," said Bert, slipping out of the garment and wincing. "That's not to say that we shouldn't, ah, accelerate our departure."

As the companions scrambled aboard, Aven stood at the aft of the ship, arms crossed in defiance of the spears being flung at her by the huntsmen.

"Enough of this," she said tersely. "Take us out."

No oars were lowered into the water, and strangely, the sails were billowed in precisely the *opposite* direction of the wind—but the instant Aven gave the order, the ship pulled away from the dock and began to pick up speed.

A howl behind them scored the chill harbor air, and the young woman's eyes widened. "Wendigo? He sent Wendigo after you?"

"Yes," Bert nodded. "Stellan—the professor—was dead before anything could be done."

"You had the *Geographica,*" said Aven, casting a wan glance at the companions. "He needn't have waited, only to be killed."

"His choice, Aven," Bert admonished her. "I could just as easily blame myself, for having left it solely to him while I traveled. . . ."

"Or Jamie," she shot back. "If he hadn't given it up just for that woman and her children . . . He's even in London! Why aren't the Wendigo chasing *him?*"

"They don't want him," said Bert. "They want this," he finished, patting the *Geographica.* "That's why we're here. That's why we came. And now, that's why we have to leave."

"Also," said Charles, "we're being chased by creatures that want to kill us—"

"—eat us," interjected Jack.

"Kill us and eat us," Charles corrected. "So, might I suggest we finish this discussion somewhere farther out of range?"

"Yes," said Jack, whose eyes had not left Aven since they'd stepped onto the ship. "And, ah, perhaps an introduction is in order."

"Of course," said Bert. "Lads, may I present the captain of the *Indigo Dragon*—my daughter, Aven."

Charles stepped forward, bowing slightly. "A pleasure. I'm Charles."

She nodded, eyebrow still arched.

"I'm Jack," said Jack, pushing past his companion and offering his hand. "If there's anything you need a hand with, please don't hesitate to ask."

"Do you know how to work aboard a ship?"

"Ah, well, no, not exactly," admitted Jack. "I'm a scholar."

Aven rolled her eyes and sighed in exasperation. "Another scholar. Heaven spare us from fools and their books."

She looked at John. "And you?"

"I'm John. Pleased to meet you."

She didn't respond, but held his gaze a long moment before turning abruptly and saying something just softly enough for him to hear.

"You had better be worth this."

For the first time, the companions got to have a direct look at their pursuers, who were amassing on the dock, howling and flailing their weapons about in a rage.

The Wendigo were not unlike men. Only those that crouched,

showing their disfigured, animalian hindquarters, were obviously something more. They were hairy; rough at the edges. Indistinct, as if they were part of an improperly processed photograph.

The cloaks they wore to disguise their bodies and to conceal weapons were now being flung aside to reveal strange dress from a dozen cultures.

"How unusual," said John. "I count several different costumes among them—Egyptian, Indian . . . Is that one Norse?"

"Not costumes," said Aven. "Did you think a man who turns evil and eats the flesh of his friends had to have a Cockney accent?"

John and the others shuddered and were turning away when he caught sight of another figure on the dock, passing among the furious Wendigo. He was not certain, but the man looked like one of the passengers who had been on the train with him earlier that day. If he was, it was further proof of Bert's claim that John was more deeply involved in the events of the evening than he had realized.

The *Indigo Dragon* continued to accelerate, and in moments the dock and their pursuers had receded into the dark behind them.

Given time to catch their breath, the companions now turned their attention to the strange vessel they had boarded. It was indeed a galleon, but of a most unusual design. It was a bit dirty, a bit creaky, but there was no question—it was a ship crafted for grand adventure.

At the fore of the ship was the masthead, a great head and torso of a dragon. It had eyes of gold and was colored a deep, rich purple. "Indigo," Bert corrected, hearing Jack suggest the color. "We don't want to offend her."

John thought, but couldn't be certain, that he saw the dragon breathe.

There was a cabin in the aft of the ship, and cargo holds below with a most unusual feature: They were much larger on the inside than they appeared to be on the outside.

Around them the ship's complement of some twenty sailors, all thickly clothed against the moist night air, busied themselves at their tasks under Aven's orders.

"Have you noticed," Jack ventured to the others, "that we're each and all a good two feet taller than every member of the crew?"

John had processed all of the goings-on in the background as the usual ship's business, but now that it was pointed out, he realized Jack was right. Not a single crewman stood taller than four feet, and the bulk of them were smaller than that.

"I say," said Jack to one of the passing crew, "would you happen to—"

He froze, eyes wide.

"Jack?" said Charles. "What is it?"

The crewman, eyes glittering, ignored him and went about his task. But Jack managed to lift his arm and point at the departing sailor's feet, which were not feet at all.

They were cloven hooves.

The crewmen gave no notice that they even cared if they were being observed, and Aven and Bert were deep in discussion over the *Imaginarium Geographica*. Charles, John, and Jack drew closer together and moved to the opposite side of the cabin.

"Did you see that?" said Jack, finally able to speak. "Did you see . . . ?"

"Quiet," said Charles. "I did. There is something strange about all of this, and I for one am about to be done with the whole matter."

"Agreed," said John. "We've gone a good distance from that row with the—whatever it was hunting us. We should be able to stop here along the river somewhere and contact the authorities—perhaps inspector Clowes can deal with all this. Anyroad, it's not our job."

"Right," said Jack, shivering. "We're just about to pass the bridge. They'll have to slow up at the shallows, and we can ask them to let us off at the docks just beyond."

"We have a plan, then," said Charles. "I'll speak to them."

In moments the *Indigo Dragon* had passed beneath the bridge, but instead of slowing as Jack had predicted, it began to fly across the water with an even greater velocity. The ever-present fog of the river began to coalesce and draw close to the ship. Even the rain had ceased. Something more was beginning to happen.

In the distance behind them, from beneath the shadows of London Bridge, a second ship, dark-masted and black as a nightmare, lifted anchor and silently began to follow.

Charles hastened to make his point. "We seem to have lost our pursuers," he said to Aven. "And I for one am most grateful for your assistance and intervention. Now that the danger is past, can you tell me at what part of the city you intend to leave us?"

"Yes," Jack agreed, looking askew at the ship's crewmen. "We'd like to get off, please."

Aven gave her father a knowing look before answering. "I'm sorry, but that's just not possible."

"Why not?" asked John.

In answer, Aven gestured at the glowing city lights on the not-distant shore, now dim and hazy through the fog.

As they watched, the mists drew closer, thickening around the ship, until in mere moments the lights of London had vanished. When the fog began to clear, the city was gone, and the storm had stopped. Above a thousand stars were shining, unfettered by the clouds that had blanketed them just minutes before. And around them, open ocean, no sign of shore in sight.

"B-but that can't possibly be!" Charles said, stammering in disbelief and no small amount of fear. "We haven't been at sail for more than a few minutes! There is no possible way we could be in open waters!"

"Right," said Jack. "I've been down the river plenty of times. We still have—had—at least twenty miles to go before reaching the Channel."

"Oh, I see," said Bert. "You misunderstand—we left England the minute the ship pulled away from the dock. We're nowhere near the Channel, or London, or even Europe, for that matter. In fact, we are not even sailing in the same ocean any longer."

"Then where are we?" said Charles. "Where are you taking us?"

Aven tilted her head at John. "Ask *him*. He knows."

John stood at the railing, looking out into the darkness as they let the question hang in the air, shimmering with the promise they all knew would be fulfilled if he would just speak the words. Finally, he answered.

"The Archipelago," John said, his voice muted with a mix of disbelief and wonder. "That's where we're going, isn't it? We're going to the Archipelago of Dreams."

Chapter Four

Avalon

Whatever personal misgivings they may have had, John, Jack, and Charles had to accept the evidence of their senses. Like it or not, they were at sea. And until a destination was named, traveled to, and safely arrived at, they were fully at the mercy of the captain and her unusual crew.

"This is all your fault," Charles said to Bert, his voice shaking with anger. "If you hadn't convinced us to leave the club—"

"If he hadn't convinced you to leave the club," Aven interrupted, "you'd be three kinds of dead. Or didn't you notice those weren't accountants and bankers chasing you?"

"She's right," said Jack, kicking at one of the spears on the deck. "Those things weren't for show. They're crusted with layers of dried blood. I think they really would have killed us, Charles."

"I agree," said John. "Whatever situation we're in now, it's better than if we'd remained in London. Although," he added, looking askance at Bert, "it would be nice if we had an idea when it would be safe to return."

"That is the question, isn't it?" said Bert. "One of several that I suspect you have. And as I have questions of my own, then perhaps we should make landfall and discuss our next course of action."

The statue was wrapped in vines and overgrowth . . .

"Landfall?" asked Charles. "Is there a place to land if we're in fact sailing toward your 'Imaginary Geography'?"

"There is indeed," said Bert. "It's an island that actually straddles the border between the waters of the world you know and those of the Archipelago.

"I don't know what it was originally called—the professor could have told you, John—but for the past thousand years, it has been known as Avalon."

Aven estimated that they were still at least an hour out from Avalon, and she suggested that her reluctant passengers try to settle in and enjoy the ride. The night air was cool but not chill, and the calm waters made for mellow sailing.

Bert noticed that John seemed to be avoiding going anywhere near the *Imaginarium Geographica,* choosing instead to observe the others from the foredeck, where he could watch for the island. Charles was shaking his head every few moments, as if doing so might wake him from the undigested-mustard-and-cheese nightmare in which he found himself. And Jack acted as if whatever danger or inconvenience he had to endure would be worth the trouble, as long as he could remain in close proximity to Aven.

The crew of the *Indigo Dragon* were, as it turned out, fauns: the half-men, half-goat creatures of myth. Aven explained that while their short stature made them rather disagreeable, their inborn ability—from the goat half of their heritage, John had no doubt—to scale mountainous terrain also came in handy on a tempest-tossed deck.

"It's an amazing sight," Aven said. "Twenty-foot waves, decks as slick as ice, rain all but blinding, and these fellows walk about as if they were strolling in the park."

"Actually," said Jack, "I would've thought satyrs would be better—larger and stronger, you know?"

"Satyrs, fft," Aven hissed. "Stronger, sure—but they spend all their time drinking, and when they're not drinking, they're chasing women. More trouble than help."

"Fauns don't drink?" asked Jack.

"Not like satyrs," said Aven. "The strongest thing fauns drink is a flaming rum punch. Usually it's nothing more potent than a nice mulled wine."

"You do realize you're arguing about mythological creatures that can't possibly exist," said Charles, waving his arms. "There are no such things as fauns and satyrs!"

As if in answer, one of the crew dropped a heavy spare mast bracing on Charles's foot, then picked it up and tipped his hat in mock apology before passing through to the cabin.

Charles howled and sat on the deck, massaging his injured foot.

"I think that nonexistent mythological creature just broke some of your toes," Jack said.

"Oh, shut up," said Charles.

It was not long before the crewman in the crow's nest signaled to the captain that land was in sight. On the near horizon, shrouded in fine mist and standing in high relief against the darker thunderheads beyond, was Avalon.

The *Indigo Dragon* slowed and made its way through the shallows to rest against a tumbledown dock. There, a pebbled beach slowly gave way to a grassy slope and a tangled thicket of growth around what had once been a grand and eloquent structure.

John, Jack, Charles, and Bert disembarked, with Jack taking the lead ahead of his more cautious and reluctant companions. Aven stayed behind, occasionally casting suspicious glances back in the direction from which they had come.

Atop the slope were ruined pilasters all about; broken arches, shattered foundations, crumbling stone. In the dim twilight, the young men could almost imagine the great cathedrals that may have once stood on the island—but that age was long past, and nature had since reclaimed it for herself.

Ruined though it was, there was an undeniable atmosphere of magic and mystery about the island that permeated the ground, the trees, the very air itself. None of them had truly thought for an instant that they were actually traveling to King Arthur's Avalon of legend, but there, in that moment, they could almost believe.

Scattered throughout the ruins were several marble pedestals, and here and there they could see the occasional intact statue. A tallish one stood on the pedestal nearest what was once an entry hall. The statue was wrapped in vines and overgrowth, almost as if it were a shrub that had grown up in the form of a knight-at-arms.

Jack squinted at it and was startled to see it squint back. "That statue," he said, turning to summon the others. "I think I saw it move."

"Ah," said Bert, who had anchored the group and was still some yards back, "I meant to tell you . . ."

Before he could finish the thought, the object of Jack's attention stepped off the pedestal and with a creaking of joints and metal swung his sword directly at the young man's head.

"Jack, get down!" John yelled, diving to pull his friend out of harm's way. The sword passed in a sharp arc through the space where Jack had been standing as he and John collapsed in a tumble. They rolled to their feet some distance away, fists at the ready.

They needn't have worried. The statue—actually a knight in armor that had gone mottled green with rust and decay—could not lift the sword again for a second swing. Even stepping closer into the soft light was an effort, and they saw that his face was deeply creased with age. Age, and something more. . . .

"Speak," the knight said, rasping. "Speak and be recognized."

Bert hurried forward and spoke for all three of them. "It's just me, old friend—it's Bert, and company."

A glint of recognition flashed in the knight's eyes. He lowered his sword and lifted his head, peering at the intruders.

It was plainly evident that the old sentinel was no danger. John, Jack, and Charles moved closer, but John was the first to realize what was odd about their assailant.

"Your flesh," he said, amazed. "It's wood, isn't it?"

"Lads," said Bert, who stepped aside and put a supporting arm around the old knight's midriff, "I'd like you to meet the Green Knight. The Guardian of Avalon."

The Green Knight's limbs and torso were hardwood—stout oaks and maples; his joints and face, soft, lined pine. His hair was a bird's-nest tangle of bark and leafy twigs. When he spoke, it was with the creaking susurrations of an ancient willow swaying in a night breeze.

"Forgive my hasty estimation," he said to Jack. "If I had but known you were friend, I would not have tried to remove your head from your shoulders."

"He understands," Bert interjected. "You were simply doing your job."

"You were French, if I am to judge by your accent," said Jack.

"*Are* French," Charles said, underscoring the correction with a scowl at Jack.

The knight responded with a deep, respectful bow. "*A votre service, monsieur,*" he said. "My strength, such as it is, is yours to command."

"Call me Charles—and thank you," Charles said.

"Charles?" the knight said with a spark of surprise in his eyes. "I was called as such, once upon a time, in another life."

"Pleased to make your acquaintance," said Charles. "These are my friends, Jack . . ."

"Hello," said Jack, offering his hand, then examining it briefly after the knight took it in his barklike grip.

". . . and John," finished Charles.

"Ah," said the knight. "The Caretaker."

John blinked back his surprise. "So Bert tells me," he said. "But how would you have known?"

"The Morgaine," said the knight, as if that explained everything. "The Three Who Are One foretold your coming, and the dark troubles that are to follow."

In answer to the others' questioning looks, Bert rubbed his chin and sighed. "This bodes ill," he said, morose. "This bodes not well at all."

He turned to the Green Knight. "Take us to the Morgaine.

We must know what they know—or at least, what they are willing to tell us."

"The Green Knights are compelled to service," Bert said as they followed the knight's lead and began walking counterclockwise around the perimeter of the island. "The first of them was a Crusader, who assumed the duty in exchange for a gift of great value. Others were summoned as a means of penance, or to avenge a wrongdoing. Of the twenty-five Guardians of Avalon that have served, only our friend here and one other have chosen to do so of their own will."

"I'll not argue with you, old friend," said the knight, nodding back at Bert, "but one might say I was as compelled as all the rest."

"How so?" asked Charles.

"What year is it," the knight asked in response, "back in the world?"

"You refer to 'the world' as if it were a different place," said Jack. "But it isn't really, is it? After all, despite what Aven claims, we did set sail in the waters of London, and as far as my senses can tell, we never left them. Surely an ocean of the world is still an ocean of the world, regardless of the strange nature of some of the lands that reside upon it."

"Ah, my young friend, but this world *is* a different place," said the knight. "The fields you know are those of Adam and Eve, and the children who followed. The fields we walk now are far, far older."

"It's 1917," Charles put in, answering the knight's question.

"Ah," the knight sighed. "Has it truly been so long, then?" He sighed again, a deep, regretful sound. For a few moments they walked along in silence before he spoke again.

"I chose to serve as Guardian of Avalon," the knight began, "to repay a debt I could not otherwise settle. A place in Death's realm had been reserved for me—and another man took it in my stead."

"A relative, perhaps?" asked John. "Or a close friend?"

"He was an Englishman," the knight said. "A commoner, of humble birth, and he sacrificed himself for a matter of principle.

"I believed, having escaped my fate, that my life would be a happy one. But his sacrifice plagued me. I was restless, unsettled. My wife and daughter, delights both, brought me no joy, for I felt it was not I who had paid the price to live in their world.

"Then, one day, I became acquainted with one of your predecessors—a Caretaker of the *Geographica*. And as I told him my story, he shared one in return: that of the last Green Knight, who had grown weary of the job, weary of guarding this place, and yet had seen no relief in the offing."

"Not much to guard here, is there?" said Jack, glancing around at the ruined heaps of stone they seemed to be constantly passing. "Someone obviously wasn't up to the task."

"Jack!" Charles chided. "That's quite rude."

"Sorry," said Jack, reddening. "But, to be fair . . ."

"No, the young man is right," said the knight. "On the surface of things, it seems there is little here of value. But sometimes, it is not about guarding something of value that is important, but rather, being a valuable guard, so that when that thing comes along that needs guarding, there is no question."

"And did that thing ever come along?" asked John.

But the knight did not reply; or if he did, it was lost to the wind rushing in from the west.

The western side of the island was a stark contrast to the spot where the *Indigo Dragon* had landed. Steep, sharp crags of porous volcanic rock jutted up into the side of the hills from the pounding surf below. The spray of saltwater filled their nostrils and dampened their clothes.

"This part of Avalon lies on the Frontier," said Bert, gesturing to the thunderheads that lined the horizon. "The actual boundary of the Archipelago. Many a ship has been lost to the storms and tidal forces here."

The knight led them along a winding path worn through the scrubby grasses that had taken root among the riddled stone, at points coming dangerously close to the steep dropoff to their right.

Ahead in the gloom, nestled within the crags, was the reddish glow of a fire. On it sat an immense black cauldron, around which were seated three old women who were chanting loudly as the group approached.

"Witches," breathed John.

"The Morgaine," the knight said, nodding.

Each witch spoke in turn, as if singing a refrain.

"By the pricking in my breast—"

"They come o'er East, into the West—"

"Though tempest bar and block the way—"

"The Mapmaker's heir shall seek the day—"

"'gainst evil's might, he will persist—"

"To restore th' power of Arthur's throne—"

"Twine Paralon with the World of men—"

"If here be dragons once again."

Bert and the Green Knight exchanged curious glances. Had they overheard a prophecy? Or was it simple coincidence?

"Boy!" the third witch screeched, having finished the chant. She wore a heavy cloak and cowl, and she motioned for the companions to come closer to the fire. "Boy! Where are you? Ah there you are. Bring that over here. Quickly, quickly now!"

A young man—or a tall boy on the verge of manhood—appeared at the mouth of the cave on the far side of the firelight, copper pot in tow.

He was sandy-haired, dressed in simple clothes, and his face was smudged with soot, but his mouth was screwed up in an expression of determination. He may have been a servant, but it was obvious he was a good worker.

"Boy, bring the kettle—we have visitors, rare enough to be sure, but if we don't feed them proper and true, then they're not likely to return," said the first witch.

"Right," Jack whispered to Charles. "As if not feeding us would be the only reason."

"Perhaps not the only reason," said the second witch, who had long white hair tied neatly under a scarf and a wicked grin that indicated she could hear better than Jack gave her credit for. "But perhaps our hospitality is not what you should be seeking."

"Uh, pleased to meet you," said John. "And how should I address you, ah, ladies?"

"Now there's a question, if ever I heard one," said the first witch, who wore dozens of ornate necklaces and had bright eyes that flashed with intelligence. "We haven't been asked our names since . . ." She scratched her head with a bird skull on a stick. "How long *has* it been?"

"Since *he* came to Avalon," said the second witch, hooking her thumb at the knight. "Seventy, eighty years, maybe?"

"Yes," the third witch nodded in agreement. "I remember. It was a Tuesday."

"Today is Tuesday," offered Jack.

"Well, that makes things easier, doesn't it, my duck?" said the first witch. "On Tuesdays I am Ceridwen. She's Celedriel," Ceridwen said, gesturing at the second witch, "and she," she continued, pointing at the sullen third witch, "is called Cul."

"Don't want to be Cul," the third witch pouted. "Want to be Gwynhfar."

"Now, Cul dear," Ceridwen admonished. "For one thing, you could only be Gwynhfar on a Sunday, and it's Tuesday. And for another, she left us long ago to marry that Wart fellow, so you wouldn't be Gwynhfar anyway. Besides, one of us has to be Cul."

"Well," Cul grumbled, "why does it have to be me?"

"You are the youngest," Celedriel clucked. "Can't be a Ceridwen until you've been a Cul for at least another century or three."

"This is all very confusing," said Charles.

"I just call them all 'milady,'" the knight offered. "I don't think it matters which one answers you."

Jack stepped to the fire and helped the boy lift the kettle atop the cooking stones. The boy nodded, grateful, then returned to the cave.

"Good errand boy, that Bug is," said Ceridwen. "So glad we decided not to eat him."

Charles couldn't suppress a shudder. "Is that what the, er, big cauldron is for?"

"Oh, no, my dear," said Celedriel. "Can't put a living being in that one—not if you want to use them afterward."

"You're thinking of the other one, dear," Ceridwen corrected. "The pot with the ravens and writings on it—the one that was stolen by that Maggot fellow, remember? It was just a year or three before we got our Bug."

"Maggot," said Cul. "Heh. Have to pay the price for that someday. That was my favorite kettle."

"That's just because you could keep all sorts of unusual things in it," said Ceridwen. "Misfortune and spirits, specters and shadows."

"Putting things into it was easy," said Celedriel. "It was taking them out again that was hard—because once it was open, there was no telling what would escape.

"But—forgive me!" she exclaimed. "We're neglecting our guests!"

"The chant you were singing as we approached," Bert began. "You mentioned Paralon. . . ."

"Paralon!" exclaimed Bug, who had been listening at the mouth of the cave. "That's where the king lives! And his knights!"

"Now you've gone and done it," grumbled Cul. "Once you get him started on knights and chivalry and whatnot, can't shut him up for days."

"I'm going to *be* a knight," the boy stated proudly. "A *real* knight—not like, um, you know."

The Green Knight scowled affectionately. "Brat."

John smiled and tousled the young man's hair. "I'm sure you will, Bug."

"If miladies can spare him," said the knight, "I would like the young squire"—Bug beamed at hearing this—"to resupply the *Indigo Dragon* with fresh water for its long journey to come."

Bert began to say that they had no need of additional supplies, but the knight cut him off. "A caution is better before than after." He turned to the boy. "Well? What are you waiting for?"

Without another word Bug took off down the path at a full run, and an odd expression of contentment came over the knight's face. Bert gave the knight and the departing Bug a curious look, but said nothing.

The Green Knight turned back to the Morgaine. "We have come to seek your counsel," he said.

"We've already given it," said Cul. "Or weren't you listening?"

"No hand is at the rudder in Paralon," said Celedriel. "No human hand, at least. What was lost, must be found; what was cloven, must be mended."

"But without the Mapmaker's heir, all is lost," said Ceridwen.

"Then it's not too late," Bert said with obvious relief. "I've brought John just in time."

To this the Morgaine did not reply, but merely stared into the fire. After a moment the Green Knight motioned for the companions to leave, and they began to make their way back to the ship.

While Bert made his good-byes to the knight, John climbed aboard the *Indigo Dragon* and looked around for Bug. "So, Aven," he said. "Are we all stocked up on water, then?"

Aven fixed him with a puzzled look. "Of course. Why should you ask?"

John waved it off. "Never mind. Forget I asked."

As the crew readied the ship to depart, Jack and Charles (who was somewhat more reluctant than his younger friend) took up their usual post near the cabin. Bert gave Aven a report on what had transpired with the knight and the Morgaine. Her expression darkened, but she said nothing.

"We're not returning to London, are we?" Charles said to his companions. "We've been drafted, whether we like it or not."

"I think *he's* been drafted," Jack said, referring to John. "We get to come along for the adventure. Cheer up, Charles. This could be great fun."

"Someone's got to be an anchor to reality here," Charles said as the ship began to pull out of the small harbor. "It's not that I mind falling down the rabbit hole—I just don't want to lose sight of the door."

The Green Knight kept his arm raised long after the *Indigo Dragon* had passed from sight. Eventually, he lowered it, his breathing gone quick and shallow.

"At last," he murmured to no one in particular. "At last my duties have been dispensed. And perhaps my soul can be at peace."

Sitting at the shore, the knight passed the final hours of his last night of service in meditation, until finally the sun began to rise. He raised his eyes to the shimmering sky of the Archipelago's dawn and drew a deep, final breath. "Ah, my Lucie . . . Finally, I come to join you in that far better place, that far better rest. . . ."

The knight's last words faded into the mist as eddies of dust began to swirl about his limbs. Slowly, gently, his aged body began to fragment into ash as he folded in upon himself, leaving nothing but the helmet and breastplate to settle into the grass. In moments he was gone.

Part Two

The Archipelago of Dreams

". . . it seems I have a battle to fight."

Chapter Five

The Corsair

The storm line past Avalon was more roiling clouds and ominous thunder than rain and wind, although there was enough fury in it to push the *Indigo Dragon* across the waves like a toy. The crew was experienced, and it was obvious they had traversed this passage before. They went about their duties as usual, occasionally checking to make sure none of their passengers had been flung overboard, and in a matter of minutes they were once more through to calmer waters.

On the formal crossing to the Archipelago, there was a different timbre in the atmosphere. They still appeared to be on open ocean, with no land in sight, but the gray morning light revealed a number of varying depths in the water below. Shallows, where there should be none.

"Is it a reef?" John asked. "Like those in Australia?"

"It doesn't appear to be," said Charles. "More like submerged islands."

"These are the Drowned Lands, called by some the Lost Lands of the West," said Bert. "You'll not find them in the *Imaginarium Geographica*, for as old as it is, there are lands older still."

"I wouldn't do that, if I were you," Aven said to Jack as he leaned over the railing to catch some of the spray in his hands. "Not here, anyway—not if you want to keep your hands."

Jack quickly leaned back and looked at Bert, puzzled.

"Look into the deeps," said Bert. "You can still see the shapes of noble towers and cities that once adorned the islands here. Legend says that these islands were the proudest of the world once, when the lands of Man and those of the Archipelago were not divided as they are now."

"What happened to them?" asked Jack. "And what does that have to do with my putting my hands in the water?"

"No one knows," said Bert. "Some think they destroyed themselves by seeking too deeply into the mysteries of life itself. Some say they were destroyed by the gods for the same reason. One theory is that it was the fault of an inattentive angel who had been assigned by Heaven to watch the developing civilization. For all we know, it was simply a natural disaster.

"Regardless, my boy," Bert concluded, clapping Jack on the back, "it was not a gentle passing, nor one of good portents. And some say that when the lands were destroyed, not all of the inhabitants perished with them. Those drowned children of a great culture may still live in the murky deep, and they would be human no longer. Their hearts would be blackened, their limbs transformed to fins, their lungs gone to gills . . .

. . . and their teeth, razor sharp."

Jack's eyes widened, and Aven suppressed a grin as he moved squarely to the middle of the deck.

Charles and John peered over the side, and in fact it did seem as if they could see the outlines of what may have been cities once, a long, long time ago.

"Bert," John said, overcome with a sudden clarity, "could this be . . ." He paused, biting his lip. "Is this Atlantis?"

Bert took a breath before replying, his expression more wistful than remorseful. "It was, my boy. It was."

"Paralon is the seat of government here," Bert began, in explanation of the Morgaine's prophecy. "It has ever been so, since the reign of the first king to unite both worlds: the High King—Arthur Pendragon.

"The descendants of his bloodline ruled justly and well for centuries, until the last king was murdered nearly two decades ago. Ever since, the leadership of the Archipelago has been in question. That's one of the reasons you are needed now, John. A crisis is at hand—and the resolution will have repercussions both in this world and in your own."

"Why is it only now that I'm needed?" said John. "Surely Professor Sigurdsson could have done whatever was needed years ago, if the situation is as dire as you say."

"He could have, true," said Bert, "save for two conditions that have never before been present. To start, this is not the first time a king has been killed. As in your world, it does happen—usually by a relative who aspires to ascend to the throne. But in this case, the rest of his family was murdered as well. There *are* no heirs."

"What's the second point?" asked Charles.

"You already know, after a fashion," said Bert. "His minions tried to kill you last night.

"What his true name is, no one knows. But in the Archipelago, he is known as the Winter King.

"In the absence of a High King, a Parliament of minor kings

and queens govern Paralon," said Bert, "while a successor is determined. But with no apparent heir, it has been an ongoing debate—one that the Winter King is determined to end by eliminating all other challengers to the throne.

"There are kings of other races who could assume the Silver Throne of Paralon—but tradition is not easily dismissed. The Winter King is human and is still subject to the ruling of the Parliament. What is occurring today is a Great Council—all the kings of all the races of the Archipelago are coming together with the Parliament to determine who should assume the throne."

"Well, then," said Charles, "you ought to trust the Parliament. They've held him off this long—can't they continue to do so, until a successor can be chosen?"

"No," said Bert. "They can't wait any longer, because of *that*," he said, pointing at the southern horizon. There was a black smudge against the water, below the cloud line. It was as if someone had taken a paintbrush to the landscape and obliterated some of the scenery.

Jack said as much, and Bert nodded in agreement. "More true than you know, young Jack.

"We call them the Shadowed Lands—the islands conquered by the Winter King. When he and his armies take them, they disappear from the cycle of life in the Archipelago—and then they disappear from the *Geographica* as well."

"If he's in the process of erasing it," said John, "then why is he willing to kill us for it?"

"No one knows," said Bert. "It is the greatest mystery of the Archipelago. But we do know that he is amassing power—power that would give him greater influence than any other king or ruler in this land, or," he added, "in others."

"Do you mean . . ." Charles began.

"The worlds are separate, but what happens in one affects the other," said Bert. "Arthur knew this, and established a throne to rule them both. Do you think it coincidence that in the time the Silver Throne of Paralon has been empty, your world has erupted in war?"

"Speaking of Paralon," said Aven, "it's about time our 'Caretaker' gave us some direction. The morning light is coming up, and while the *Indigo Dragon* can find the way, it'll be easier to navigate if she can be given a few specifics."

"Oh, uh, yes, of course," said John when he realized she was talking about him. At Bert's urging he unwrapped the *Geographica* and began thumbing through the pages. After a few minutes, he came to a large page of parchment with a heading that translated roughly to "Paralon," along with extensive annotations that included nautical instructions. He furrowed his brow in concentration. "It's, ah—it's all in Old Saxon."

"Is that a problem?" asked Aven.

"Ah—no, no, not really," said John. He examined the annotations for a few moments more, then looked around at the expectant faces. "It says, ah—it says we should be going, ah, that way," he finished, waving vaguely to the starboard side of the ship.

Aven raised an eyebrow in surprise, but Bert nodded to her, and she began instructing the crew to turn the *Indigo Dragon* in that direction.

Nervously, John wrapped up the *Geographica* and tucked it under his arm.

* * *

"You're one of the three Caretakers," Charles said to Bert. "So why did you need John? Why couldn't you simply have left London once you had it?"

"Being the Caretaker Principia requires a lifetime of study," said Bert. "I myself have some skill and knowledge, but honestly, I simply don't have the training—which is why Professor Sigurdsson retired, so that he could begin to train his eventual replacement. You, John."

"What about the third Caretaker?" said Charles. "You said there were always three."

Aven cursed and spit. "Useless as a buck centaur in a dairy, that one. If he had taken his responsibilities more seriously, then *you*"—she pointed at her father—"wouldn't be in danger, and *your* mentor"—pointing at John—"wouldn't be dead, and you"—again jabbing a finger at John—"would still be doing whatever it is you do."

"Now, Aven," Bert chided, "Jamie has his own life to lead, and we can't begrudge him that. Not everyone is made for this sort of adventure."

"That's what makes me angry," she said. "Jamie *was*. He *was* suited to this, father. And he gave up a lifetime in the Archipelago for playacting in Kensington Gardens."

"Is it me," Jack confided to Charles, "or do I sense a hint of spurned romance in her anger?"

Jack wasn't quiet enough; Aven overheard him and shot him a venomous look before flinging her father's arm off her shoulders and storming into the cabin.

An instant later they heard her curse loudly, followed by a flurry of shouting and banging. Before anyone could move, she reemerged from the cabin, breathing hard and red faced from exertion.

"Some men weren't made for adventure," Aven snorted, "and some boys don't know when they've had too much."

Under her arm, face purpling from the headlock in which she had him, was Bug.

They had a stowaway.

Having an extra person on board did not present any particular problems, although Aven did suggest throwing him overboard, just to save the debate. Bert suspected that the errand to fetch fresh water had been a ruse to allow the boy to sneak on board, and said so.

Charles shook his head. "Frenchmen."

"To what end?" said John. "If the knight thought Bug should go with us, why not simply ask?"

"I beg your pardon," said Aven. "I don't recall giving you any authority to say what does or doesn't happen aboard *my* ship."

"Well, he's here now," said Charles. "What do we do with him?"

"Just what we need," grumbled Jack. "A child to look after."

Bug's eyes narrowed. "I'm no younger than you."

"Young enough, potboy," Jack shot back.

"That's enough," said John. "I'll take him on as my, uh . . ."

"Squire?" offered Charles.

"Whatever," said Aven. "Just keep him out of the way." She leaned down as one of the fauns whispered something in her ear. "No," she said, straightening up and looking at Bug. "You can't feed him to the mermaids. Yet."

Bug looked at John. "She's joking, surely?"

"Probably," said John. "But keep close to me anyway."

A shout from the crew brought them all to the port side of the ship, as the water began to roil with activity. Something large was rising from under the sea.

"A whale?" asked Jack.

"Too big," said Charles.

"Just watch," Bert said, smiling, as the shape, now obvious as some kind of construct, rose from the water.

Jack and Charles stood speechless in the embrace of the growing shadow. Rising alongside the *Indigo Dragon* was the magnificent, gleaming, golden hull of a ship that was unlike anything they had ever seen. It had no masts or sails and seemed enclosed, like the submarines they'd heard of from the American Civil War. There were huge fortified portholes along the sides, and various openings below the waterline that both drew in and expelled water. And fore, on the hull, was the upper body and head of a dragon. A metallic gangplank slid seamlessly from an opening in the hull and attached itself to the railing of the *Indigo Dragon*. Above, a panel slid silently open and an impressive figure filled the open doorway.

"Dear God in Heaven," John said as he tried to take in the remarkable sight before them. "Is that what I think it is?"

"It is indeed," said Bert. "Boys, I would like to introduce you to the captain of the greatest ship to sail on the oceans of any world—the *Nautilus*."

A swarthy, bearded man with glistening, dark skin stepped off the gangplank and put his hands together, inclining his head in the Hindu fashion.

He smiled, and while not unfriendly, it was undoubtedly the smile of a predator. "Captain Nemo, at your service."

Everyone was introduced, including Bug, who got a long, curious look from Nemo.

"We're going to the council at Paralon," said Bert.

"As am I," Nemo replied. "There are restless forces growing in the lands to the north and the south, which must be quelled if we're to unite against the Winter King.

"A caution, though—you're going to catch the currents off the Shadowed Lands if you keep heading in this direction, and you'll miss Paralon altogether. I thought your captain was better trained than that."

Aven blushed and scowled at John and her father in turn. "How far off are we?"

"Five degrees to the south should correct your course."

Aven withdrew to change the course of the ship, and Nemo's eye caught sight of the *Geographica* under John's arm.

"Would that parcel hold the *Geographica*?" he asked.

"The *Imaginarium Geographica*, yes," said John.

For the first time, Nemo spoke with a slight hesitation in his voice. "May I—may I touch it, Master John?"

"Certainly."

John again unwrapped the *Geographica* and proffered it to Nemo, who accepted it as if he were holding a fragile parchment that would crumble if he breathed on it the wrong way.

"It's been through a lot," Charles said. "It's sturdy. Won't break, I assure you."

"You misunderstand my care," said Nemo. "To those of us in the Archipelago, it is a holy book. Here in these lands there are a thousand different worlds, a thousand cultures. Some are united by fealty, some by commerce. But the only thing that unites us all, the only Grail that can strengthen us by drawing the disparities closer, is the *Imaginarium Geographica*."

"Then every time the Winter King conquers a land . . . ," Charles began.

"Yes," Nemo said, nodding. "The corresponding map vanishes, and we take another step backward to the barbarian cultures that gave birth to us."

"You could always just destroy it," Bug offered, before being silenced by Jack with a poke in the ribs.

Instead of responding in anger to the suggestion, Nemo nodded his assent. "It's been suggested, boy, and tried. As valuable as it is, it may be better for the lands to lose it, if it means the Winter King cannot have it."

To underscore his answer, Nemo suddenly stepped in front of Aven and dropped the *Geographica* on the hot brazier that sat mid-deck.

There were shouts of dismay and disbelief, and John leaped forward to retrieve it before it burned.

But there was no need to worry. The coals were blazing, but they did no more than singe the outer layer of oilcloth.

"Magic," breathed Jack.

"Yes," said Nemo. "The *Imaginarium Geographica* cannot be destroyed—which makes proper stewardship of it both a blessing and a burden.

"Guard it well, lad," Nemo continued, dusting off the ash and returning the book to John. "It is a great responsibility to be the heart of the compass. But I knew your teacher, and while I mourn his passing, I sense that he chose his successor wisely and well."

Nemo turned to Bert and gripped his forearms, then kissed Aven on the cheek before leaping back to the gangplank.

"Be well, my friends," he said as the ship pulled away. "I'll see you soon."

As the *Nautilus* departed, Aven cornered John and demanded an explanation. "We're lucky he came along," she said, eyes flashing with anger. "Five degrees would have put us in the North Sea. We would have lost an entire day and missed the Council at Paralon altogether."

She gestured brusquely at the *Geographica*. "Can you read that thing or not?"

"Of course he can," Bug said. "He just needs some practice, right, Sir John?"

Aven snorted at the honorarium, but Bert voiced his agreement with the boy. "He's had a rough time of it, daughter. But he'll be up to the task in short order, of that we can be sure."

Wordless, Aven went back about her work, followed eagerly by Jack.

"Perhaps you should spend some time in the cabin studying the *Geographica*," Bert suggested to John. "Just to become better acquainted with it."

John nodded. "That's not a bad idea. At least then maybe then I'll look smarter if Phileas Fogg stops by to correct my navigation."

"Never happen," said Bert. "Fogg hates sailing."

"Speaking of which," said Charles, who was looking aft, "I daresay Nemo must have forgotten something—he's coming back."

"What?" Aven said. "He's ahead of us. He wouldn't be approaching from the east." She shoved Charles roughly aside and peered through a spyglass toward where he'd been pointing.

"That's not the *Nautilus*," Aven said. "It seems our enemy has decided to step out of the shadows and make his intentions clear."

The fog parted, and a massive hull, broader and more forbidding than the *Nautilus* came into view.

It was the *Black Dragon*—the ship of the Winter King. And it was pointed at the *Indigo Dragon* at ramming speed.

"What do we do?" said Charles.

"Find something that's bolted down and hold on," said Bert. "Let Aven do her job—there's nothing the rest of us can do now."

"In London the ship pulled away from the docks against the wind," said Charles. "Can't it just, ah, twist out of the way and avoid being struck?"

"She's a ship, not a cat," said Bert, "and the fact that she has a will of her own doesn't mean she can pirouette on demand."

Aven was running back and forth across the deck and shouting orders, a frantic note in her voice. The ship of the Winter King was five times the size of the *Indigo Dragon*. The smaller craft would not survive a collision. But that, John surmised as he wrapped his arms around a section of rigging, was the point.

The only chance to even survive the initial impact would be to turn the ship as the *Black Dragon* reached them—but there was no way to reorient the sails to do so. Not in the seconds that remained.

This was apparent to everyone but Jack.

In his youth he'd spent a summer with a tutor who sailed, and who loved to play just such a game of daring, only to tack into the wind at the last instant and avoid the collision.

Easy with a skiff—not so easy with a galleon. Still, Jack thought it was worth a try.

Leaping atop the cabin, he grabbed a short cutlass from a surprised crewman and began severing the lines that held down the starboard side of the sails.

Aven looked on, incredulous. "Are you insane? If you cut those, the sails will . . ."

She realized suddenly what he was doing and ordered all of the crewmen to help him.

The gleaming black hull was bearing down on them with terrifying speed, but in seconds all the lines had been severed and the sails snapped around from the force of the wind. "Now!" Jack screamed. "Tack into it! Hit the rudder, hard as you can!"

At once Aven, John, and Charles threw themselves onto the wheel and yanked it around. With a horrible groan of straining wood and metal, the ship wrenched around to face the *Black Dragon* just as it reached them—and passed by, with only inches to spare.

"That was the stupidest thing I've ever seen in my life," Aven called out to Jack. But while her tone was harsh, she was smiling as she said it, and his heart soared.

The companions looked up as the nightmare ship glided by, its deck populated with the worst sort of brigands and scoundrels—including Wendigo—all too surprised that the ship was still there to sling spears and fire arrows.

As it passed, Aven's stern countenance returned. "Jack saved us for the moment, but it's going to take time to repair the riggings, and they'll have wheeled about by then, even at that speed. Then they'll have us."

"I'd hate to be wrong about this twice," said Charles, "but now I'm quite certain that the *Nautilus* has indeed come back."

Approaching at a speed greater than that of the *Black Dragon,* Nemo's ship had in fact reappeared to the north of them and was swiftly drawing alongside the *Indigo Dragon.*

"I will never again disparage the work of Jules Verne," said Charles.

"Right there with you," said John.

"Were you this much trouble when you were first mate aboard the *Nautilus?*" Nemo called out to Aven, grinning.

"No," Aven shouted in response. "But it was only called the *Yellow Dragon* then, and neither of us had developed our delusions of grandeur."

"Get your crew working on the riggings. What happened to them, anyway?"

Aven gestured at Jack. "That idiot cut the lines. It never would have occurred to me, but it saved the ship."

Nemo tipped his head at Jack. "Well done, young warrior. And now," he concluded as, in the distance, the *Black Dragon* had turned and was regaining speed, "it seems I have a battle to fight."

"Nemo," Aven began.

"No," he said, cutting her off. "You carry the *Geographica.* Get it and the Caretaker to Paralon. I'll keep the Winter King occupied long enough to let you escape."

Nemo held a clenched fist across his chest—a gesture of respect, captain to captain.

Aven returned the gesture and, shouting orders to her crew,

turned the *Indigo Dragon* back with the wind. The ship, intuitive as ever, called upon her unique motive power and made full speed away from the fray.

Several leagues away from the battle, the damage to the ship had been assessed, and to everyone's relief, it was minimal. With the repairs underway, Aven turned her attention, and her fury, to John.

"Enough of this! This is the second time I've risked my ship for you, and I've yet to see the reason why."

Bert tried to intercede, but she was having none of it. "Not this time, Father. You've made all the excuses for him I can stomach.

"Every captain has maps of their own lands in the Archipelago, as well as of adjacent islands. Every captain, including the Winter King, can find their way around by trial and error. But only one atlas exists that contains them all, and only it can get us to where we need to be, when we need to be there. And only one person alive has been schooled and trained in the ancient languages and cultures that will allow him to interpret the directions in that atlas.

"Well," she said, thumping a fist on the *Geographica*, "*this* is that atlas. And *you*," she said jabbing a finger at John, "are the Caretaker. So can you read it or not?"

Defeated, John lowered his eyes in shame. "I can't. I don't know how."

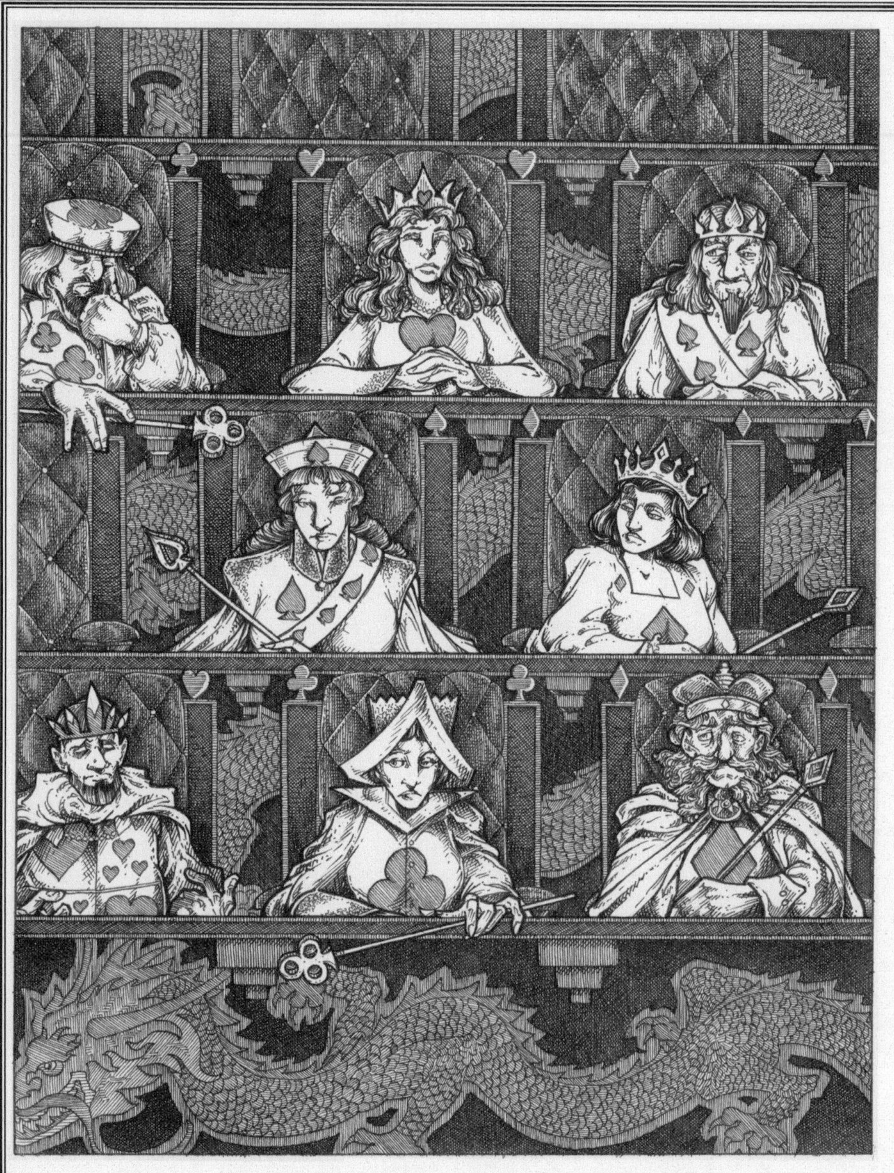

. . . the members of the Parliament filed in and took their seats . . .

Chapter Six
The Tick-Tock Parliament

"If that is true, then we may be lost," said Bert. "Only a trained Caretaker can properly navigate a ship through the Archipelago of Dreams. The maps and notations are in a dozen languages, many of them long dead. There are very few people living who could make any sense of it at all."

The lines could not have been more clearly drawn: Aven, Bert, and, and surprisingly, Jack on one side; John, Charles, and Bug on the other.

"Jack?" Charles said, a note of astonished surprise in his voice. "You can't be siding with them. After all . . ." He began to say something, then seemed to reconsider, adding only a soft admonishment. "Bad form, Jack."

"But Aven's right," said Jack. "We were chased out of London, running for our very lives, all because of him and that book. His teacher was killed for it. The entire *Indigo Dragon* was nearly just destroyed for it. And this entire . . . wherever we are, may be going to war over it. And he's supposed to be the only one alive who can read it, and he's failed."

"Jack!" Charles said. "That's quite enough."

"But he's right," said John. "I have failed."

Aven swore and reached for her broadsword, but Bert interceded and held her arm. "There has to be an explanation, Aven. I'm the one who chose him.

"John," Bert said, unable to hide the pleading in his voice, "I have read your work. You have the gift, I know it. And Stellan knew it too. That's why he agreed to take you on. Why, I've seen the correspondence myself—he *was* training you."

"Yes," John said, "he was. But I wasn't learning—not as I should have, at any rate."

He turned to Charles and Jack, resigned. "It never seemed to be important," he explained. "Ancient languages that no one else could read . . . Who could have imagined there would ever be a need? My friends at home, even my wife—they all questioned the wisdom of spending so much time on what seemed to be impractical pursuits."

"Not so impractical now, is it?" Jack said.

"For God's sake, Jack," said John. "There is a war on! I could hardly be expected to spend what little free time I had reading and translating manuscripts in Old Teutonic."

"Men will die because you didn't," Aven said. "And perhaps already have."

"He doesn't care," Jack said.

"Yes, I do!" John shouted, grabbing Jack by the coat. "I do care, you fool! I have seen men die! I have felt the spray of their blood on my face as men I laughed with, ate with, sheltered with, died in front of me! Can you say the same?"

They were both shaking. John's face had broken out in a sweat, and his breathing was fast and shallow. After a moment he released Jack and dropped his head into his hands.

"I'm sorry, Jack," John said after a time. "I do feel as if I've failed all of you—but the professor most of all. Believe me, I didn't know . . . I never knew what—"

"Enough, John," said Charles, putting his arm around his companion's shoulder. "Let's all take a little while to compose ourselves, and then maybe we can have a look and decipher it together. Three heads are better than one, and all that. What do you say, Jack?"

But when they looked up, Jack and Aven had already moved to another part of the ship, commiserating. Bert stood in the doorway of the cabin, eyes downcast, caught in the middle of his hope and his fear. Only Bug remained with them, wanting to help, but obviously swept up in something bigger than his experience could provide for.

The fellowship had been broken. And there was nothing any of them could do but continue sailing toward Paralon.

Despite his positive demeanor, after an hour with the *Geographica* even Charles had to admit he was at a loggerheads with it. His editorial position at the Oxford University Press had allowed him a great deal of experience with Latin, so those passages and some of the Greek phrases were not totally undecipherable—not that it helped much.

"I also get a smattering of Old English, and a few words of Hebrew, but the rest is dead impossible," said Charles. "There are a great deal of annotations in modern English, but there's no hierarchy to it, no order, other than a rough chronological one."

This pronouncement did little to assuage John's melancholy mood, or Jack's defiant one. Bert was still subdued, but hopeful.

"Look," he said, "since Paralon is the 'capital' of the Archipelago, its map has been extensively annotated in English.

"I myself have added to the listing, so I can read most of it myself from past experience. Besides," he added, "we're already pointed in the right direction, so we should make it that far without incident. After we're there, then perhaps we can locate a scholar, or appeal to the Parliament for access to the king's archives and library for help.

"Cheer up lad," he finished. "We still have options."

"Maybe," Bug offered from the nook in the cabin where he'd been observing, "the Council will decide on a new king, and you won't have to worry about it anymore."

"Think good thoughts, lad," Bert said as he left the cabin, closing the door behind him.

The sun was nearing the apex of its arc across the sky when the crewman in the crow's nest called out, "Land, ho!"

They had arrived at Paralon.

The island was far larger than Avalon, or any of the Shadowed Lands they had passed. In the distance a mountain range could be made out, as well as the dark greens of what could only be great forests. The vista was stunning enough that even the taciturn fauns paused in their labors to watch as they approached.

The harbor toward which they sailed was formed around a natural river basin that emptied into the sea, just deep enough for ships to moor. The ground beyond sloped up gently to a landscape of low rolling hills and fields, then abruptly shifted to a domineering ridge of plateaus that rose straight up from the valley floor.

On the tallest of these stood a massive stone fortress, gray and forbidding: The Castle of Paralon, wherein sat the Silver Throne of the High King of the Archipelago.

This was not Camelot, as they had suspected it might resemble, but something far more primal, which shimmered with the raw energies of living myth. It was the archetype of archetypes; Paralon was the reality that the legend of Camelot aspired to be.

"Dear Lord," Charles breathed. "It's magnificent."

John and Jack both nodded in agreement. Even Mad King Ludwig had never imagined a castle such as this.

"There are a number of ships in the harbor," Aven noted. "The council may already have begun."

"So this Paralon," Charles said as they began to disembark, "is the largest military power in the Archipelago?"

"Why would you think that?" Bert said in surprise.

"How else would it become the locus of power?"

"See those forests in the distance?" Bert asked. "Apple orchards—hundreds, if not thousands, of years old. Military might is transferable, losable, comes and goes. But good produce," he finished with a wink, "good produce is very difficult to attain."

Jack busied himself trying to be helpful to Aven, who did her best to ignore him without seeming to. His reckless but successful move during the encounter with the Winter King, as well as his sympathetic distancing from John, had emboldened him, much to her dismay.

Bert helped a still downcast John secure the *Geographica* inside a sturdy leather case with straps that could be slung over his shoulders for easier carrying, which Bug offered to do. He took his role as John's squire seriously and was attentive to any ways he might be helpful. Besides, there was no way to suggest that he stay behind—not when the prospect of seeing real knights and kings lay before him.

Charles was already at the far end of the dock, where a small figure was cursing and banging at the insides of an odd contraption that appeared to be the offspring of a clockwork automobile and Cinderella's pumpkin carriage.

"Keep at it," Charles said. "I'm sure you'll get whatever the trouble is sorted out."

"I'll do my best, which is all any of us can do, in't it?" came the reply.

Charles yelped and jumped back as he realized the creature that had answered him was not a man, or even one of the fauns.

It was a badger. In a vest and waistcoat, walking upright, with a pince-nez in one eye and spats on both furred feet.

Charles was still stammering in disbelief as the others came up behind.

"A waistcoat, but no trousers?" John asked.

"It's very impolite to take notice," said Bert.

"Be ye royalty types, or officious emissaries?" the badger asked.

"Scholars," said Charles. "We be . . . ah, that is, we *are* scholars."

"Scowlers, are ye?" said the badger. "And whereabouts do you do yer scowlerin'?"

"Ah, Oxford, actually," Charles said.

The animal seemed to take this as a matter of course. "Oh yes, Oxford. A place of scowlerly knowledge and Druidcraft. Lord Pryderi of the race of Man was an Oxford scowler."

"And you," said Jack. "What's your name?"

"Pardon my manners, young scowler," said the badger with a gesture that was halfway between a squat and a bow. "I be called Tummeler, and Tummeler is me."

"Pleased to meet you, Mr. Tummeler," said Jack, who, to the badger's delight, shook his proffered paw. "I'm Jack. These lot are my friends and fellow, ah, 'scowlers,' John, and Charles, and our captain, Aven. The fellow with the hat is Bert."

"Welcome, scowler Jack and all," said Tummeler. "Be ye here for the Council?"

"We are," said Bert. "Has it begun?"

"Not yet," said Tummeler, "as a number of designates such as y'rselves are only just arrived, and the Council at Paralon asked ol' Tummeler to escort any last-minute princely sorts and emissaries as may be expectin' to attend."

He beckoned at them with a paw and turned away. "This way, if you please, young scowlers and company. The Council awaits."

In short order Tummeler had the vehicle running (with a discreet assist from Aven, who didn't want to embarrass the small mammal in front of visitors by pointing out that a clump of badger fur was obscuring one of the contacts in the engine) and they started across the valley to the castle.

"We calls 'em principles," said Tummeler, referring to the steam-belching vehicle in which they traveled. "As in, 'you can get from here to there, but it's easier to do it with principles.' That's in general. This 'un," he continued proudly, "I calls the Curious Diversity."

"Fascinating," said Charles. "How does it run?"

"Well enough for all practical porpoises," said Tummeler.

"No—I mean, what gives it motive power?"

"We gots to go somewheres," Tummeler replied. "What gives *you* motive power?"

"I—I just decide to go where I need to, and then I do," Charles stammered.

"Well, it's the same with principles," said Tummeler, "'cept I do the decidin'."

Aven smiled. "It's a design manufactured by one of *his* predecessors," she said, tilting her chin at John. "There is an element of steam involved, and often electricity, but no one truly knows how they run. Bacon only passed on the secret of their construction to certain animals and to Nemo. The animals can't explain it well enough, and Nemo has never shared."

"Bacon?" said John. "Do you mean Roger Bacon, the Franciscan friar? He was a Caretaker too?"

Tummeler nodded. "As I be telling you—always good eggs they be, those Oxford scowlers."

The Curious Diversity passed through an immense stone gate, bracketed by two equally massive statues. The statues' left hands were outstretched in a gesture of warding; their right hands were held closer to the breast in a gesture of beckoning.

"Th' Great Kings of Paralon," said Tummeler. "There be two outside each of the gates as th' compass spins—east, west, north, and south."

"Incredible," said John.

"Hah!" said Tummeler. "Wait'll y' see th' Great Hall."

When the Silver Throne was first established, Bert explained as they traveled, Arthur ruled from a modest castle on the island of Avalon. It was his eldest son, Artigel, who moved the seat of rule to Paralon, where he enlisted the Dwarves to build a great city.

The streets were paved, and as they entered they saw a number of other principles, each of their own unique make, chugging along the roadways. The buildings they passed were white stone and glass, and all were topped with soaring roofs and towers.

The main castle, which they had sighted from the harbor, was not built atop the plateau, but carved from it, into it, through it. It was a remarkable feat of engineering. Tummeler parked the Curious Diversity on a broad avenue at the intersection of streets below the towering edifice and motioned them to a bridge that led to two great applewood doors.

"Here," he said, gesturing with a paw. "I'll be waitin' here f'r when all's said an' all's done. One word of warning," the badger added. "Watch out for one in partic'lar. Th' one called Arawn, that is. Eldest son of the old Troll King Sarum. He's a bad 'un. Bad from the get-go, and bad to the core. He's been calling for a full council for several years, and he has made it no secret that he thinks the time of Men is past, and a new High King should be chosen from one of the other races.

"It don't take a scowler," Tummeler finished, "to guess who he thinks should get the job. Good luck to you all, master scowlers."

There were a thousand different races in the Archipelago, Bert explained—more if you included the animals. But only the four great races were allowed to send formal emissaries to the Council: the Trolls, the Goblins, the Elves, and the Dwarves.

The fifth race, Men, convened the council out of sheer tradition.

Despite the occasional conflicts that arose, all of the races respected Arthur's lineage, and had accorded that respect to the Parliament during the years since the murder of the old king and his family. But they had grown restless, and each race wanted to claim the Silver Throne for their own.

"Are we going to be allowed?" Charles asked. "We are neither royalty nor emissaries."

"We'll be allowed," said Bert. "I have some standing with the Parliament, and *he*, after all," he said, tapping John on the shoulder, "is the Caretaker."

Aven rolled her eyes and cursed under her breath.

"At least," Bert added, "he is the bearer of the *Imaginarium Geographica*. That alone gives him, and you all, a degree of status."

John sighed and looked at Bug, who smiled supportively.

Together, they entered the Great Hall of Paralon.

Tummeler had not overspoken. The Great Hall was a sight stunning in its grandeur.

Each entry from the four points of the compass opened through arches a hundred feet high, bracketing a great gallery of boxfront seats. Far, far above, the ceiling ended in a crystal window that may have been set atop the plateau itself. Carved into all of the pillars were alcoves bearing torches, illuminating the entire hall in a brilliant white light. It was, in a word, spectacular.

"The Winter King will never get the throne," Jack murmured to Charles.

"Why not?"

"Because," said Jack, "he'd have to repaint everything *black*."

About half of the seats in the gallery were taken. Bert led the companions to a staircase behind one of the pillars on the left, and they climbed to an open cluster of seats about a third of the way up.

"The central seating is reserved for the human Parliament," Bert explained. "They've yet to arrive, which is good—we've not come too late."

The elves took up the seats to the right of center; they represented the largest number of delegates from any race. They were slender, fair-haired, and fair-skinned, and they bore the aloof demeanor of a race that rarely saw death.

The dwarves sat to the left, above and around the companions. They were shorter and stocky, and well armed. Not a single delegate carried less than two short swords, as well as bows and braces of arrows.

"Keep on their good side," Bert warned. "They're a testy lot. Like to pick fights—mostly with elves, though. It's a height thing."

"So, uh, you lot built this place, eh?" Jack said to the dwarf sitting three seats over.

"Yes," said the dwarf.

"Uh, nice work," said Jack.

"Humph," snorted the dwarf.

Bert raised a hand in greeting and saw the gesture returned by a greasy, gnarled man dressed in elaborate silken robes sitting high in the center of the gallery.

"Uruk Ko, the Goblin King," said Bert in explanation. "And entourage."

"A Goblin King?" John whispered in distaste.

"Oh, he's an affable enough sort," said Bert. "Stellan—Professor

Sigurdsson—and I once shared a long voyage with him in the southern isles on a ship called the *Aurora*. It was meant to be an exploratory expedition—mapping for the *Geographica* and whatnot—that somehow turned into an adventure all of its own.

"But," he concluded, shrugging, "that's the sort of thing that happens when the captain is a talking mouse."

Directly opposite the goblins in the great hall, sitting low in the gallery, was a bulky, dark-visaged personage that could only have been a troll. Thick, corded arms were folded against a massive chest, which was further plated with heavy leather armor. His bearing and manner, as well as the number of supplicants crowded around his elevated chair, indicated that he was in all likelihood a creature of high status, if not the Troll King himself.

"I don't know him," Bert said. "Those of the Troll race tend to keep to themselves in the eastern isles of the Archipelago."

"One guess," said John. "I'll bet that's Tummeler's Arawn."

"Quiet," said Bert. "The Parliament is arriving."

Entering from a fifth entrance between the east and north gates, the representatives of the Parliament were dressed according to the suits in a deck of cards: clubs, spades, diamonds, and hearts. Somberly, they marched in, looking neither right nor left.

Bert's brow furrowed as the members of the Parliament filed in and took their seats with the rest of the Council.

"What is it?" John whispered.

"Can't say," Bert replied. "Something is amiss, although I can't quite put my finger on it."

They watched in silence as the elaborately dressed men and

women settled into their places in the gallery. At length a shifty yet officious-looking man—the Steward of Paralon, Bert said—strode to the center of the hall and called for order.

"As Steward of Paralon, I shall oversee these proceedings," he began. "In the absence of a legitimate heir to the Silver Throne, the Parliament, under my guidance, has ruled Paralon and with it, the Archipelago.

"Now a claim has been made on the throne. A claim of birthright and blood."

At this there was a great deal of murmuring from the gallery. "What's that about?" John whispered. "I thought all the heirs were dead."

"I don't know," said Bert. "Listen."

"The claim," the Steward continued, "has been approved by the Parliament. If none dissent, by the end of the day we shall have a new High King."

Calls rang out to the Steward, who waited for the cacophony to die down before addressing them again.

"The claim," he said, "has been made by one of Arthur's own kinsmen, and as such ought not to be disputed. While he has had no previous standing with this body, he has nevertheless come to be known by most of you . . .

". . . as the Winter King."

"Wait," boomed a voice. It was Bert. "May I speak?"

The Steward grimaced. "The Parliament . . . ," he began.

"The Parliament," said Bert, "called a council to debate the matter of succession. Whether or not there is an heir, as you say, we should be allowed to address them."

"By what right," asked the Steward, "do you speak?"

"I am one of the Caretakers of the *Imaginarium Geographica*," said Bert, "and the other sits beside me."

This brought many nods, mostly friendly, from the throng. The Steward shook his head. "I appreciate your desire to participate," he began to say.

"Let him speak," came a gruff voice. It was Uruk Ko, the Goblin King.

The Steward could bluff and bluster past most of those assembled; he could not, however, stare down an actual king of an entire race. Reluctantly, he bowed and stepped to the side of the hall, casting nervous glances up at the Parliament members.

Bert stood in the center of the Great Hall and faced the gallery. "Ladies and gentlemen of the Parliament," he began, "I have had direct and recent experience with the man called the Winter King. . . ." But before he could continue, he was cut off by the King of Diamonds, who stood and shook his fist at the other man.

"Unacceptable," said the king. "The Parliament cannot accept the proposal."

"Did he make a proposal?" John whispered to Charles. "If so, I missed it."

Bert seemed similarly puzzled. "Your Majesty, if I have presumed too much—"

"Yes, entirely out of the question," the king continued, as if he had not heard Bert at all. "A Walrus as High King is preposterous. And everyone knows a Carpenter cannot be High Queen—if we allowed that, then who would organize all of the dances?"

"This is very strange," said Charles.

"Shush," said Jack. "Look—another king is rising to speak."

The King of Spades raised a hand. "Please don't fire the

cannons," he said, "or I shall never be able to remove the potatoes from my ears."

The dwarves had begun to murmur, as if they too sensed all was not well.

"They're all mad," said Jack. "What is this?"

"I don't know," said Aven. "Something is very wrong."

The Steward was about to escort Bert off the floor, when the Queen of Clubs's head caught fire. The flames shot high into the air, and yet she remained seated, hands folded, a gentle smile on her face, as if nothing were amiss.

The murmuring that began with the dwarves had now spread to the elves and goblins. And the trolls were beginning to unsheathe their weapons.

The Queen of Hearts, a portly, dark-haired woman, picked up a croquet mallet from under her seat and smashed the King of Hearts in the chest. "I hate roses," she said. "They never speak when spoken to."

Bert looked around, but the Steward had disappeared. All throughout the seats, the delegates were rising to their feet, shouting.

One of the trolls overcame his forced decorum and threw a mace directly at the Queen of Hearts. With the impact, her chest split open and spilled a cascade of wheels and cogs onto the floor of the hall, showering the nearby delegates in an explosion of sparks.

The Parliament members were not human at all. They were clockwork constructs.

"A fraud!" boomed the Troll Prince Arawn, standing and shaking his armored fist. "The Council is a fraud!"

In moments the entire Great Hall of Paralon had erupted in chaos.

"Quickly!" Tummeler shouted. "Master scowlers! Get in, get in!"

Chapter Seven

The Forbidden Path

The smoke was acrid, and it filled John's nose, mouth, and lungs. Desperately, he covered his head with his arms and burrowed more deeply into the muddy French soil.

The shelling had been relentless. And just as it seemed the travails could grow no worse, the telltale fog of the Gas came wafting malevolently through the shattered trees.

Screaming, John leaped to his feet and began to run, only to be caught up in the rolls of concertina wire that had been strung along the rear trenches. All around him were bloated bodies of the dead, lying in a landscape blackened, stripped bare of life. Helplessly, he could only watch as the Gas crept closer, accompanied by the increasingly thunderous sound of the artillery: *Boom. Boom. Boom . . .*

Boom.

"John!" said a voice he knew, but it was not that of any soldier in his battalion. "John, for God's sake, pull yourself together!"

John shook his head, blinking, as he came to his senses and his vision cleared. Charles was grasping him by the shoulders, shaking him and shouting his name. His other companions were making their way to the exit under the sparse cover of the boxfronts of the seats. Incredulous, he looked around at the maelstrom of weapon play, flames, grappling bodies, and furious shouting that had moments before been the Grand Council.

There was no sign of the goblins; and the last of the elves were just departing under the cover of the northern arch. The dwarves had spread across the gallery and had begun hurling explosive bundles at the troll delegates, as more and more trolls flooded through the southern and eastern entrances. The trolls had clambered into the center seats and had smashed the members of the Clockwork Parliament to pieces. In the uppermost part of the gallery, bellowing directions to his arriving reinforcements, was the Troll Prince Arawn.

More than one treachery had been planned for that day, it seemed.

"That's why there were so many ships in the harbor," Aven said to Bert. "The Trolls planned a revolt no matter what happened in the Council."

Bert nodded in agreement, as he and Charles supported the dazed John under his shoulders and moved lower toward the western arch. "The Steward of Paralon just beat them to the punch," he said. "This may be the Archipelago's undoing."

"What's wrong with *him*?" Jack said, scowling at John.

"The explosions," Charles said. "He's gone into a bit of battle shock."

"I'll be all right," John said, attempting to regain his footing. "Really."

Aven glared and Jack's eyes narrowed in disgust as John shook off Charles and Bert's assistance. "Let's get out of here," Aven hissed through gritted teeth, "before the whole place comes down around our ears."

• • •

The companions raced down the corridor toward the avenue where they'd left Tummeler and his vehicle. Around them members of all the races ran about, trying to ascertain what had happened. Behind them, in the Great Hall, there were more explosions, and the smell of smoke.

"The trolls will almost certainly have blockaded the harbor," said Aven. "Our best bet is to try to get out of the city proper, and then circle back when the tumult's died down."

"*If* it dies down," said Jack.

"What of the *Indigo Dragon*?" asked Charles, panting. "Will it be torched?"

"No," said Aven. "She can take care of herself. She'll already be out of harm's way."

They reached the end of the corridor, bursting through the doors and into the open, where Tummeler already had the Curious Diversity waiting, its engine running.

"Quickly!" Tummeler shouted. "Master scowlers! Get in, get in!"

In a confusion of limbs the companions threw themselves into the seats of the principle. "North!" Aven shouted. "Take us north!"

Tires squealing, Tummeler pulled onto the northern thoroughfare and sped away from the towers.

It took several minutes to actually escape the confines of the walled city, and several minutes more to pass the last of the outposts where they might have been stopped. As luck would have it, all of the guards and sentries that might have held them in their flight had gone toward the heart of the conflict at the Great Hall.

John's earlier panic had subsided into a feverish slumber, interrupted only by occasional shakes of his limbs.

"Fever dreams, that is," Tummeler said, looking over his shoulder and clucking his tongue. "What ails master John?"

Talking in turns, Bert and Aven explained to Tummeler what had taken place at the Grand Council. When they got to the part about the Parliament, the small mammal cut in and changed the subject.

"Ah, I knowed there be trouble afoot, once I heard it wuz Arawn come t' speak fer th' Trolls," said Tummeler. "But enough of th' worries. I be taking you somewheres calmer, somewheres safe."

As he said this, he steered the Curious Diversity off of the main road and onto an unpaved tributary that sprouted off to the west. It led to the mouth of a canyon that creased the upper part of the plateau line, and was, Bert pointed out, supposed to be off limits to everyone.

"Not t' th' animals," said Tummeler. "This be a road known to us and few others, and since the royal family was kilt, only to us."

"A forbidden path?" said Charles. "Why is it forbidden?"

"Because," said Bert, "it leads to the remnants of the old city, the first city, which was built when Artigel sat upon the Silver Throne. The greater city was expanded upon and through the mountain when the first alliance with the Dwarves was made, but the original still exists—in fact, it houses the royal archive and library, unless I'm mistaken."

"But," said Charles, "won't we get into trouble?"

"Heh," Aven snorted. "More trouble than what we just left? I doubt it. Besides, I don't think there is anyone left in power who will care, forbidden or not."

"The advantage of following forbidden paths," Tummeler said, nodding, "is that no one will follow after."

"That's terrible logic," said Charles.

"No," said Tummeler. "That's animal logic."

John awoke to the sound of something snuffling loudly around his face, and he sat up with a start. The snuffling was Tummeler, who was kneading his small paws and peering closely at him.

"Master John, be ye awake?" the animal said, a note of genuine concern in his voice. "Be ye all right, master scowler?"

"I be, ah, that is, I'm all right," said John, attempting to lift himself up on his elbows. He was lying across the rear seats of the Curious Diversity. Nearby, Bert and Charles were talking closely, and Aven and Jack were also keeping counsel of their own a little farther on.

They had stopped near a spring, in a clearing that was sparsely wooded with thin, scraggly trees, at the cleft of the canyon. The sun was still high in the sky. The entire fiasco of the Grand Council and their flight from the city had taken scarcely an hour.

Bug sat in the front seat of the principle, face tense with concentration.

"The others," he said without turning. "They said you were a knight, back in the world you come from? That you saw battle, and that's what's making you sick?"

"I'm a soldier," John said, sitting upright. "That's like a knight, I suppose. And yes, I became sick during the war. It still troubles me at times."

Bug turned to look at him. "They said the memory made you ill. How can a memory make you sick?"

John paused, unsure how to answer. "I had friends," he said finally. "Friends who died, right before my eyes. And I feared for my own life. That kind of fear, once a man has experienced it, never fully goes away. Do you understand?"

Bug didn't reply, but swallowed hard and turned away. John got the feeling that yes, the boy did understand—perhaps more than any of them could know.

At Tummeler's direction, the companions began to walk through the canyon, heading west. "This is a continuation of th' road," Tummeler explained, "that leads to where we be goin'."

"We should be continuing north," argued Aven. "We don't have time for this."

"And when we get back to the ship, where then?" Bert admonished. "We have no guide, and the Winter King can only be strengthened by the chaos of the Council. He'll still be looking for the *Geographica*—and us. Perhaps here we can find someone to translate the *Imaginarium Geographica*—and maybe restore some semblance of order to the lands before all is lost."

The others nodded in agreement, save for John, who hung his head in shame. He had never felt so useless, and would have said so, if it weren't for the fear that not one of his friends would dispute it.

As they walked, Bert explained that when the Silver Throne was created, alliances had yet to be formed. "There was a loose fealty to Arthur, but his children had a harder row to hoe," he said. "The Dwarves were first to form a pact with the king, then the Goblins. The Elves were next, in an alliance formed by marriage—and then, much later, the Trolls. During that time, Artigel found it useful to have a seat of power that could be defended and protected. This canyon was the ideal place.

"The consent of the Four Kingdoms, represented by the four major races—the Trolls, the Elves, the Goblins, and the Dwarves—to be ruled by Men was predicated on the continuity of rule," said Bert. "It's because of the Parliament that they have allowed an empty throne for so long. And even then, only because the Steward was governing at their behest."

"The Steward of Paralon," said John. "He seemed familiar somehow."

"After all of the assorted characters we've seen," said Jack, "any human would seem familiar."

"Not like that," said John. "I'm quite certain I've seen him somewhere before. I wish I'd gotten a closer look. . . ."

"Never mind," said Bert. "He fled before anyone else. It's all but certain that he had something to do with the deception of the Clockwork Parliament."

At this, Tummeler clicked his teeth nervously but kept his eyes on the path ahead.

"There," said Tummeler at last. "There she be."

He gestured ahead at the steep rock face of the canyon, where an enormous edifice seemed to have been carved into the stone itself, in much the same manner as Paralon. It was rougher, cruder, but bore the same unmistakable craftsmanship. A great framework of stone and iron was inset into the southern wall of the canyon, and two huge wooden doors within that. Above, wrapped protectively around the upper part of the doors, was a stone bas-relief of a dragon, surrounded by exotic golden lettering.

"Elvish," Tummeler stated, as Bert nodded in agreement.

"How do we get in?" Jack asked, examining the doors. "There doesn't seem to be a handle or keyhole."

"Perhaps the inscription is a magical instruction," said Charles. "Remember where we are, and how things work in this place."

"I don't suppose *you* can read that," Jack said to John, who scowled, face reddening.

"Jack," Charles admonished. "Mr. Tummeler brought us here—I'm sure he can facilitate our entry."

"Oh, drat and darn," said Tummeler. "I've forgotten the magic word again."

"What does the writing say?" John asked, not quite daring to touch the inscriptions, which were deeply engraved into the granite, yet were worn smooth with extreme age.

"It's Elvish," Tummeler repeated. "It says, basically, 'Declare allegiance, and be welcomed.'"

"Well, doesn't it perhaps mean that the magic word that opens the door is 'allegiance'?" said Jack. "In Elvish?"

"That's a stupid idea," said John. "Then anyone who spoke Elvish could get in."

"Pr'cisely," said Tummeler. "No, it be an actuated magic word. One of the oldest magic words there be. It was made so by one of th' great Elven Kings of old, called Eledin, he be."

"Eledin?" said Charles. "That's close to 'Aladdin,'" he said, waving his hand across the doors. "If only it was that easy—to simply say, 'Alakazam.'"

With a low groaning of wood and metal, the giant oaken doors cracked apart and slowly began to spread open.

"Y' know the sacred magic word," said Tummeler, eyes wide with respect. "Y' be a true scowler, master Charles."

"Good show, Charles," said Jack.

"Bravo," said Bert.

"That shouldn't have worked," said John. "It was supposed to be Ali Baba and 'Open Sesame.'"

"Oh, for heaven's sake," said Charles.

There were several skeletons strewn about the entryway, robed in various styles of clothing. A few of the remains were misshapen, the bones either too short or elongated and overly large. It was Jack who realized that not all of the remains were human.

"Does everyone still think this is a good idea?" Jack said. "It looks as if other adventurers weren't entirely successful at getting very far."

"Oh, don't mind the bones," said Tummeler. "The Archivist keeps 'em about to give th' place atmosphere."

"Scared, Jack?" Aven said with a mischievous grin.

He straightened his posture and stepped forward. "No."

With Jack leading the way, the companions moved down the corridor, which was as tall as the doors and lit by the supernatural glow of runes engraved in the walls some ten feet above their heads.

"More Elvish," said Bert.

The corridor opened into a broad cavern that was honeycombed with holes, each of which was filled with books, or artifacts, or in some cases, gold and jewels.

"Hello?" said Tummeler. "Is anyone there?"

"Welcome," rumbled a deep, smoky voice. "I hope you've come by for a cup of tea, because those are the only kind of visitors I permit here anymore.

"Otherwise," the voice continued, "I'm going to have to kill you all."

"Will you drink with me? Or do you want to plunder, and die?"

Chapter Eight

An Invitation to Tea

Even the light from the Elvish runes seemed to recede as an immense red dragon rose slowly to its feet and moved toward them from the shadowed recesses of the cavern.

"My name is Samaranth," said the great red beast, "and all those you see around you declined my invitation, opting instead to help themselves to the treasure. So, Sons of Adam, choose. Will you drink with me, or do you want to plunder, and die?"

"Are you serious?" said Jack. "Tea or death? Of course we'll take the tea." The others all nodded in enthusiastic agreement. "What kind of fool would choose death?"

"Bet they wuz Cambridge scowlers, eh, master Charles?" said Tummeler with a wink.

"Undoubtedly," said Charles.

The stone floor was covered with an assortment of Persian rugs of varying sizes. The largest lay squarely before them, where the dragon indicated they should sit.

"This is quite an honor," Bert whispered to John as they seated themselves in a semicircle at the feet of the dragon. "There are no other dragons left in the Archipelago. Haven't been since the old king died. But to share tea with Samaranth . . ."

"What's special about Samaranth?" John whispered back, keeping a wary eye on the dragon, "as opposed to, well, regular dragons?"

"He's the first," Bert replied. "The oldest. The original dragon of the Archipelago. In fact, he may be the oldest creature alive."

"Perhaps you are correct," Samaranth said, smiling. "I may indeed be the oldest. But time, as you well know, Son of Adam, is relative."

Bert reddened at this and folded his arms, bowing. "I meant no disrespect, Samaranth. I am indeed honored to meet you. And, ah, to partake of your hospitality."

The dragon bowed his head to Bert in acknowledgment, then to each of them in turn, pausing only at Bug, to whom he bowed a bit more deeply, and for a moment longer than the others. Bug, for his part, blushed visibly.

Samaranth straightened and gestured toward the badger, who was standing to one side, beaming. "And you, Child of the Earth—will you join us?"

"Certainly," said Tummeler. "Y' wouldn' happen t' have those crackers I fancy, would y'?"

Samaranth made a huffing noise not unlike a steam engine, which after a moment the companions realized was laughter.

"Yes," said Samaranth. "I have the Leprechaun crackers. One moment, and I'll get them."

"They ain't made from real Leprechauns," Tummeler confided to Charles. "I just calls 'em that."

The dragon returned with a silver tea service delicately balanced on one arm, and a small bundle of crackers on the other.

"Mistress," he said to Aven. "Will you do the pleasure of serving?"

Aven began to retort something about not being servile to men, but the dragon's tone and manner was so respectful that she could not refuse. She took the tray from him, and Jack rose to his feet to help, taking the parcel of crackers.

"These are tea biscuits," he said, puzzled. "Just like we have at home."

"There are those who trade with your world," said Samaranth, "and they in turn trade with the animals, who in turn trade with me."

"Umm-hmm," Tummeler said happily through a mouthful of crackers.

"What do you trade?" Charles asked. "Jewels? Gold?"

Samaranth turned to him. "Is that all you see of worth here, O Son of Adam? The riches of the Earth?"

Charles shrank back. "Ah, just wondering."

"Knowledge," Bert interjected. "You trade in knowledge."

"Hurm," the dragon growled in satisfaction. "A Caretaker of the *Geographica* would understand this."

"That's the second thing you've said that indicates you know me," said Bert. "Pardon my asking, but have we met before? Because I'm certain I would not have forgotten, I assure you."

"No," said Samaranth, "but it is in my interests to keep abreast of what occurs in the Archipelago—and those who seek to influence its affairs. And to that end," the dragon continued, "tell me what it is that has brought you here to have tea with an old dragon."

It took them the better part of an hour to recount everything that had happened, from the murder of Professor Sigurdsson to the flight from London, to the prophecy of the Morgaine, the battle with the *Black Dragon,* and the Grand Council at Paralon. They also recounted, much to John's embarrassment, his failure to translate the differing languages of the *Imaginarium Geographica,* and the urgent need to do so, that they might find a way to defeat the Winter King.

The dragon said nothing but merely listened, pausing only to refill the teapot with fresh tea and to replenish the Leprechaun crackers for Tummeler, who had not stopped munching them the entire time.

When the companions finished their accounting, Samaranth said nothing, but sat, considering. When he finally spoke, it was about the past.

"Ages ago," Samaranth began, "the Archipelago of Dreams was guarded by thousands of dragons. The skies were filled with them. Then, not all that long ago, they began to disappear, until they were all gone, save for myself. And the only knowledge that remained of them was found in myth, and legend, and in books." This last was said with a rather pointed look at John.

"We guarded the boundary between the Archipelago and the world beyond, using flame and fear to turn back travelers that ventured too close. But I have not seen another dragon for almost twenty years, and men like the one you call the Winter King have risen to power—men who would learn the secrets of the lands not to rule justly, but to conquer cruelly."

"He has already placed many lands in Shadow," said Bert, "and for some reason, he believes that possession of the *Geographica* will aid him in his efforts."

"Why he wishes to possess the *Geographica,* I cannot say,"

mused Samaranth, "but there are already too many plans afoot in the lands, and were it to fall into his hands, it would not bode well for the Archipelago."

"Then what can we do?" said Bert. "There is no king, and not even a real Parliament to give counsel. Worse, there apparently hasn't been a real Parliament in some time—and the revealed deception ended the possibility of unity in the Archipelago."

"Yes, that is a problem," said Samaranth, turning to face Tummeler. "Would you care to tell us, little Child of the Earth, just what the animals were thinking?"

Tummeler froze, a half-eaten Leprechaun cracker hanging out of his mouth.

"The animals?" said Aven. "Do you mean to say that they built those imposters in the Parliament?"

"It makes sense," said Charles. "They are the only ones aside from Nemo who know how to build the vehicles, and the clockwork kings and queens were at least as complicated as that."

The companions turned to look at Tummeler, who was twisting the ends of his vest and twitching his whiskers mournfully.

"Aye, 'tis true, I be afeared to say," Tummeler began. "We—the animals, that is—built them several years back, to avoid just this sort o' calamity."

"But why did you build them?" Jack asked. "There are plenty of humans on Paralon who could have served."

"Not kings and queens," wailed Tummeler. "Th' Parliament must be kings and queens of the greater islands of the Archipelago, and none wuz left alive."

"*None* of them?" Bert said. "That's not possible."

"Both possible an' true," said Tummeler. "With no High King, no royal heirs, an' no real kings an' queens in Parliament, it were only a matter o' time before the other kingdoms would start to fight for th' Silver Throne.

"So it were decided that we—th' animals—should build replacement-likes, to keep a Parliament t'gether so's a new High King could be decided on."

"Who decided that you should build the replacements?" Bert asked.

Tummeler wiped a paw across his snout and shrugged. "I don't know. I never saw. Ol' Tummeler never did anyfing but drive supplies to and fro in the Curious Diversity."

"The Steward," said Charles. "Was he clockwork too?"

Tummeler shook his head. "I don't know."

"It stands to reason," said Charles. "If no one knew the other kings and queens were being murdered, as the High King's family had been, then they could be replaced with fakes."

"But why would anyone want to do that?" Jack asked.

"Consensus," said John. "Only the continuity of human rule kept the other races in check. And a consensus of Parliament and the delegates of the other kingdoms could put someone on the Silver Throne—someone like the Winter King, which is exactly what the Steward was trying to do."

"And Bert stopped him," said Charles. "Well done, Bert."

"Of course, now the capital city is on fire, and the entire Archipelago may be at war," said Jack. "But let's not dwell on the past."

"So what do we do now?" asked Aven. "Whatever is occurring among the races, the Winter King will still be pursuing the *Geographica*, and we can't let him find it."

"Agreed," Samaranth said. "As much as it pains me to suggest, the *Imaginarium Geographica* must be destroyed."

"We tried that," said Jack. "Nemo threw it on a brazier, but it wouldn't burn."

"No," said Samaranth. "Only he who created it can destroy what he has wrought. It must be taken," the dragon finished with a smoky exhalation, "to the Cartographer of Lost Places."

"That brings us full circle to our original problem," Aven said with a contemptuous glance at John. "We don't have any way to read all but the most basic maps and annotations in the *Geographica*—and with no way to translate the rest of the maps, we can never find our way to the Cartographer's island, even if he still really exists."

"Oh, he still exists," said Samaranth. "He created maps constantly for the Caretakers in years past, although he has since come to distance himself from contact with anyone from either world."

Bert nodded in agreement. "I never met him myself," he said, "but Stellan did on several occasions, very early on in our Stewardship of the *Geographica*. The last three maps were all added under our watch. Unfortunately," he added, "they are all for islands on the outer edges of the Archipelago, and will be of no use to us in finding the Cartographer."

"So," the dragon said, turning to John, "you were not properly trained as a Caretaker?"

"I was trained, but I never knew the import of my studies," said John. "I have a basic functional knowledge of several languages, but know almost nothing of the rest of them."

"Nothing?" snorted Samaranth. "Not even a single letter?"

"Single letters, sure," John said, "but not enough to translate from map to map."

"Nothing?" the dragon repeated. "Not even a single recurring phrase?"

"That's right," John said. "But wait, I forgot—there was one thing I *could* translate right away."

He took the oilskin-wrapped book from the pack on Bug's back, unwrapped it, and flipped to a map near the center of the book.

"There," he said, pointing to an engraving of a dragonlike creature and the annotation below it. "It's much like the caution on an old mariner's map I once saw: 'Here, There Be Dragons.'"

"Correct," said Samaranth. "With one difference."

The companions crowded around John and the *Geographica*, but none of them understood what point the dragon was making. Finally, the realization dawned on John.

"It's to the east of the lands depicted," John said. "On the mariner's map at the British Museum, the caution is on the western edge—the outermost edge of the world as it was known then; but all these," he continued, paging through the maps, "are on the eastern edge."

"Correct again," said Samaranth, leaning closer to John. "One more gives you the tournament."

John studied the maps, paging from one to another before he saw it. "It's on every one," he said.

Samaranth bowed his head. "That same phrase, in one variation or another, is on every map, and," he concluded, "in every language."

"A primer," Charles said. "John, you said you'd studied all of the languages, at least a little."

"Yes," said John. "I see where you're going. I can use the

common phrase as a primer to work out grammar and syntax, based on the differences between versions."

"If you work from the back of the atlas forward," offered Bert, "you can also unravel the languages chronologically. Most recent languages first."

"What do you say, John?" Charles asked. "Do you think you can do it?"

John looked doubtful, but he was quickly becoming absorbed in the maps. "Old English to Teutonic, to Italian, and . . . mmm, Latin . . . ," he murmured, more to himself than anyone else.

Aven and Jack exchanged skeptical glances, but Bert smiled broadly, as did Bug. Charles offered a pencil from his vest pocket, and without another word, John sat on the rug and began to make notes, now fully absorbed in his task.

"Well," said Samaranth. "It seems as if you had your translator with you all along."

As John worked, Bug and Aven cleaned up the tea service while Bert, Charles, Jack, and Tummeler discussed their strategy with Samaranth.

"The seas will be treacherous," said Bert. "The trolls will be out en masse, if they are not already."

"Arawn," Samaranth said with a hiss, spitting embers across the rugs that Jack hurried to stamp out. "Spoiled brat of a troll. His father is a diplomat—but that one would burn a tree to cook an apple. And then he'd discard the apple, and beat his servants for not putting out the fire."

"If only something of the old Royal House of Paralon

remained," sighed Bert, "then we could simply have a coronation and get back to business."

Samaranth laughed in that huffing way and arched an eyebrow at the little old man.

"If only it were that easy," the dragon said, "you'd already be done." Bert started to ask what he meant by this, but Samaranth continued speaking. "Quests are never easy—at least, any that are worth their while.

"You want a coronation?" Samaranth said, rooting around in one of the honeycomb caches in the walls. "Take this—maybe you can put it on anyone foolish enough to sit on a throne, who seeks to rule a kingdom."

With that, the dragon tossed a small object to Bert, who looked at it briefly before tossing it back, eyes wide.

"Hah!" Samaranth snorted. "So quick to turn away a kingdom, are you, little Traveler?"

"What is it?" Charles asked.

"A ring," said Bert. "The High King's ring."

"Indeed," said Samaranth. "It was I who made it, and I who gave it to each king in turn as they assumed the Silver Throne. And it was I who took it back, when the last king demonstrated through the choices he had made that he was no longer worthy to bear it."

"But it's just a ring, isn't it?" asked Jack.

"The High King's ring—called by some the Ring of Power—was the symbol of his office," said Bert, "and was said to be the source of his power in the Archipelago."

Samaranth seemed surprised by this. "You think so? There are many rings in the Archipelago. The Elves bear rings, as do the Dwarves. And Men. Is it the ring that makes the wearer, or the wearer that makes the ring? It makes no difference to me whether you take it," he finished, proffering the ring in his open claw.

"Although," the great dragon added, considering, "it may not be what you—or the Winter King—expect it to be."

"That's all right," Jack said, reaching to take the ring from the huge palm of the dragon. "Maybe we'll discover its power along the way."

"Power is a thing earned," Samaranth said, "not something that may be passed along with the possession of objects like thrones . . . or rings, for that matter.

"Power, true power, comes from the belief in true things, and the willingness to stand behind that belief, even if the universe itself conspires to thwart your plans. Chaos may settle; flames may die; worlds may rise and fall. But true things will remain so, and will never fail to guide you to your goals. Isn't that so, Master John?"

As they talked, John had come up behind his companions. There were graphite marks on the corners of his mouth, and oddly, on his forehead, but his eyes were shining, and there were a dozen strips of cloth with scribbled notations sticking out of various parts of the *Geographica*.

"John, dear fellow," said Charles. "What is it?"

"I've done it," John said, his voice trembling in triumph and excitement. "There's still a lot of footwork to do, but Samaranth gave me the key, and I've been able to make sense of most of the maps."

"Does that mean . . . ," Bert began.

"Yes," said John. "I've found the island. I know how to find the Cartographer of Lost Places."

The companions' farewells to Samaranth were considerably less strained than their introduction. The great dragon showed them how to reach a northern inlet where the *Indigo Dragon* would most likely be waiting, far removed from the fray at Paralon, and then saw their provisions for the ship restocked from his own stores.

Each of the companions thanked him in turn for his assistance and hospitality, save for Bug, who jumped when Samaranth winked at him, and John, who was too consumed with notetaking and translating to notice they were leaving until they were actually sitting in the Curious Diversity. A short ride later, and they were once more out of the canyon and approaching the inlet. Sure enough, the *Indigo Dragon* was there, gangplank at the ready.

In less than an hour, they had unloaded their supplies and were prepared to set sail for the Cartographer's island. Somewhat shyly, Tummeler tugged at Charles's coat.

"Master Scowlers?" said Tummeler. "I—I have somethin' I'd like t' be givin' y', if you don't mind."

Charles and John knelt down next to the small animal, as he offered them a largish book that smelled of crisp ink and freshly bound leather. "What is it, my good fellow?" said Charles.

"I wrote an' published it myself," Tummeler said, twisting the ends of his vest in his paws. "It's a cookbook."

The cover was embossed with the title: *Mr. B. Tummeler Esquire Presents Exotik Foods of the Lands and How They Is Cookt.*

"Very impressive," Charles said with genuine sincerity. "How's it doing for you?"

"Oh, y' know how it goes, bein' an Oxford scowler an' all," said Tummeler. "I published it durin' th' high season, and set up shop on Rivington Lane down at th' merchant district. I even had a sign what said 'Locale Author' on it, but, ah . . ."

"Haven't sold any?" said Jack.

"Not a one," admitted Tummeler. "But I've got *prospects.*"

"Well, I think it's an admirable effort," said Charles. "Thank you, Tummeler."

"Y'know," the badger said, "bein' as I've not sold any, I'd have more than enough f'r you all t' have copies of y'r own. . . ."

"No, no, one will be fine," said John. "We already have one very important book to look after, remember? Having one more will be as much as we can handle."

Tummeler beamed so much at the compliment it seemed the buttons on his vest were about to pop off. "Very wise, Master Scowler. Be well on your journey."

The badger stood on a small rise, waving his farewells, as the *Indigo Dragon* pulled away from the inlet and headed for open waters, and he continued to wave long after the ship had disappeared from view.

Part Three

The Children of the Earth

"Arm yourselves, and prepare to be boarded."

Chapter Nine
Into the Shadows

Jack stood near the prow of the ship, a bit put out at John's newfound confidence. Aven and her crew were taking direction from the Caretaker as if the fiascoes of the previous days had never occurred. It was bad enough that the potboy from Avalon acted as if John were a knight and not just a mediocre scholar from Oxford, but Jack couldn't understand why Aven seemed to forgive and forget so quickly. He didn't resent the fact that as captain, Aven had to consult with John about the navigation. He just couldn't understand why she had to keep *smiling* at him as they conferred.

The fauns seemed to have the ship's operations well in hand, so Jack excused himself from the group and went belowdecks to do whatever it was that could be done on a ship to look productive and kill time.

"There are a few gaps in the order," John was explaining as Jack elbowed his way past to the hatch, "due to the Shadowed Maps. I don't think the maps have disappeared entirely. If we knew what caused them to vanish, we might be able to reverse it—but it may be that the only one who does know that is the Winter King, and I'd rather avoid asking, if we can help it."

"When the Winter King conquers a land, its map disappears from the *Geographica*?" Bug asked.

"Yes," said John. "The outlines of the lands themselves remain, but they are covered in shadow." He thumbed through several pages until he came to one of the vanished maps. It was a yellow-tinged sheet of parchment, like many of the others, but taking the place of the illuminations and notations were several large, indistinct smudges, as if the drawings had been hastily rubbed out.

"What happens to the people?" said Bug. "The ones who live in the Shadowed Lands?"

"They become something called 'Shadow-Born,'" said Bert, "although I've rarely seen any myself."

"Is that like a Wendigo?" asked Charles.

"Worse, if you can imagine that," said Bert. "Wendigo, as bad as they are, are little more than mercenaries. Shadow-Born have long been rumored to be the darkest of the Winter King's servants. They are shells, living without true life—dark, cloaked figures, mute, who do his bidding without question. Or remorse," he added. "How it is done, I cannot tell—all I know is what the stories say: that the Winter King somehow steals and traps the shadows of his victims, and forever after compels them to serve *him*."

"What do you mean, 'true life'?" said Charles.

"That's another rumor," said Bert. "It's said that the Shadow-Born cannot be killed. If it's true, then they would be worse than any Wendigo."

Aven looked at John. "How many maps in the *Geographica* are Shadowed?"

"Perhaps a quarter of them."

No one had anything to say after that.

John estimated that the Cartographer's island was maybe a full day's sail away, give or take a few hours. Aven conferred with Bert, while Jack and Bug pretended to examine one of the ramshackle cannons near the cabin—where they could also keep an eye on Aven.

Aven glanced around and caught Bug staring at her. He blinked and immediately began examining knots in the rigging—which came loose, much to the dismay of the fauns.

"Sorry," said Bug, who moved quickly to the other end of the ship while the crew re-drew the rigging.

Aven smiled, then frowned and furrowed her brow.

"What is it?" asked Bert.

"There," she said, pointing behind them.

On the horizon, moving fast from out of the setting sun, was the shape of a ship. The *Black Dragon* had found them once again.

The crew quickly mobilized, and in moments there was no question: It was definitely the ship of the Winter King.

Aven continued watching through the spyglass, as if confirming something she hadn't expected to see.

"What is it?" asked John.

"Trouble," said Aven.

"Really?" John said. "I hadn't guessed."

Aven shot him a poisonous look and turned to her father, handing him the spyglass. "That's not what I meant. He has Shadow-Born on board the ship. Four of them."

"Four!" Bert exclaimed, peering at the pursuing ship. "I've never heard of more than two ever being together at any time. If he's brought four Shadow-Born, that bodes very badly for us."

"You can stop trying to cheer us up now, Bert," said Charles. "I think I'm about as happy as I'm going to get."

"Our only hope is to outrun him," Aven said, "and I don't think that's possible—not without Nemo to buy us time."

"I've been examining the weapons stores below," said Jack. "We don't have much, do we?"

Aven shook her head. "We're stripped for speed—and we were never really equipped for battle to begin with."

"I have an idea," said Jack. "Hey, potboy," he called to Bug. "Give me a hand belowdecks."

"What are you thinking, Jack?" said Aven.

"No time to explain," Jack shouted. "Just get the fauns to prepare a cannon on the aft deck."

"Aft?" Aven exclaimed.

"Just do it!" said Jack, as he disappeared below.

In moments Jack and Bug had brought up a massive cannonball and were loading it into the cannon.

"A few of those would show them what's what," said Charles.

"It's the only one we have," said Jack.

"Oh. Well then," said Charles. "Aim like an Oxford man, Jack."

"That's my plan," said Jack. "Turn us around," he called to Aven. "Quickly!"

"They'll be prepared for that," she yelled back, "since your stunt the last time."

"That's what I'm counting on," said Jack. "Turn us around! Quickly!"

The crew turned the ship and pointed it at the *Black Dragon*. As Jack had predicted, the bigger ship slowed down so as not to lose too much distance when the *Indigo Dragon* passed.

A hail of arrows and spears showered the deck as they sped past the *Black Dragon,* and Aven climbed onto the rigging to get a better look at their adversary.

"That's our advantage, used and gone," she called down to Jack. "They'll not let us get the distance to turn again, and they're too fast to evade."

"It won't matter if they're faster if they can't steer," said Jack as they passed the aft of the *Black Dragon*. "Fire! Now! Now!"

The fauns lit the fuse, and an instant later a booming cough erupted from the cannon, expelling with it their solitary cannonball.

The iron ball shot through the air and found its mark, exactly where Jack had intended it to hit. The *Black Dragon*'s rudder shattered in an explosion of splintered wood and iron.

The crew of the *Indigo Dragon* let out a cheer and hastened to raise the sails for speed. John, Charles, and Bert clapped Jack enthusiastically on the back, and, best of all, Aven climbed down from her perch and kissed him on the cheek. Only Bug was nonplussed.

"I don't want to be a wet blanket," he said, "but I don't think this is over yet."

He was right. Despite having lost their rudder, the crew aboard the *Black Dragon* were making no efforts to even respond to the loss. They were still milling about, cursing and waving weapons, and looking for all the world like they hadn't even completed the preamble to this nautical overture.

Suddenly, inexplicably, the *Black Dragon* turned sharply, and, picking up speed, began to come straight at the *Indigo Dragon*.

Jack was incredulous. "But—but his rudder is gone! How in heaven's name did they turn like that?"

"Only one answer," said Bert. "The *Black Dragon* is not such in name only, but a true Dragonship—although how he managed to get his hands on one I cannot imagine. Dragonships are alive and have wills of their own—and more powers available to them than ordinary vessels."

"So what do we do now?" said Jack.

In answer, Aven drew her sword. "We do whatever we can. Arm yourselves, and prepare to be boarded."

While the fauns worked to coax more speed out of the *Indigo Dragon*, Bert, Bug, Jack, and Charles divvied up the remaining weaponry, which was old and rather shopworn. John had disappeared.

"Sure," said Jack, "the only soldier among us, and he's hiding somewhere. It's no wonder he got sent home."

Charles looked disapprovingly at his younger friend but said nothing, instead turning his attention to the rapidly approaching ship.

With the ease born of a superior motive power, the *Black Dragon* glided alongside the *Indigo Dragon* and aimed a brace of cannons at her.

"Oh, dear," said Bert, as the cannons erupted in echoing thunder and masses of hot iron began screaming through the air above their heads.

"He's not aiming to sink us?" Charles shouted.

"He can't risk losing what he's after," Jack shouted back. "He still wants the *Geographica*. Where is John and that damned book, anyway?"

"I saw him go into the cabin," Charles yelled.

"It figures," said Jack, as the *Black Dragon*'s cannons continued their relentless fire.

Bert and Aven were arguing as to strategy (she advocating more offensive maneuvers, he advocating flight), and John had just reemerged to take up a sword and join the fray when a well-aimed cannonball shattered the mainsail mast and ended any debate. A second destroyed the rudder. And a third, to their horror, sheared the masthead itself—the soul of the Dragonship—cleanly from the prow. The *Indigo Dragon* was dead in the water.

It took only moments for the smaller ship to become completely overrun by Wendigo. Whatever bravado the companions' swords had birthed was swallowed up by common sense, and they dropped their weapons.

The Wendigo forced them to their knees, tying their hands behind their backs, and then lined them up along the far railing.

The Winter King's servants had begun to light torches, which cast fearful shadows across the deck; as against Aven's vehement protestations, the fauns were herded aboard the *Black Dragon*, casting back mournful glances as they went.

"I suppose they'll be put to service for the Winter King now?" Charles asked.

"Not quite," Aven said, looking at the ravenous stares the Wendigo were giving their new shipmates. "Less service to him than served to his crew."

"Dear God," breathed Charles.

"They may still have the better end of the licorice whip," said Bert. "Look—we have more company."

Two of the Shadow-Born had stepped onto the deck, bringing with their presence a chill to the atmosphere. Where they moved, the color seemed to drain out of the air itself. The robes they wore were featureless and black; hoods covered their faces. Only the hands, pale and ethereal, which extended below the draped sleeves, bore witness that the Shadow-Born had once been human. Even the Wendigo stepped aside as they passed.

"That's a Shadow-Born?" Jack whispered to Charles. "They don't look very terrifying to me. I don't know why Bert and Aven got so worked up about them."

Just then, one of the fauns broke free from its captors and ran squealing back across the gangplank to the *Indigo Dragon*. Moving with incredible speed, the first of the Shadow-Born stepped in front of the fleeing creature. The faun stopped in its tracks.

The Shadow-Born reached out and grasped the poor beast by its own shadow. The faun began to jerk about as if it were a puppet on a string, letting loose a shriek that was cut short as its shadow ripped free in the specter's grip.

The Shadow-Born clutched its prize to its chest, and as they watched, the shadow of the faun wavered and disappeared, and the substance of the Shadow-Born seemed to grow darker.

The faun dropped to the deck, glazed eyes rolling back in its head. The color had been drained from its flesh and fur along with its shadow, leaving it all but dead. Or worse. The limp body on the deck would normally have been too tempting for the Wendigo to resist, but they all stayed well clear of the motionless form.

None of the companions had anything to say about the Shadow-Born after that.

Then a third figure came aboard, and for the first time, the companions got to take a good look at their pursuer, their adversary, the man called the Winter King.

He was not tall; rather shorter than they might have expected. His countenance and dress was that of a Mongol, but of a high caste—more Genghis Khan than Attila the Hun. His skin was swarthy and gleamed with the sweat of the battle. He wore a slight mustache and wispy beard in keeping with the upper Asian bent of his appearance, but even his stride bespoke power. Even John had to admit reluctantly that the bearing and manner of the Winter King, enemy though he was, exuded a regal nobility that demanded attention, if not respect.

Also, disturbingly, the Winter King cast no shadow.

Still, the most distinguishing characteristic of his appearance was his right hand—or rather, his lack of it. Where his hand should have been was a gleaming steel brace that ended in a sharp, curved hook.

The Winter King stepped across to the deck of the *Indigo Dragon* and surveyed his captives. Aven spit at him, hitting him on the cheek.

He drew his left hand across his face, wiping off the spittle, then licked it, much to the disgust of the companions.

"Not the reception I'd hoped for—but not unexpected, either."

His voice was vaguely European, with an accent that was difficult to place. The inflections and tone seemed to be equal parts British and Roman, in the old sense of the term. Nevertheless, the

Winter King spoke with a timbre of authority that would brook no opposition.

"You sailed with the Indian, didn't you?" he asked Aven, almost casually. "His first mate, as I recall. You should have stayed with him. Better for you that you had."

"He escaped you, didn't he?" said Aven.

An almost imperceptible sheen of anger flashed across the Winter King's features. "For the moment. But there will be a reckoning, I think, in the future. It was my mistake to engage the *Yellow Dragon* in combat—the delay it caused was just long enough that I missed returning to Paralon and the Council, else I would be your king now."

"Not bloody likely," said Bert. "You should have built a better Parliament."

The Winter King moved on to Bert, smiling in what was almost an expression of old camaraderie. "Ah, yes—my old friend the Far Traveler."

"We are not friends," said Bert.

"Too true," said the Winter King. "Thank you for pointing it out." He moved again to face John, Jack, and Charles. "And who might you three be? More Caretakers drafted from the Children of Adam and Eve?"

"I'm the Caretaker," John said quickly. "They're just friends of mine."

"So noble," said the Winter King, "to try to draw attention to yourself. Not that it will help them, mind you, but a noble effort, nonetheless. And you," he continued, turning to Bug. "What are you?"

"I'm his squire," Bug said, nodding at John.

The Winter King's eyes widened in surprise. "His squire?"

"Yes," said Bug. "But I plan to become a knight."

"Really? Have you any knightly training?"

"I thought I killed a dragon once," said Bug, "but I recently found out I was mistaken. So, no, not really. But I think I'd be good at it, and I'm getting much better with a sword, so you should let us go now, before Sir John and I have to get really upset and take you and your crew prisoner."

"Oh, ho, ho!" The Winter King laughed. "I think I like this one best. He has more mettle than the rest of you put together."

He turned back to John. "You are outnumbered, outgunned, and outmaneuvered. And I can kill you all with a word. But you know what I really want."

"Yes," John said.

"Oh, my boy . . . ," said Bert.

"It's all right, Bert," said John. "If we give him what he wants, he won't hurt any of us. Isn't that right?"

"I said no such thing," replied the Winter King. "But there's no question of what will happen if you fail to cooperate."

John nodded. "It's in the cabin, wrapped in oilcloth, inside a buckled leather bag."

Aven hissed something unintelligible and looked away. Charles and Bert visibly drooped, and Jack stared straight ahead, focused on the *Black Dragon*. Only Bug seemed to act as if John had done the right thing—and in truth, done the only thing he *could* do.

One of the Shadow-Born moved swiftly through the cabin door and emerged a moment later with the oilcloth-bound parcel, which it handed to the Winter King.

"The *Imaginarium Geographica*," the Winter King murmured

with what was almost a purr as he stroked the oilcloth. "Magnificent. There are countless wonders to be found in this book, if you but know how to discern them—but you don't, do you? Otherwise, I would never have been able to catch up to you."

John's face burned with shame, but he remained silent.

"I think our business here is almost concluded," said the Winter King, "save for one or two loose threads."

He gestured with his hook, and a clutch of Wendigo brought a whining, struggling figure across from the *Black Dragon*. They thrust him to the deck alongside the companions, and when he lifted his head, they all gasped with the shock of recognition.

It was the Steward of Paralon.

"Please!" the Steward begged. "You have to help me!"

"Is he asking us, or asking him?" Charles said to Bert. "Because I'm not feeling very charitably toward him right now."

The Steward overheard the whisper and threw himself to the deck, wailing.

"I don't have any further need of you, Magwich," the Winter King said to the prostrate man. "But another may come with me, if he wishes." He had moved down the line of companions and was now standing directly in front of Jack.

"What?" said Jack. "Me?"

"You," said the Winter King. "In our earlier encounter, I saw enough to realize that it was due to your ingenuity that the *Indigo Dragon* escaped. And in our battle just concluded, you again proved yourself to be resourceful, courageous, and a more than worthy adversary."

"Pfft," said Aven. "You can't be serious."

"I am," said the Winter King, who had not taken his eyes off

Jack. "Not all of my servants are Shadow-Born. Some of them—the greatest of them—have chosen to seize greatness, to forge their own path. . . ."

"Their own path as your lackeys, you mean," said Bert.

"Keep a civil tongue, Far Traveler," the Winter King retorted. "As I recall, you have been less than successful with your own protégés. They seem to either quit on you or come into the job with half a heart.

"Be honest with yourself—you define yourself as 'good,' and me as 'evil,' but it seems to be my followers and not your own who live by the courage of their convictions."

"Is that why you had to kill the kings and queens of the Parliament," Bert said, "and replace them with clockwork constructs?"

The Winter King shot a poisonous glance at the cowering Steward. "Those toys were not meant to engage in debate, much less function indefinitely," he said, "just to keep a semblance of order until I could assume my place on the Silver Throne. But you are mistaken about one thing—I didn't kill the kings and queens. They continue to serve—merely in a different capacity."

He gestured with his hook, and the two Shadow-Born removed their hoods. Both Aven and Bert gasped in recognition.

"The King of Hearts," Bert began.

"And the King of Spades," finished Aven.

On the *Black Dragon,* the other Shadow-Born also removed their hoods, and a nod from Bert confirmed that they were the other two kings, Clubs and Diamonds.

"They wouldn't join you, so you stole their spirits and compelled them to serve you," said Bert.

"The exceptions that prove the rule," the Winter King

shrugged. "It makes the others who do that much more determined not to disappoint me.

"Still, they are merely servants, and as powerful as they are, not always as useful as the Wendigo, who have more . . ."

"Life?" said John.

"I was going to say, 'substance,'" said the Winter King, "but yes, life. Which is what I'm offering to young Jack: life eternal. The chance to never grow old. Willingly cast aside that which makes you human, and weak—set aside your spirit, and become truly Shadowless, and you will discover a power that makes you greater than any king."

He looked again at Jack. "So what's it to be? I know you are conflicted, but that's what life is—the choices you make, and the consequences they bring. Do you want to become a pirate king, and take a path of adventure with me? Or do you want to stay with this broken-down old vagabond and become one of his lost boys, spending your days entombed in stacks of dusty books?"

"I—I have to think about this," said Jack.

"Jack!" Charles hissed. "You can't possibly be considering . . . He—he murdered the professor!"

"Jack," said Aven, an uncommon sincerity in her voice, and oddly, a gentleness, too. "Please. Don't listen to him. You're better than he is—you know this."

Jack looked at the earnest, pleading faces of his companions, then drew himself up and looked at the Winter King. "Thanks anyway. But I can't go with you."

The Winter King looked at Jack and stroked his chin with the gleaming hook, considering. Suddenly he moved closer, and Jack puffed up his chest in what he hoped looked more like a gesture of defiance than fear.

Jack could feel the hot breath of their captor as the Winter King leaned in and began to whisper in his ear. He spoke too quietly for the others to hear, and Jack's face gave no hint as to the content of the words.

A moment later, the Winter King straightened, spun about on his heel, and crossed back to the deck of the *Black Dragon*.

One of the Shadow-Born gestured at the *Indigo Dragon* and their captives, indicating a question as to what to do with them.

The Winter King hefted the parcel in his hand and snorted, giving the order without even a cursory backward glance.

"Break it. Break it into pieces, and let them drown."

"I know all of the Children of the Earth."

Chapter Ten

Marooned

"*Well, this is* a fine how-do-you-do," said Charles. "Although I think I may welcome being drowned if I don't have to listen to this wailing."

The Steward of Paralon had taken up with a high-pitched keening, punctuated by frequent snorts and gasps. Charles kicked him, which only made the terrified man wail louder.

"Leave him be," said John. "He's useless anyway."

"It's your own fault," Bug said to the Steward. "You're not a Shadow-Born, or a Shadowless. You're not even a Wendigo. Didn't you think your master might someday just get rid of you?"

"That's pathetic," said Charles. "He's not even the Devil's right-hand man. He's just the lackey who runs to the corner to buy him tobacco."

The Steward took a handkerchief from his pocket and blew his nose. "I'm just a contract worker—I don't deserve to be treated this way."

"Bloody hell," said Charles. "Your hands are free, you fool! Untie the rest of us!"

"Don't want to," sniffed the Steward. "You'll hit me, or pummel me, or something equally nasty. And I think, all things considered, I'd rather just drown without taking a beating first."

"You idiot," said Aven. "Can't you swim?"

"No."

"If we're free, none of us will drown—including you!" The others all nodded enthusiastically, each of them keeping a watchful eye on the departing *Black Dragon*.

"Promise?" said the Steward, looking warily at Charles.

"I promise," said Charles. "Untie us, and there will be no pummeling until we're all safe on dry land."

"Okay," said the Steward. "Now, if I can just get that in writing . . ."

Charles screamed and kicked Magwich in the head. The Steward of Paralon dropped to the deck, out cold.

"Great," said Jack, as the other ship wheeled about and began speeding toward them. "He was our only chance."

"Sorry, sorry," said Charles. "But can you blame me?"

"Not really," Jack admitted.

"Brace yourselves," said Bert. "Here comes the *Black Dragon*."

The companions had hardly any time to react further before the great black ship had rammed the defenseless *Indigo Dragon*, cracking her in two.

They were thrown violently into the water as the aft section of the ship began to sink almost immediately. The fore was still buoyant, but sinking fast, and more torches were extinguished with each passing moment, plunging the companions into darkness.

The *Black Dragon* had already begun to move away. The Winter King was apparently confident that there would be no recovery for the helpless companions.

His mistake was one that any of them might have made themselves—he'd underestimated Bug, whose hands were free instants after they hit the water.

Swimming swiftly among them, Bug freed first John, then Aven, who untied her father and Jack. Jack freed Charles, who then realized he'd have to take responsibility for the unconscious Steward, lest he drown.

"Drat," said Charles.

Jack and Aven swam away from the sinking pieces of the boat, while John swam toward it, disappearing into the cabin moments before it was completely submerged. He reappeared moments later. "Got my coat," he said, smiling broadly.

"You really need to readjust your priorities," said Charles.

"Look who's talking," Jack said, pointing at the hapless Steward, who was beginning to awaken.

"Point taken," said Charles.

Bert was faring the worst. He had more clothes on than the rest of them—clothes that had become immediately waterlogged.

"I've got you," said Bug, lending assistance to the older man.

"Thank you," said Bert. "How did you manage to free yourself, anyway?"

Bug grinned. "Easy. Swimming lessons on Avalon. The Morgaine used to tie my hands behind my back every morning and make the Green Knight row me to the middle of the pond, where I'd have to free myself and swim back."

"That's terrible," said Bert,

"Naw," said Bug. "The only really hard part was getting out of the burlap bag."

"Jack!" Aven shouted. "John needs your help!"

John was indeed in trouble. He was treading water, but he had his arms wrapped around his coat, which he'd folded into a bundle that he was clutching tightly to his chest. This position made it all but impossible to keep his face above water.

With strong, sure strokes, Jack reached his companion in seconds and flipped him over into a dead man's carry. John refused to relinquish his coat and continued swallowing water for his trouble.

"I think he's gone into some kind of shock again," said Jack. "He's not going to be much help, and I can't carry us both for very long."

"I don't think you'll have to," said Bert, pointing into the moonlit night sky. "Look."

High above them, circling, observing, were several immense birds, each with a wingspan as broad as the deck of the *Indigo Dragon*.

"Are they birds?" said Charles. "I've never seen the like."

"Bloody big birds," said Jack.

"Steady on, lads," said Bert. "They're friends—I think," he added quickly.

Seven great crimson and silver cranes glided down at an angle crosscurrent to the breeze, and one by one picked up each of the companions in tapered claws that were enormously strong. The rescue complete, the great avians turned and flew swiftly toward the southern horizon, while below, the last remnants of what had been the *Indigo Dragon* sank beneath the waves.

The companions awoke one by one to find themselves on a beach, both cooled and drying from a gentle breeze that blew from the south. There was no sign of the giant birds that had rescued them from the water.

They were spread across some fifty yards of sand, well away from the high-water mark. Their rescuers had obviously intended for them to be safely up out of harm's way, where they could sleep without fear of being pulled back in by the receding tide.

John was lying outstretched, drowsing, his head resting on his jacket and his face pointed toward the rising sun.

Bert was several yards to his right, snoring peacefully, and had even somehow managed to retain his hat.

A bit farther on to the left, and much to Jack's chagrin, Aven had fallen asleep with her head nestled in the crook of Bug's arm, while in between, he and Charles were clustered with the Steward of Paralon, who was watching them from half-closed eyes.

"All right, you git," said Charles, sitting upright and grabbing the Steward by the lapels. "Awake is awake and asleep is asleep, but I'll bash your head in with a coconut before I'll let you spy on us for that king of yours."

At this the Steward set up such a mournful howling that everyone was soon awake, and even feeling a bit sympathetic.

"You've put quite a scare into him, Charles," said John, yawning, "but can't you get him to shut up?"

"What was it the Winter King called him?" said Jack. "Maggot?"

"Magwich, if you please," sniffed the Steward. "It's Magwich. And I was his prisoner, just as you were."

Aven had awakened and blinked sleepily a few times before realizing what position she'd ended up in and with whom. Quickly she and Bug stood up and stretched, hoping the others wouldn't notice that they were both blushing.

"So, uh, how did you sleep?" asked Bug.

"I'm wet," said Aven. "I hate sleeping in wet clothes."

"You look good in wet clothes," Bug offered.

"Oh, shut up," said Aven, unable to hide the quick grin as she spoke. She walked over to the loose circle that was forming around the Steward. "What is this idiot yammering about?"

"He claims he was a prisoner of the Winter King," said Charles. "Which doesn't explain why he wasn't tied up like the rest of us. Nor does it explain the comment about having been 'useful.'"

"What are you all looking at me for?" said Magwich. "I was his hostage, not his collaborator!"

"Mmm-hmm," said John. "As if we're likely to believe *you*."

"He used me!" Magwich wailed. "I didn't want to do it, but he made me!"

"It is possible," John admitted. "After all, Tummeler and the animals were used in just that way too."

Bert nodded. "There's would be little point in hiding his allegiance to the Winter King now," he said. "Whatever has gone before, it's obvious he was intended to die along with the rest of us."

"Sure," said Aven, "because the Winter King no longer needed him. He said as much. I say we just kill him and spare ourselves the trouble of watching our backs."

"Seconded," said Charles.

"Kind of bloodthirsty, don't you think, Charles?" said John.

"I'm an editor," said Charles. "I have to make decisions like that all the time."

"You should be looking to that one, if you want to root out a traitor," the Steward said, pointing an accusing finger at Jack. "The Winter King obviously had something particular to say to *him*."

"I don't even understand what he whispered to me," Jack retorted. "And you saw the rest—he asked me to join him, and I told him no."

"But you thought about it," Magwich said.

"I didn't see you tied up," Jack retorted. "Your hands were free. If it was so bad aboard the *Black Dragon*, why didn't you just throw yourself overboard?"

"I hate the water," said Magwich. "Can't swim. Hate all this business with ships. If the Winter King hadn't needed me for that little deception at Paralon, he could just as well have left me in London—and believe me, I'd have been much better off."

"Speaking of Paralon, you seemed more like an advocate of his than a hostage," said Charles. "And . . . wait. Did you say you were in London?"

"I knew it!" John exclaimed, jostling Charles aside and coming nose-to-nose with Magwich. "I knew I'd seen you before."

He turned to his companions. "He *was* in London—and Staffordshire before that. He was on the train with me, and I saw him again at the docks, with the Wendigo."

Another puzzle piece fell into place. "You were the one who led the Wendigo to the club," John said to the cowering Magwich. "We had to flee for our lives, and it was all your fault!"

The terrified Steward stammered in protest. "Not to kill you! Just to find the book! That's all! All he ever wanted was the book!"

"Did you also lead him to the professor?" said Bert. "Did you help him murder my friend?"

"Oh, no," Magwich said with some relief. "I was only supposed to lead him to this one—John—but he didn't have the *Geographica* either. You all managed to escape from him anyway, so what's the problem?"

John turned to Charles. "I've changed my mind," he said. "Go ahead and kill him."

Magwich shrieked again and started to run until he realized John's suggestion wasn't intended to be taken seriously—mostly, anyway.

"None of this matters," said Aven, "because he got what he was looking for. The Winter King has the *Imaginarium Geographica*."

"No, he doesn't," said John. He took his bundled jacket from underneath his head and began to unfold it.

"If you hadn't been so determined not to lose your coat," said Jack, "I wouldn't have had to save you, you know."

"Don't think I'm not grateful, but wasn't the coat I was trying to save," John retorted. "It was what I'd wrapped inside."

John pulled open the flaps to reveal a slightly damp but otherwise unharmed *Imaginarium Geographica*.

All of the companions crowded around him with exclamations of surprise and astonished whoops, save for Magwich, who stood a distance away, sniffing in disdain at the camaraderie of the others.

"My lad," Bert said, beaming, "today you have done the role of Caretaker proud."

"Bravo, John," said Charles.

"I'll admit, I'm impressed," said Aven. "But if you had the

Geographica, what was wrapped in the oilcloth the Winter King stole?"

Jack realized it before the others, and convulsed with laughter. "Of course! It was the right shape, the right size . . ."

John grinned. "I thought it might buy us a few minutes, but I never really expected it to work.

"I gave him Tummeler's recipe book."

"So for the moment," Charles said, "we appear to have regained the upper hand, at least with regard to what he wants and what we have. But the question still remains: Why does the Winter King want the *Geographica* so badly that he would destroy the Archipelago to get his hands on it?"

As one, the companions all turned to look at Magwich, who sighed in resignation.

"The Ring of Power," Magwich said sullenly. "He needs the *Geographica* to find the High King's ring."

The companions exchanged astonished looks, and Charles crouched down in front of the pouting Steward of Paralon. "What does he need with the High King's ring?" he asked. "What makes it so important?"

"The dragons," said Magwich. "It says as much inside your book there. The proper summoning, read by the High King while wielding the Ring of Power, calls the dragons."

"So *that* is the real power of the Silver Throne," said Bert. "The ability to control the dragons *would* be the ability to control the border between the worlds, if not the entirety of the Archipelago itself."

"Precisely." Magwich nodded. "The Winter King believes the location of the ring is hidden within the *Geographica*. Used together with the summoning, he thinks the dragons would return to the service of the new High King—himself."

"Well, he's out of luck twice then," said Jack, tossing a bauble from his vest pocket into the air and then catching it again, "because I have the High King's ring right here."

"What?" Magwich shrieked, abruptly standing up. "You mean you've had it all along?"

"Since that mess at Paralon," said Jack. "We were given it by—"

"By an ally of the old king," Bert interjected. "But remember—we were warned that it may not be what we think it is."

"I wonder if that's why the Winter King tried so hard to convince you to join him," Charles said to Jack. "Maybe he sensed that you had it."

"Not likely," said Aven. "He thought he was taking the *Geographica*. Why leave the ring behind when that was part of the reason he needed the *Geographica* to begin with?"

"I think I've found the summoning he's talking about," said John, who'd been leafing through the *Geographica*. "It does say something about a 'Ring of Power,' and calling on the dragons, but it's in some combination of Latin and Egyptian. It's going to take a while to work it out."

"What else is new?" said Aven. "At least you kept him from getting the atlas," she finished in what was practically a compliment. "You're not nearly as stupid as I thought you were."

"Thanks a lot," said John.

"Not to interrupt your discussion, Sir John," said Bug, who'd been observing the proceedings from a distance, "but a very, very large cat is watching us."

An immense golden creature, mane flowing to and fro with

the breeze, was sitting just inside the treeline about thirty feet away. It watched them with a lazy, disinterested expression, as if it came across marooned travelers every other day.

"That's not a cat," Jack said, his voice as still as he could manage. "That's a lion."

"Oh!" Bug said. "The Green Knight told me about them. He said lions were called Kings of the Forest."

Before any of the companions could stop him, Bug strode quickly toward the great cat, hand outstretched. Instead of turning the boy into an opportune snack, as they half expected would happen, the lion allowed Bug to stroke its mane, then scratch behind its ears. A low rumbling sound began to emanate from the beast, and after a moment they realized it was purring.

"I hit my head," said Charles. "I hit my head in the wreck, and I'm seeing things again."

The companions' attention had been so drawn by the lion that they only just realized it was not alone. Throughout the woods, under trees and in them, were hundreds of cats, and they were all watching the arrivals on the beach.

"I can't tell if we're in trouble or not," said Charles, "but I'm glad Bug made friends with the big one first."

"Cats . . . ," Bert mused. "An island of cats . . . That sounds very familiar to me. John? May we consult the *Geographica?*"

"Sure."

They opened the book, and John handed it to Bert. "I know it's here somewhere," said Bert. "It'll be among the pages in the back, near the map to the Cartographer's island—if I'm right, this is one of the elder islands."

As they looked, the others tried not to notice the fact that the cats came in all shapes and sizes—including more than a few in the predator class, a fact that Jack mentioned to Charles.

"Aren't all cats predators, though?" Charles responded.

"Probably," said Jack. "But this is the first time I've ever wondered if I classified as *prey*."

After a few minutes, Bert thumped a triumphant fist on an open page. "There! I knew it!"

He summoned the others to where he and John were examining the *Geographica* and pointed to a map of a roughly oval-shaped island. "I think I know where we are," he began.

"You are on our home," a voice, amused but welcoming, said from the trees. "Uninvited, but welcome nonetheless."

The cats parted like clouds of dust in a monsoon, and an ancient man, gray-haired and white-bearded, moved through them to the beach. He was carrying a gnarled staff, which spouted a flame from its top. Seven other men, the youngest of whom seemed of an age with Bug and Jack, were also approaching from the treeline.

"I am Ordo Maas," said the ancient man. "Welcome to Byblos."

It was a tradition common throughout cultures of the world to revere the elders of a society, and since the days of Methuselah, it had simply been assumed that the older a person was, the more life experience they'd had: Therefore, they were probably wiser than anyone else.

By that measure, John surmised, Ordo Maas might have been wiser than every other living being on Earth. He emanated the aura of such advanced age that one could suppose he might have predated the great Mesopotamian cities of antiquity, the Chinese Empire, and several of the lesser mountain ranges like the Andes and the Alps (being merely a contemporary of the Himalayas). At the very least, he was probably wiser than anyone John had ever met, or was likely to meet, short of Adam himself.

If there had been any question as to whether or not Ordo Maas deserved a large measure of respect, it was obliterated by Bert's response to his appearance. He whipped off his hat and threw himself prostrate on the ground in front of the ancient man. Even Samaranth had not received this measure of outright worshipfulness.

Aven hesitated only an instant before dropping to a slightly more dignified kneeling position, which Jack, John, Charles, and Bug quickly emulated. Only Magwich remained standing, but he seemed to be frightened out of his wits and was hunched over, trembling (which Charles figured was just as good).

Ordo Maas frowned and covered his eyes. "This is why I gave up being a king," he said, shaking his head. "Everyone wants to waste time bowing, and scraping, and 'if-you-please'-ing, and at my age, that just won't do. Please," he finished, tapping Bert with the torch-topped staff he was holding, "do get up."

"My apologies," said Bert. "I didn't think it would hurt to start with the formalities, just in case."

"Formalities?" said John.

"This is the island of Byblos, my boy," Bert said. "I'd heard of it since the first day I became a Caretaker."

"Begging your pardon," said Charles, "but we've been to Paralon, and as impressive islands go, it's a pretty hard act to follow."

"Paralon?" said Ordo Maas. "Tell me, how is my good friend Mr. Tummeler? Is he still writing books?"

"You know Tummeler?" said Charles.

"Very well," said Ordo Maas. "I know all of the Children of the Earth."

"How is that?"

"Because," said the eldest of the seven men accompanying Ordo Maas, "all of the Children of the Earth—the animals—are descended from those he brought here, thousands of years ago."

"Yes," said Bert. "That's what I was trying to say. While there were wilder lands, occupied by creatures that were the precursors of the other races scattered throughout the islands, the true beginning of the Archipelago was here, on the island of Byblos. What Samaranth is to the dragons, Ordo Maas is to men."

"Well, now I really feel old," said Ordo Maas. "Raising the animals was easy—teaching them to speak was much harder."

"In that case," said Charles, "I'm very pleased to meet you indeed."

"The feeling is mutual," said Ordo Maas. "Please," he continued, gesturing with the staff toward the slight path in the woods from which they had come, "let us repair to my home, and you may rest, and sup. And as we walk, you can tell me about what my friend Tummeler has been up to."

Chapter Eleven

The Shipbuilder

Ordo Maas and the seven men—all his sons—led the companions through the thickly forested trail to a small compound of pale-wooded cottages in the center of the island, trailed by cats all the while.

"Interesting homes," said John. "Were they made of wood from another part of the island? It doesn't look like any from the trees we passed."

"Our original ship was quite large," said Ordo Maas, "and we never expected to use it again, not in the same manner we originally did. So we used the timbers from its hull to build our homes, and one or two other useful things."

"That's an understatement," said Bert, "if the rest of the legend of Byblos is true."

"There are lots of legends," said Ordo Maas, "but yes. What you've heard is true."

"What are you talking about?" said John.

"He built the ships," said the youngest son. "All of them."

"Hap," Ordo Maas chided. "Do not be boastful."

"Ships?" said Charles. "You mean the Dragonships, don't you? Did you really build them?"

"My sons . . . came across a small, badly battered boat."

Ordo Maas nodded, a small smile playing at the corners of his mouth.

"I, and my children."

"Your sons?" said John.

"I have many children, but these seven are those who helped me, in the beginning, to build the first of what you call the Dragonships, yes."

The companions (plus Magwich) were shown to an expansive room in the largest cottage, where they sat on overstuffed cushions scattered across the floor. Jack noticed that the cushions smelled slightly of livestock—a thought that went with the fact that the broad double doors were large enough to admit a horse, or more likely, a lion.

The house was plain, but in a manner that was simple rather than drab. Ordo Maas's sons served them cups of hot tea and a platter of bread thick with pepper, which they needed little encouragement to devour. They noticed that dozens of saucers of tea—several of which were already being attended to by the cats that had followed them—had also been set along the walls.

The companions were curious as to what Ordo Maas would say about the Dragonships, but they held back from asking for details while their host was so graciously serving them. And to be honest, they were grateful for the respite and sustenance, stretching luxuriously on the cushions and drinking a large quantity of tea.

Once the companions had sated their hunger and thirst, the dishes had all been cleared away, and everyone was comfortably settled, Ordo Maas began his tale.

• • •

"A very, very long time ago, when this world and your own were much younger, and not so different, the boundaries between them were as gossamer, and could be freely passed.

"I traveled to the lands herein often, most frequently to those islands now called the Drowned Lands, but then, we lived in *your* world—"

"Where father was a very wise king," interjected Hap.

"Where I was already very old," Ordo Maas continued, "and was relied on to remember things that others had forgotten. I discovered that the world would soon be engulfed in a cataclysm. It would be covered in water, in a great flood that would last for a year, and many of the empires that then existed would be destroyed.

"I was mocked by the other elders and forbidden to reveal my beliefs to any over whom we ruled, nor to take steps to protect myself and my beloved wife. So, under the cover of darkness, we fled to a vast desert, and it was there that she and I began our family. And together, my sons and I started to build a great ship. It took us many years, but finally, it was complete, and we started to gather into it all the things that would be needed to rebuild the world."

"This sounds very familiar," said Jack.

Charles nudged him. "Don't interrupt. Keep good form, Jack."

"It should sound familiar," said Ordo Maas. "The gods have been destroying mankind by flood since time began. It was necessary until the point that men had learned enough to begin destroying themselves all on their own.

"To begin on the paths of the gods, one must first perfect one's weaknesses.

"When the ship, which we called the ark, was complete, we took into it the power of the gods, which had been stolen from them by my father, to be given to me, so that when we once more emerged into the world, we would begin with one of their strengths."

Ordo Maas gestured with his staff, and the flame danced with movement. "He brought it from the home of the gods with his own hands, and ever since, it has never left mine," he said. "And, when someday I must pass, as all things do, into the Summer Country, I shall give it on to my own sons."

"We also had with us one other object of power, the last great gift of our gods—given, we believed, to aid us in rebuilding the world. But it was a burden as much as a gift, and more than one man—or woman—could be expected to bear.

"As I was given Fire, so that we could make tools, so was my wife given a gift: a great kettle of iron, emblazoned with the symbols of Creation, lidded with the shield of Perseus, and sealed with wax.

"We were told that within the kettle were the Talents of Man—everything necessary for the world to be reborn when the great waters of the flood receded—and that it must never be opened until the world was prepared. But, believing ourselves to be the equals of the gods, we did not listen. She opened the seal, and the world paid a heavy price—for within were not only the Talents of Man, but all of the Vices as well. All the evils of the world, held captive in the kettle, and freed by a moment's hubris."

He sighed heavily, and one of his sons placed his hands on Ordo Maas's shoulders.

"She was cast from the Archipelago," the ancient man continued, "and the kettle was given into the safekeeping of another. Not," he added, "that we believed such a caution would be a permanent remedy—for it is the mandate of Men to seek after change. Even if that change is not for the better.

"But I digress—I was telling you about the ships," said Ordo Maas. "When the flood had passed, we found ourselves here, on the island we came to call Byblos. Much of the geography of the world had been changed—but the Archipelago had remained largely unaffected by the flood, and we came to realize that it was not truly a part of the world from which we had come. Connected, but not in full.

"The Frontier had protected the lands herein and had barred passage during the flood to all vessels but our own. It was the Flame, you see," he said, pointing to the staff. "It was a living manifestation of divinity, and it was what allowed passage through to the Archipelago.

"In time, as the world began to heal, our children began to cross back and forth, sometimes successfully, others, less so. That was how I realized what it was that had allowed the passages, and I determined that I would try to create another ship that might pass freely throughout any waters in which it was guided.

"In time I came across a shipwreck—a ship from your world, which nevertheless had that touch of divinity. And I rebuilt it, slowly, laboriously, and then made a gift of it to a distant descendant."

"The *Red Dragon*," Bert said. "That was the *Red Dragon*."

"Yes," Ordo Maas said, nodding. "The first of the Dragonships. There had been a masthead sculpted to its prow, which had been battered away in a storm. And so when I remade it, I fashioned it after the protectors of the Archipelago, the bearers of divinity in this world—the dragons.

"It seemed appropriate that those ships that followed after were not constructed wholly new, but were instead rebuilt from ships that had already seen much service—ships that had a soul, so to speak.

"Then, more than a thousand years later, when it seemed that the world was on the edge of destroying itself yet again, a great king came to the Archipelago—Arthur Pendragon.

"Arthur had the ability to command the dragons—the protectors of the Archipelago and guardians of the Frontier—and also had created a great empire in your world. It was an opportunity to reunite the two worlds under a protector who would rule with wisdom and strength. And so with him, and him alone, I shared the secret of the Dragonships that I had created."

"Begging your pardon," said Charles, "but after a buildup like that, I do hope you're going to share it with us, too."

"Their eyes," said Ordo Maas. "The Golden Eyes of the Dragons are what allow passage between the worlds.

"I tell you this now, because you are the Caretakers of the *Imaginarium Geographica*, and as such, would have use of one of the ships—the *Indigo Dragon*, I believe. So how is it that you came to be floundering without her, in the waters near my home?"

"That," said Bert, "is where our story begins."

And, with occasional contributions from the others, Bert told Ordo Maas all that had happened.

◆ ◆ ◆

"The *Black Dragon*," mused Ordo Maas. "It isn't one of ours. I haven't built any new ships in more than four centuries—not since the *Indigo Dragon*, bless her heart. At present, I am simply a Cat-Herder."

"How can you be a Cat-Herder?" said Jack. "They never come when you call them one at a time, so I don't know how you can control an entire, ah, herd."

"Simple," replied Ordo Maas. "You just have to call them by their true names. Cats are very secretive and reveal their names to but a few—but those who do know may summon them at will. And cats always come when called by their true names."

"Oh, for heaven's sake," said Jack.

"Knowing the true name of a thing gives you power over that thing," said Ordo Maas. "Sometimes a small power, not a great one, but power nonetheless."

"Can you tell us the Winter King's true name?" asked Jack. "That's one fellow I wouldn't mind having a bit of power over."

Ordo Maas shook his head. "I cannot give you the true name of the Winter King. It is one of his greatest secrets."

Jack drooped. "It was worth asking."

"You didn't hesitate in telling us *your* name," said John.

"I have had many names," said Ordo Maas, "and hope to live long enough to add many more."

"It seems strange to have more than one name," said Charles, "much less a true name instead of a false one."

"There are those of your own fellowship who do not go by their true names," said Ordo Maas.

"It's a diminutive," Bert began.

"Not you."

"You see," said Jack, explaining, "I hated my given name, so my brother began calling me—"

"Or you," said Ordo Maas.

He was looking at Bug.

"But," the young man said, stammering, "I've always been called Bug. That's what the Morgaine named me. . . ."

"No," Ordo Maas corrected. "That's what the Morgaine *called* you. You were named before you came to them."

"How do you know that?"

"Because," said Ordo Maas, "this is not the first time you have taken shelter on my island."

"A number of years ago—almost twenty, in fact—my sons were fishing in the southerly waters and came across a small, badly battered boat. In it was a young woman, who was barely older than a child herself.

"Her name was unknown to me, but I knew she was the old King's youngest daughter, and the only one to escape the slaughter at Paralon. She had been at sea for many days and barely clung to life—and when we removed the blanket that was covering her, we discovered why.

"Nursing at her breast, given life by the last few drops of milk her thirst-ravaged body could provide, was a child—an infant boy. And as we lifted him from her arms, the last spark faded from her eyes and she died, having held on to the last, so her son would survive.

"We buried her here, atop the island, and then turned our attentions to the child. There was no family left to claim him, and all that remained to him of his heritage was the medallion he wore around his neck. It read 'Artus.'"

"What did you do with him?" Charles asked, looking around at Ordo Maas's sons.

"Oh, I couldn't care for him here," said Ordo Maas. "Perhaps in years past, when the mother of my children was still here . . . But alas, I am too old, and my sons have too much work to also add the duties of caring for and raising a small child to manhood.

"No, I decided the upbringing of the last heir to the Silver Throne required a more . . . maternal touch. So I took him to someone who could provide that for him. To three someones, to be exact.

"It was someone I knew from your world, who had a spiritual connection to both—called by some the Three Who Are One. I knew her—them—as the Pandora."

It was John who made the connection first. "The Morgaine. You took the child to the Morgaine."

Ordo Maas nodded. "Yes. I suggested that they call him Artus—after all, it was the child's true name. Two agreed with me, but the third wouldn't hear of it."

"Probably Cul," Charles said to Bert. "Very disagreeable, that one."

"She said the child was too small for a proper name like Artus," said Ordo Maas, "so she suggested they just call him Bug."

"Hey," said Bug. "That's *my* name."

The companions turned and looked at their stowaway in stunned silence.

"I don't believe it for a second," said Jack. "You're telling me that this potboy is the heir to the Throne of Paralon?"

"Jack," said Charles. "No need to be mean."

"I'm a squire now," said Bug, "not a potboy."

"Hah!" said Jack. "A squire to whom? To *him*? He's not even a real knight."

"Don't bring me into this," said John.

"Hang on," said Charles. "Bug—ah, Artus—can what he's saying be true?"

Artus shrugged. "I don't know. The Morgaine never said anything about it to me. But the Green Knight said once that I had a great destiny—I always thought he meant that I might someday be a knight."

"Greater than that, lad," said Bert. "You are descended from the blood of Arthur himself—making *you* the true king of the Archipelago."

With that, he bowed deeply, followed in turn by John and Charles. Aven hesitated slightly before bowing herself, but Jack and Magwich refused to do it at all and watched the scene with bewilderment.

"See?" Ordo Maas whispered to Artus. "Once they get started with this sort of thing, they want to just keep doing it."

"Get up, please," said Artus. "I don't think I like you bowing to me—even if I am the heir, I'm not a king. Not yet." He thought a moment, then turned to the old shipbuilder. "That means my grandfather was the king who killed my family. And he would have killed me, too, if he'd been able."

"Yes."

"That makes you very powerful," said Aven. "If an heir is alive to sit on the Silver Throne, then the Winter King is no longer a threat. We have the *Geographica,* a descendant of Arthur, and the Ring of Power. He's lost, plain and simple."

"That's right," said John. "I'd forgotten about the ring. Do you still have it, Jack?"

Reluctantly, Jack took the ring from his pocket and proffered it to a hesitant Artus, who finally took it and placed it on his finger.

"Hey," he said brightly. "It fits."

"There is one more thing to consider," said Ordo Maas. "Having a king, and the trappings of the office, may not be enough to overcome the Winter King. He still possesses a talisman that may yet turn the events in the Archipelago in his favor. And despite all you have done, it is a power you may be unable to defeat."

"What talisman?" said Bert. "He's searching for the *Geographica,* which we have, in order to find the ring, which we also have. How can he possibly be a threat now?"

"He murdered a king before," said Seti, the eldest of Ordo Maas's sons. "He can do so again."

"Yes," said another of the sons, called Amun. "And in the years since, he has amassed great power, conquering many lands without the ring or the *Imaginarium Geographica* to help him."

"That's right," John said, crestfallen. "I'd forgotten. He's taken over the Shadowed Lands without being able to control the dragons. At best, we haven't stopped him—we'll just be keeping him from making things worse."

"How has he done it?" said Jack. "Where does his power come from?"

"He has found a way to harness the evil within men," Ordo Maas said. "You have seen them with him on the *Black Dragon*. He calls them Shadow-Born."

✦ ✦ ✦

"What do you know of the old king, Archibald?" asked Ordo Maas. "Of his rule, and his decline?"

"We know he turned evil," said John, "and murdered his family."

"Essentially," replied Ordo Maas, "but that is not the whole of the story.

"Archibald ruled over the Archipelago during a very tumultuous time in your world. There had been several great conflicts there, and that upset the balance here. For the first time in a number of generations, there was unrest in the Archipelago, and Archibald was bearing the brunt of it.

"He had the best of intentions, right before the fall—but intentions cannot pay the price for the actions that follow. Several times he called upon his allies from the Four Races, and more than once on the dragons themselves, to maintain peace. But Archibald was always seeking after a way to make the peace *permanent*. He wished for a more compelling force with which to rule his subjects. And then finally, after many years of searching, he found one.

"He discovered a record of an ancient mythical object that could draw out the spirits from living men, leaving them as stone, trapped in a living death.

"Worse, their spirits—their Shadows—would then be compelled to his service. With enough of them, he could create a deathless army that no force on Earth could defeat."

"I thought he was a good king," said Charles. "It sounds like he was a villain all along."

"Archibald's intentions were good," said Ordo Maas. "Where he erred was in believing that he could replace free will with his own. But he was determined to achieve peace at any cost—and this talisman was the object that he believed would help him to do it."

"Something that dangerous would not be unknown," said Bert. "One of the Caretakers would have known of it, surely? Or Samaranth?"

"It's well known," said Ordo Maas, "in both this world and your own. In fact, we have spoken of it here, today, in my house. But no one believed it existed, much less how to use it. It has had many names, but the one by which it is known best comes from those who had it when it was stolen: Pandora's Box."

"The kettle you brought aboard the ark," said John, "which held all the evils of mankind."

"Yes," said Ordo Maas. "It remained on Avalon for centuries until an agent of King Archibald found it and stole it.

"Archibald opened it again and discovered how to use it to create the Shadow-Born; and then he made his great mistake—he attempted to use it to steal the spirits of the dragons, to create the most powerful servants of all."

"I take it that didn't work," said John.

"Not at all," said Ordo Maas. "The dragons were of an age and power equal to that of the box and could not be trapped within it. But in that moment, they saw the king for what he was becoming.

"Samaranth took his ring and declared Archibald no longer worthy to summon the aid of the dragons. And that was when they began to leave the Archipelago.

"Soon after, the king went mad and slaughtered his whole family. None escaped, save for the youngest daughter—young Artus's mother—and Artus himself.

"This was when the Winter King began his rise in the

Archipelago. He killed Archibald and took Pandora's Box—and in the years that followed, when one after another of the lands of the Archipelago fell under Shadow, I realized that Pandora's Box was still open, and that he was using it to create an army of Shadow-Born. And thus began his conquest of the Archipelago."

"The Morgaine—or as you called them, the Pandora—are not easily tricked," said Charles, "and they were able to keep the box hidden and protected for a very long time. How did Archibald's lackey manage to make away with it?"

"An excellent question," said Ordo Maas. "Especially since you're keeping company with the thief."

"What?" said John. "The thief is here?"

In answer, Ordo Maas lifted his gnarled staff and pointed it at Magwich.

"Where's Magwich?"

Chapter Twelve

The White Dragon

"That's right, that's right," Magwich wailed. "Blame everything bad in the world on the poor Steward."

Jack and Aven stood up and cornered the Steward, who seemed coiled to spring and flee. Resigned, he flopped back onto his cushion and nodded his head.

"Yes, yes," Magwich said. "I took it. I'm not proud of it, you know, being ordered around by someone like Archibald, who was weak—and then having to follow the Winter King, just so that he would spare my life."

"You just go from bad to worse," said Charles. "What kind of man are you?"

"I tell you," said Aven, "if we don't just kill him, sooner or later we're going to regret it."

"You can't kill me!" sputtered Magwich, grasping at Jack's trouser legs. "I'm one of you! A man from the real world! I came here, years ago, with another Caretaker who abandoned me! All I've done since is just try to survive!"

"Which Caretaker?" asked Bert.

"Does it matter?" said Magwich. "I went to a lecture he gave, and he talked me into coming here with him."

"You were an apprentice Caretaker?" said Bert. "I don't believe it!"

"You should," Magwich sniffed. "He even named a character in a book after me, so I couldn't have been as bad as you want to make me out to be."

It hit them all at once. "Dickens," said Bert. "Charles Dickens recruited you."

"Why did he abandon you, if he was training you and even brought you into the Archipelago?" said Jack.

Magwich waved his hands. "A total misunderstanding, I assure you."

"He probably stole something and got caught," said Charles.

"I was never indicted," said Magwich. "But he left me here anyway. I always knew it was a mistake to leave Cambridge."

John slapped his forehead.

Jack looked at Charles. "Don't say it."

"I won't," said Charles. "But I know you're all thinking it too."

"You're the one who told him," Bert said, rising to his feet and pointing at Magwich. "You told the Winter King about the *Geographica*—and the little training you did have from Dickens is how you were able to translate the passage about the Ring of Power and the summoning of the dragons."

"You'd have done the same," said Magwich, "if he was threatening to make you look into the kettle and take your shadow."

"Well, it's clear what we have to do now," said Aven. "We have to find him and close Pandora's Box—or this may never be over."

"Agreed," said John, "especially if the conflict here truly does affect the war in our own world."

"The Morgaine certainly had *you* pegged," said Charles. "So,

Maggot, tell us this, since you're the one who stole it: How do we close the box?"

"You can't," Magwich said. "No man can. Because you would have to look into its abyss, and when you do, you're lost. It cannot be closed."

"We'll cross that bridge when we come to it," said John. "We still have another task to finish first—to destroy the *Imaginarium Geographica.*"

"What?" Magwich and Bert screamed at the same time. "Destroy it?" Bert exclaimed. "But why, my boy?"

"Of course we're still going to destroy it," said John. "By now the Winter King will have realized that he doesn't have the *Geographica* after all—and how long do you think it will be before he has a hundred ships scouring the sea for us?"

"He has a point," said Jack. "The Winter King won't stop until he's found us, and it."

"Samaranth thought it was a good idea to destroy the *Geographica,* however regrettable," said John. "The only reason we have not to is Magwich's word that finding the ring was his sole purpose in searching for it."

"That does it for me," said Charles. "We must find the Cartographer's island and destroy that damned book. After that, we can decide what to do about Shadow-Born and boy kings."

"Before we go anywhere," said Artus, "may I ask a favor?"

"Certainly," said Ordo Maas.

"May I see my mother's grave?"

Together the companions felt a sudden mix of shame and sympathy—they had all been so immersed in talk of legends, and floods, and empires, and ships, that they had overlooked the fact that their friend Bug, young Artus, had just learned everything he'd never known about his family—including the story of the mother who loved him enough to die protecting him.

"Of course, lad," said Ordo Maas. "Please, follow me."

Hor, one of Ordo Maas' younger sons, led the way through a fern-shrouded path to a small clearing above the cottages. Great barkless trees towered above, curving up in odd angles high into the air.

Ordo Maas stopped, pointing into the clearing. "It's there, marked with the seal of Paralon," he said to Artus. "Do you want to go in alone?"

"I'd like Sir John to go with me, if it's okay," he added, casting a quick glance at John.

"Of course," John said. "Lead the way, Artus."

"I'll keep an eye on Maggot," said Charles.

"It's Magwich," said the Steward.

"Right—I keep forgetting," said Charles. "So tell us, how did you get the kettle away from the Morgaine, anyway?"

"It was simple," said Magwich. "American whiskey. Put them right out."

"You got them drunk?" Bert said.

Magwich shrugged. "It was efficient and nonconfrontational. One of them kept fighting it off, though, and I had to give her a backrub to get her to sleep."

"I hope for your sake it was Ceridwen," said Charles, "or Celedriel."

"No," Magwich said with a shudder. "It was Cul, all right. I couldn't get the smell off my hands for months."

When Artus and John rejoined them, Bert raised the question of how they would get from Byblos to the Cartographer's island.

"I thought perhaps we might summon those cranes that rescued us," he said. "If they were to carry word to Paralon that we needed a ship, or to my friend Uruk Ko . . ."

"A good thought," said Ordo Maas, "but it would take too long. The Winter King may even now be returning to the waters around Byblos to seek you out. No, if you are to leave, it must be now, and with haste."

"But we need a Dragonship," said Bert. "Anything else would not be able to navigate as surely or as quickly, and there are only the seven Dragonships to be called on."

"No," said Ordo Maas. "There are only seven Dragonships to be called on that you *know* of."

Trailed by dozens of cats, Ordo Maas and his sons led the companions to the northern part of the island, where a great frigate was floating serenely in a small harbor.

"The *White Dragon,*" said Ordo Maas with obvious pride. "The last legacy of the great ark."

"Did you anticipate another flood?" asked Charles.

"No," said Ordo Maas. "Then again, neither did any of my friends in the Empty Quarter—but there came a time when they wished they'd had one anyway."

"Hey," said Jack. "It has a rowboat, too."

"It occurred to us when the first great ark sprang a leak," said

Ordo Maas. "It took a week to locate, and two days to mend, during which we took in a great deal of water. For a while, it seemed a very real possibility that we would sink—and, the animals notwithstanding, I suddenly wished I'd thought to build a rowboat, just in case of an emergency."

He turned to John and Artus, bowing. "To the Caretaker of the *Imaginarium Geographica*, and the High-King-in-waiting, I present my ship," he said. "Use it as you will, and go forth to seek your destiny."

"We will," said John. "Thank you."

"And remember," said Ordo Maas, "when the time comes, you shall not be alone. There are allegiances greater than any that bind the Winter King and his servants. Allegiances not bound by fear and pain, but by ancient promises of Spirit and Living Will.

"When the time comes, those allegiances will be called upon, and you will not fight alone."

With that he bowed deeply and stepped aside to allow the companions to board the *White Dragon*.

"Come look, lads," said Bert. "Come look, and see a sight such as you have never seen in your lives."

The companions moved to the railing as the *White Dragon* eased out into the channel and looked in the direction Bert was pointing.

High in the center of Byblos was a mountain with a crown. The skeletal remains of a great ark, come to rest atop the mountain thousands of years earlier, threw the spars of its frame high into the air on either side of the peak, framing it as if resting on the brow of a giant. End to end, the ship spanned half the diameter of the island itself and was fully as broad.

It was not hard to imagine that if they had wished it so, Ordo Maas and his family might have also taken with them everything they needed to begin anew after a deluge great enough to cover the Earth.

Everything they needed to restore the peoples of the Earth, and the flora, and the fauna.

A scattering of raindrops hit the deck of the *White Dragon*, a forerunner of the storms that loomed on the horizon—the very horizon toward which they were sailing.

And suddenly, the *White Dragon* felt very small. Very small indeed.

Ordo Maas and his sons watched the ship until it had disappeared in the distance.

"Father," said Amun. "There's one thing I don't understand. If you knew Magwich was their enemy, why did you speak so openly to them in front of him? Why give secrets to one who wished them harm, and may still?"

The ancient shipbuilder chuckled. "You are truly your mother's son. No one else thought to ask.

"Yes, it was a choice that had risks. But to try to talk to the Caretakers in secret might have warned him that I knew the depth of his treachery. And then he would truly have been the Serpent in the Garden, waiting to strike.

"No," he continued, "better that they know him as their enemy, and that *he* know that they know it. Secrecy is the weapon of those like the Winter King—they have power only so long as the secrets are kept."

His sons did not fully understand, but they nodded in agreement, for they believed their father to be wiser than themselves.

"My sons," said Ordo Maas, "I have a request of you.

"There will be a great conflict. Greater perhaps than any we have seen in this world. And those who go to fight against the evil Shadows do so with little hope of survival. They are brave, and their hearts are pure. But they cannot prevail without help, and there is no High King to draw together those who might come to their aid.

"There are those who may help turn the tide, but there is only one way to summon them in time, if at all."

The sons of Ordo Maas did not reply, for they knew what it was their father was asking of them, just as he knew they would not refuse.

"That will take longer than one night," said Sobek. "We will have to remain changed into the day to reach—"

"Yes," said Ordo Maas.

"But if we have not changed back by sunrise . . . ," Aki began.

"Is there no way?" asked Amun. "There was a way, once, to allow the change to be reversed."

"It is lost to us," Ordo Maas said. "It left the Archipelago with your mother, Pyrrha. Should you choose to do this—"

"We will not be able to change back," said Seti, the eldest, his posture resolute. "We will remain as we once were—but still honored to be sons of our true father, Deucalion. And honored to do this thing he asks."

Tears filled the ancient shipbuilder's eyes as he stood in the circle of his sons, all of whom knew what their answer would be, each bowing his head as he met their eyes.

As they nodded their assent, the transformation had already begun. Their necks grew long and tapered, as silver and scarlet feathers began to emerge all across their skin, shivering, shimmering.

One by one, the sons of Ordo Maas turned into cranes, beautiful and elegant, and took flight into the deepening night sky.

The experience of sailing in the *White Dragon* was very similar to that of sailing in the *Indigo Dragon*, with a few exceptions. For one, it was a much, much bigger boat. And for another, it was faster.

"I loved the *Indigo Dragon*," Aven said, standing at the great wheel, "but a girl could get used to this kind of vessel. I wonder if Nemo's seen her?"

"We'll make good time, that's certain," said Bert. "What's the word, John? Where in the Archipelago are we?"

John, Charles, and Artus had spread the *Geographica* out on the deck and were charting the course between Byblos and their destination. Jack was busying himself with examining the riggings and sails. No one quite cared what Magwich was up to, and for his part, he didn't care that they didn't care, as long as he could stay as far away from Charles as was physically possible. His head still ached from the earlier kick.

John bit his lip and made another quick notation before replying to Bert's question. "More to the south than I'd hoped, but farther west than I'd expected. Can you keep us about six degrees north by northwest?" he called out to Aven. "That should do the trick."

"No problem."

John put his arm around Bert's shoulders and indicated the path he was plotting among a series of the maps. "The island where the Cartographer can be found is the largest in a chain of islands," he explained. "An archipelago within the Archipelago. They seem to be the remnants of a great volcanic crater that rose up from the ocean floor millennia ago. Eventually, it settled back into itself, or the waters rose, or both, leaving only pieces of the rim remaining as a rough circlet of islands."

"How many are there?" asked Artus.

John looked back down at the *Geographica*. "Almost a dozen," he said. "The one we're looking for is ahead of us in the center—like a pendant on a necklace."

Charles had helped himself to a bag of Tummeler's Leprechaun crackers that had been included with the supplies, and he peered over John's shoulder at the *Geographica* as he munched on them. "What's it called, John?"

"I can't see that the island itself has a name," John replied. "The entire grouping is indicated with a notation that is a mixed-up version of Latin and ancient Greek. It says *Chamenos Liber*."

"A strange name," said Charles. "Does it say why they're called that?"

John leafed through several pages before shaking his head, then looked up at Bert, who shrugged. "I can't say," said Bert. "Stellan may have known, but he never told me. And I can't recall ever reading or hearing about it.

"Remember," he continued, "this is one of the oldest places in the Archipelago, and the Cartographer is the one who created the *Geographica*. If it's not in here to be found out, it may be possible that even *he* does not know."

Having set their course, Aven left the *White Dragon* to her more than able self-corrections and went into the larder to assist Artus with preparing some dinner. Like their meal on Byblos, the foodstuffs were vegetarian in nature: lots of breads and grains, and various compotes and preserves. Still, they were a welcome change of pace from Tummeler's crackers and the stale cheeses favored by the crew of the *Indigo Dragon*.

John continued to examine the *Geographica*, working through the extensive annotations dealing with the Cartographer's island.

"According to this note—if my Italian is reliable enough," he said to himself as much as the others, "the place where we can find the Cartographer is an immense tower called the Keep of Time. Inside is a winding stairway lined with doors. The Cartographer must be behind one of them."

"But it doesn't say which one?" asked Charles.

"No. But there is a caution here not to open any of the doors. I can't quite follow why. . . ."

"I suppose we could just stand at the bottom and bellow his name until he answers," said Artus, appearing at the galley door holding a tray heavily laden with food. "At least, that's how I used to call the Green Knight when he left me at the bottom of the Wishing Well on Avalon."

"They really put you through it, didn't they?" said Charles.

"You have no idea," said Artus. "They claimed it was 'knightly training,' but I think it was mostly to keep me out of the way when they didn't need any work done."

"Why do you call it a Wishing Well?" asked John. "Was it magic of some sort?"

"No," said Artus. "I just call it that because I spent most of my time in it wishing I was someplace else."

• • •

John wrapped the *Geographica* in a fresh sheet of oilcloth he'd found in the ship's stores and stowed it securely in the rear cabin. Despite the constancy of the thunderheads on the horizon, the moon was again very bright, making the weather pleasant, and in other circumstances, their simple feast on the deck would have been considered an exceptionally fine midnight picnic.

Jack and Bert joined them for the meal, but other than whining about the lack of marmalade, Magwich showed little interest in eating, asking instead when Aven planned to serve drinks.

The bread knife she threw in response struck the mast next to the Steward's head with a loud *tung*, and Artus quickly jumped to his feet to show Magwich where the water was stored, before Aven started throwing larger, sharper things.

Charles shook his head in wonder. "How did Dickens ever think that someone like Magwich could be a Caretaker?"

Bert shrugged. "He never said anything to me about it. But then, when I met Charles Dickens, he'd already retired and turned the *Geographica* over to Jules, who in turn recruited me."

"It's possible then," said John, "that you were recruited as a Caretaker because Magwich didn't work out."

Bert thought on that a moment, chewing idly on a carroway seed and stroking his mustache. "I don't know if that would be a good thing or a bad thing."

"He's certainly been no end of trouble," said Jack, as Aven agreed with an enthusiastic nod. "When you think about it, he's been a pivotal point for every bad event that's happened: the theft of the kettle; the death of Archibald; the murder of the professor; the sham Council at Paralon. In fact, if it weren't for him, the Winter King wouldn't have been chasing us at all—because he wouldn't know about the *Geographica*."

Suddenly, the *White Dragon* jerked violently, as if struck. Then again. "What the hell?" said Aven. "That shouldn't be happening."

Rising, she bolted for the wheel, which was lurching back and forth as if the ship itself wanted to change course.

"What's wrong with it?" Jack yelled.

"I haven't the faintest idea," Aven shouted back as she wrestled with the wheel. "The ship is fighting our course, as if she wants us to turn around."

Jack ran to the foredeck and quickly scanned the sea with Aven's spyglass. "I can't see anything—no ships, no islands. Not even any debris in the water."

"Could we have lost something?" said Bert. "Maybe someone fell overboard."

John did a quick head count, and a terrible realization came over him.

"Jack," he said, his voice low, "where is Artus?"

The others understood immediately.

Charles rose, glowering. "Where is he?" he said, anger rising in his voice. "Where's Magwich?"

"Worse than that," Jack yelled from the port side. "Where's the rowboat?"

John found his squire in the galley, where Artus lay unconscious and bleeding on the floor.

"He knew," John said, gesturing at Charles. "He knew—and I refused to listen. Forgive me, Artus."

The boy king-in-waiting blinked and slowly sat up. "He hit me—I'm so sorry. . . ."

"Not your fault," said Aven. "It's ours. We should have killed him. I said as much."

"At least we're rid of him," said Charles. "Did he take anything?"

"Not much, as far as I can tell," said Aven. "The rowboat, a few food stores, some water."

"It was planned, then," said Bert. "He knew what he planned to do the minute we set foot on the *White Dragon,* and he saw that rowboat. He planned to escape all along."

"To what end?" said John. "Everyone in the Archipelago hates him."

"The ring!" Jack exclaimed, looking at Artus' hands. "The ring is gone!"

John closed his eyes, and his head dropped. "Oh. Oh, no."

He moved quickly out of the galley and returned a few minutes later, empty-handed. "It's gone," he said. "He took the *Imaginarium Geographica* as well."

"That's why the ship was fighting our course," said Aven. "She knew what he'd done and was trying to warn us."

A quick assessment of the nearby seas bore no trace of Magwich's passage. Whichever direction he had taken the boat, it was impossible to tell. There would be no pursuit.

"Now what?" said Charles. "Should we return to Paralon to consult with Samaranth?"

Aven shook her head. "He already told us all he could," she said. "He made that clear."

"But without the *Geographica*," said Jack, "is there any reason to seek the Cartographer?"

"No one knows more about it than he," said Charles. "Even without it in our possession, he may still be able to tell us something we can use to destroy it. If—when—we find it again."

"It seems," Bert said, "that we have no choice. We must continue forward."

PART FOUR

In the Keep of Time

"Look," Artus said, pointing. "On the island. That tower . . ."

Chapter Thirteen
The Tower

The course had been determined well enough that no further corrections or navigation were necessary—but once again, John felt as if he'd failed them all utterly. Aven was furious and not speaking to anyone, and even Artus was keeping a protracted distance. Only Charles and Bert were conciliatory—to a degree.

"We couldn't have known," said Bert. "We had all the cards, and we thought the game was over—we didn't expect that the Steward was still playing."

"I can't believe I saved him," said Charles.

"What I don't understand," said John, "is why take the *Geographica*, too? He had the Ring of Power. If he planned to take it to the Winter King, or try to sell it, or even try using it himself, then what did he need the *Geographica* for?"

"The summoning," Jack said from the foredeck, keeping his back to them. "He needed it for the summoning of the dragons. The ring alone is not enough—the words must also be spoken. And now he has them both."

✦ ✦ ✦

Dawn eventually came, passing into morning then afternoon as the companions slept, ate, and generally stayed out of one another's way.

Finally, the *White Dragon* approached a great circular chain of islands just as the sun had begun to set. The islands were gray granite and rose prominently out of the sea like sentinels—which in a fashion they were.

There were no slopes, no low rises to the islands of Chamenos Liber—it was as if columns of stone had dropped from the sky and impaled themselves upon the glassine surface of the ocean.

In the distance the largest of them could be seen faintly through the mists. Aven tipped her head at John, and he nodded. That would be their goal. She had started to turn the ship to steer between the columns when Jack grabbed the wheel and gave it a vicious turn. The *White Dragon* came about, narrowly missing an impact with the nearest island.

"What are you doing, you idiot?" Aven said, incredulous. "I'm doing the steering here."

"Sorry," said Jack. "There was no time to argue with you—but I think it's better that we skirt the smaller islands and approach the large one from the eastern side."

"It's faster and more direct to cut straight through."

"Probably," said Jack, "but I don't think that's mist out there—I think it's steam."

The companions went to the railing and looked out into the center of the circle of islands, and they realized that Jack was right. The mist that obscured their view of the Cartographer's island was contained within the granite pillars.

"I remembered what John had said about these islands once

being part of a volcano," said Jack. "I thought it wiser to steer clear, even if we lose time."

"Well done, Jack," said Bert. "It seems as if you're the Caretaker of the *White Dragon*."

"Look," Artus said, pointing. "On the island. That tower . . ." He leaned back, toppling into Charles. "I can't see the top of it."

"The Keep," John said, his voice hushed in the night mists. "The Keep of Time."

The island was nearly a mile across and, unlike its smaller, harsher siblings, was covered with grasses that sloped gently up to the base of the tower. The tower itself was perhaps forty feet in circumference, and it was inset with windows at staggered intervals as it rose, one about every twenty feet. The frame was wood, but the walls were granite. The stone of the tower was very ancient, and of a somewhat lesser gray than that of the islands, as if it were slightly ethereal, or not in the same focus as the ground on which it stood.

Aven steered the *White Dragon* into the shallows where they could clamber off and walk to the pebbled beach that gave way to the grass. Standing on the shore, they looked at one another and realized they had no idea what they were going to do once they were inside. The entire purpose of their ordeals and long journey had been to bring the *Geographica* to the one person who could destroy it—and they had lost the book mere hours before they'd reached their goal.

Expectantly, they all looked to John to lead the way into the tower. He felt like an idiot.

The base of the tower was ringed with open arches that

led inside, as if it stood on four massive feet one could walk between. The interior was more brightly lit than could be ascertained from without. A luminosity emanated from the floor, which faded farther up, to be replaced by the light from the windows.

In the center of the floor was a raised circular platform, like a dais. On either side of it were two sets of steps that rose into the tower before curving back into each other in a great braided pattern. At each point where the braid of steps crossed was a door set deep into the stone walls, but they bore no visible hinges or handles. They were simply there.

Jack stepped into the center of the tower. "I can't see the top of it," he said. "It seems endless."

"I couldn't see the top from outside, either," said Charles. "No doubt about it—unless the Cartographer is behind the first door we open, we're in for a bit of a climb."

"Knock on wood that he is, then," said Artus, reaching out his fist to rap on the bottommost door.

Before his hand touched the polished wood, the door swung open. Inside was *outside*—the door didn't open into a room within the tower, as they had every reason to expect, but onto the broad expanse of a mist-laden forest primeval.

"It's a swamp," said Artus.

"More than that," said Bert. "I think it's a doorway into the past—to the dawn of mankind itself."

"Is that an elephant over there?" said Charles.

"That's not an elephant," said Bert, "that's a mammoth."

"A woolly mammoth?" Charles said, incredulous. "You can't be serious."

"It couldn't be a mammoth," said Jack. "They lived in colder climates—on steppes, snowy plateaus, that sort of place. This is a swamp."

"Argue with your own eyes," said Bert. "Mine see a woolly mammoth in a swamp."

"It doesn't appear to be moving," said John. "Look—nothing in here is. It's as if everything were made of stone."

It was true: The leaves on the trees did not stir; the clouds in front of the immense moon did not drift. Even the insects in the air were frozen in place, as if trapped in colorless amber. Until, that is, Artus took a step forward, past the threshold.

The buzzing of the insects was immediate, as was the tang of rotting flesh and, they assumed, mammoth dung.

The flora were swaying gently alongside the great river that lay just past the entrance, as were the fauna. An extraordinarily large head rose from the water and continued to rise, until the neck atop which it rested had grown to more than forty feet in length.

"Is that a sea monster?" said Artus.

"My old teacher, Sir Richard, called them 'dinosaurs,'" said Bert. "Regardless, I think it's time we took our leave of this place—he looks hungry, and I can't run as fast as the rest of you."

Artus quickly stepped back, pulling the door behind him. "Agreed. I don't think the Cartographer's behind this one."

"Right," said John. "Onward and upward it is."

Charles pointed to the twin stairways. "Clockwise or counterclockwise?"

"Widdershins is always the prudent choice," said Bert. "Counterclockwise."

Thus agreed, the companions began to climb.

* * *

Every few levels, one of them would stop to open a door, each time revealing a different landscape from a different period of time. It was Charles who realized that the scenes were not random, but following a very distinct progression.

"We're moving upward in time," he explained. "Each doorway is opening into a different point in the past. At the bottom, the beginnings of civilization. And as we move up, so do we move forward in time."

"What's at the top, then?" said Aven.

"Good question," said Charles. "We may yet have a chance to find out—as far as I can tell, we haven't even hit the Bronze Age yet."

"One thing about the past," said Bert, "it smells awful. My clothes still reek of mammoth dung."

Jack took the next door, which also swung open at a mere gesture. Inside, a frozen diorama like the others depicted a brutal scene of combat between what Bert claimed were Mongols and ancient Icelandic warriors. There were missing limbs, and the ground was awash in blood.

"I think this one's a 'no' too," said Jack, "but I'd say we're firmly in the Bronze Age now, if we're to judge by those axes they're swinging."

"Uh, Jack?" said Charles.

"Yes?'

"Those huntsmen," Charles said. "They're coming this way."

Jack looked down and realized he'd inadvertently stepped over part of the threshold, unlocking the scenario from its frozen state. He quickly shuffled back—but the huntsmen, scenting fresh prey, and still maddened with bloodlust, were now coming at a full run.

"You can turn it on," said Jack, "but can you turn it off?"

"Shut the door!" the others yelled together, and Jack did, just as a gore-laden bardiche buried itself on the other side.

They held their breath, but heard no further impacts.

"Apparently," said Bert, "closing the door closes the portal."

"Thank God," said Jack.

Just then, a rumbling sound echoed throughout the tower, and the floor seemed to shift beneath their feet. As quickly as it had begun, it stopped.

"What was that?" said John.

"No clue," said Bert. "But it still smells awful in here."

"Yes," said Aven, "it does. But why? That smelly prehistoric doorway was at the bottom of the stairs, and we've been climbing for hours. We have to be several miles high by now—why do we still smell it?"

Jack was looking at the door the huntsmen had just attacked. "Artus? The door you opened below—you did close it, right?"

"I'm almost certain I did," said Artus. "Almost. Certain."

Before Jack could respond, a great mucous-colored maw with rows of sharp teeth rose up between the stairwells and chewed, swallowed, and regurgitated Artus's certainty.

The head and neck of the sea monster trailed downward to a great bulbous body, supported by four enormous flippers that were braced against both stairwells, using them like ladders.

"How did it get through that door?" Artus shouted, startled. "It's too large to fit!"

"Curse it," said Aven. "I left my sword on the ship!"

Jack was casting about for a means of defense. There was nothing to be found—the walls of the keep were bare. Suddenly, he snapped his fingers. "If it came in, it can go out again," said Jack. "John! Go over and below with Charles, and stand ready! Artus! Open a door behind me!"

"Which door?"

"Any! I don't care which! Just be ready!"

The monster had turned its head to focus on Charles, who was the closest. "Well, this is a fine how-do-you-do," said Charles. "I've finally found something big enough to eat Maggot, and he's nowhere around."

"Hey!" Jack yelled at the beast, waving his arms to get its attention. "Over here!"

The sea monster scooped the air with its neck, and came nose-to-nose with the young man. "Damnation," Jack exclaimed as he cocked his arm. "That worked too well."

Jack let fly with his fist and smacked the great beast square in the left eye.

With an enraged roar, the sea monster lunged forward at Jack, who threw himself into the air across the open stairwell. John and Charles caught him by the arms and lifted him safely onto the opposite stair.

The momentum of the sea monster's attack propelled its head and neck through the open doorway, where it caught—impossibly, the beast's body constricted until it fit through the doorway. When it had passed through entirely, Artus slammed the door shut.

"That was very close," he said. "I'm sure this one is closed. Sorry about the other one."

"Bravo, lads!" Bert exclaimed, clapping his hands. "Bravo! Well done!"

"Did you get a look inside the door when he opened it?" asked Charles.

"Yes," Jack said, breathing heavily. "There were Scotsmen—Scotsmen in kilts, maybe sixteenth century."

"Well," said Charles. "A sea monster loose in Scotland. That's going to have some interesting repercussions."

The companions sat on the stairs to catch their collective breath. All of them seemed overjoyed by their narrow escape except for John, who seemed on the verge of tears.

"What's the matter, John?" said Bert. "Chin up—we seem to have a knack for beating the odds."

"Jack has a knack, you mean," John muttered. "No matter what our dilemma, it seems he can always come up with some way to resolve it."

"It seems like I can, doesn't it?" said Jack.

"Bad form, Jack," said Charles. "We're each doing our part. I'm as much to blame as anyone for not keeping a firmer hand on Magwich."

"It's more than Magwich, though," said Jack. "It's a matter of taking action when action is called for. Of just seeing something that needs doing, and doing it. And it seems as if John never does."

John stared at his friends for a moment, then stood and began climbing the stairs. With anxious glances both upward and below, the others followed.

✦ ✦ ✦

They climbed.

Conserving their breath for the exertion, they climbed in silence that was interrupted only by the strange rumbling that occurred every hour or so.

Charles had started counting levels when they began, lost count after the run-in with the sea monster, started again, and gave up sometime after counting to four hundred.

"I'm starting to see why he removed himself from the affairs of the Archipelago," said Charles. "It takes him a century just to go downstairs to greet the milkman."

"Is it me," said Artus, "or is it growing darker up above?"

Bert looked up and gave a joyful shout. "A ceiling! I see the ceiling! We're almost at the top!"

There were three more landings, and four more doors. The one at the top had no stairs. "The future," said Bert. "Unreachable. That means the next-to-last will be the Cartographer. I'm sure of it."

John, however, had paused at the nearest door below. He was looking at it curiously and sniffing the air.

"What is it, John?" said Aven. "Trouble?"

"No," said John. "Cinnamon."

Chapter Fourteen

Night Passage

The Caretaker of the *Imaginarium Geographica* had been transported by a smell—and suddenly, he was no longer responsible for the fate of two worlds, or the resolution of a war, or the many failures he felt had become chains around his neck, grown heavier with each passing hour. He was once again merely a student/soldier, whose greatest responsibilities involved reading Old English manuscripts and making sure he didn't leave his rifle in a trench.

John reached out a tentative hand and stroked the air a whisper above the surface of the door.

"John!" Charles exclaimed. "After what just happened below, I can't believe you're going to risk opening another door!"

"Agreed," said Jack. "We should proceed to the last door and find out if the Cartographer really is here. We've wasted enough time on the past—uh, so to speak."

"This one is different," John said. "Can't you smell it?"

Aven moved next to John and sniffed at the air. "Yes, I can. It's a tobacco of some kind."

"A cinnamon tobacco," said John. "A special mix."

"How odd," said Bert, scratching his head. "The only person I

"John, my dear boy. Please, come inside."

ever knew who liked cinnamon tobacco was . . ." His voice trailed off and his eyes widened in surprise. "Open the door, John."

John reached out with a steady hand and pushed. The door swung open effortlessly on silent hinges, and a fresh wafting of cinnamon-scented tobacco smoke drifted across the companions.

Through the door was a tableaux more familiar to them than any other they'd seen in the keep—because most of them, save for Aven and Artus, had been there mere days before.

It was a study, unmistakably British in decor; a library filled with books and a very familiar figure who could not possibly be sitting in his chair, examining centuries-old incunabula with a magnifying glass and calmly puffing away on a large pipe.

Unlike the other tableaux, which required a crossing of the threshold to spur into motion, this setting was already active, as if it had been waiting for someone to open the door and enter the flow. The figure at the desk noticed them through the open door and spoke; the familiar timbre of his voice left no doubt as to who it was sitting at the broad oaken desk.

Professor Sigurdsson gestured to his young protégé to enter and sit. "John, my dear boy. Please, come inside. We have much to discuss, I think.

"Are there others with you, John?" continued the professor, peering through the smoke at the doorway. "It seems I saw someone else outside."

John looked back at Bert, who shook his head. Whatever import this had was meant for John, and John alone. He stepped forward into the study and closed the door behind him. "No, Professor," he said. "Just me."

The professor stood and took John's proffered hand in both of his own, pumping it frenetically. "So happy to see you, John," he said. "Wasn't expecting you for another day or so, given the state of transportation in these troubled times."

"Believe me, Professor," John said, taking a seat opposite his mentor, "I wasn't expecting to see you, either."

It was almost too much to take in. There had barely been enough time to accept the news of the professor's death, much less come to terms with it. The adventure to the Archipelago had begun almost immediately. And since, all his thoughts of the professor had been fleeting and commingled with regret, and sorrow, and an overwhelming sense of failure.

For an instant John considered whether this visit might be the universe's equivalent of sending him to the rector's office for a reprimand, notwithstanding the fact that the rector was dead.

"I do not know why we have been given this strange opportunity," said the professor, "but I am glad we have, for I fear I shall not live out the night."

John started. Was it possible the professor had had a premonition of his own murder?

"It's true," the professor continued, keeping his own counsel as to whether or not he'd answered John's unspoken question. "Strange elements are loose in the city these days, and they involve me far more than I hoped they would at this age. But I have responsibilities, and I must see them through, whatever the cost."

"I got your note, Professor," said John. "What did you need to tell me?"

"I know from your letters that you are filled with fear, young John. Not just because of the war, but fear for your future.

"I know you are conflicted—that you are at a crossroads and

are not sure which path to take. But know this: I chose you for a reason. You have gifts, John. Remarkable gifts. And if you develop them, as I hope I have helped you begin to do, then you may yet go forth to lead an exceptional, extraordinary life."

John was taken aback—whatever he had expected, it was not this. The professor had always been friendly toward him, in the way that a mentor might be, but such directness, especially with such passionate encouragement, was more than unusual.

"I have not been entirely honest with you, John," said the professor. "The studies I have given you—I've pushed you, I know. But it was all for a purpose. A purpose far greater than I have told you. I'm ready to do so now."

John considered what was happening. Had he indeed stepped backward in time, to the night the professor was killed? Or was he experiencing some other kind of spectral visitation, a phenomenon generated by the strange energies of the keep? And if so, what might be the effect of his revealing the future to the professor? Would it change the events of the past? Or merely complicate the present to a worse degree than he already had?

John made his decision.

"You have been training me," he said, "to become a Caretaker."

The professor relaxed. "You know, then. Wonderful, my boy. How did you come to realize it?"

"I've met Bert. And I've seen the *Imaginarium Geographica*. But—"

"Excellent," the professor said, cutting him off. "Then it doesn't matter what happens to me. Not now."

"Of course it matters!" said John. "How can it not?"

Professor Sigurdsson puffed away on his pipe, filling the room with the aromatic smoke.

"Because," he said at length, "we each have our role to play, and mine was to train you, to prepare you for the mantle you've claimed. No more, no less. And I can see that I did it well enough that I can take whatever is to come with a wink and a nod and a how-do-you-do."

"That's the problem," said John. "You did do your part—but I didn't do mine. I was a terrible student, Professor! And I think I've failed you in every way that one can fail."

Professor Sigurdsson started to laugh, then realized that the young man was serious.

"Boys will be boys, John, and the distractions of life are there to color your work, and vice versa. Besides, you were called away to war, and that's bound to have an effect on your studies."

"That's not what I'm talking about," said John. He couldn't quite bring himself to admit all that had gone wrong in the Archipelago: the inability to function as a translator, followed by the actual loss of the *Geographica* itself. "Bert told me what would be expected of me as Caretaker Principia of the *Geographica*, and I'm not sure I'll be able to do it. I'm just not ready."

"Bert had the same concerns, when last we discussed you," admitted the professor. "But I assured him that when called upon, you would rise to the challenge. And that was enough for him. He never questioned it again. Although in truth, he was a supporter of you before I was. I'm a good scholar—but Bert has the imagination. Not many like him. But in you, my boy, he found a kindred spirit.

"Listen to him, John. He'll advise you well, when I'm not able to, and in ways that I cannot. Heed the words of the Caretakers who preceded you, whose wisdom can be found in the *Geographica*, for they have learned lessons you will need to learn yourself. And make note of the things you observe, so that you can pass the knowledge on to those who will come after—for you have joined a grand tradition, my boy. And once you have accepted this, it will remain forever a part of your life.

"Believe in yourself," the professor said, grasping John's hands in his own. "You have all that you need within you. You are strong enough. You are intelligent enough. You have learned more than you need to complete the tasks that lie before you. Now you must overcome the fear that is preventing you from embracing your destiny."

"The fear that I am too weak?" asked John.

"No," said the professor. "The fear that you are too strong."

John was taken aback. "Too strong? How can I be too strong? I've failed at every task I've been given."

"Because of your fear," said the professor. "Not because you were incapable. Our weaknesses are always evident, both to ourselves and to others. But our strengths are hidden until we choose to reveal them—and that is when we are truly tested. When all that we have within is exposed, and we may no longer blame our inadequacies for our failure, but must instead depend upon our strengths to succeed . . . that is when the measure of a man is taken, my boy.

"Believe in yourself. Believe that you were not meant to spend your life in dusty libraries, nor in the battlefields of war, but in doing something greater.

"Believe in yourself, John, and that you have it within you to lead an extraordinary life.

"Just believe, my boy. My dear boy. Believe."

The wind rattled the windows of the study, the first indication that the weather was shifting.

"I think a storm is coming in," said the professor. "I've said what needed saying, and I think it's time for you to go."

As if punctuating his words, a tapping sound had begun down the street outside. The professor rose and clapped his student on the shoulders.

"You'll do fine, my boy," he said as he opened the door, "and remember, whatever happens—I have been, and always shall be, very proud of you."

With that, John stepped out of the study and closed the door.

Once more he found himself standing in the Keep of Time.

"Is something wrong?" asked Aven.

"What do you mean?"

"You just stepped inside," said Charles. "Just this moment. The door closed, then opened again. You weren't gone for but a second or two."

"Impossible," said John. "I've been talking with Professor Sigurdsson for the past half hour."

"The doorways," said Jack. "They manipulate one's perceptions of time. To John, it was half an hour. To us, out here in the keep, it was no time at all."

"What did he say to you, John?" Bert pressed.

John tilted his head, then smiled. "He said we have a job to do."

As he spoke, the familiar rumbling sound started again, and as the companions watched, the floor shifted beneath their feet, and the ceiling expanded, as if the keep were taking in a breath.

"I think the tower just grew," said Charles.

"That makes sense," said Bert. "This is nearly the last room—if all of the other doorways led to points in the past, then it stands to reason that the Cartographer's room, there near the top, is constantly moving into the future, and the one above is *in* the future."

The door they had determined to be the Cartographer's was the only one in the entire keep that had a keyhole. Jack squatted down on his haunches and peered through.

"Spare me your furtiveness," said a clipped, slightly irritated voice from behind the door. "It's very rude to peep through keyholes—either knock down the door or go away."

Jack stood upright. "Do you have a key?"

"I have a thousand keys," said Bert, "but none that would fit this lock."

Charles reached out a hand and pushed. The door didn't budge. "Solid," he said. "Not like any of the others. Maybe we're *meant* to try to knock it down?"

"Perhaps we could pick the lock," Artus said, as he reached out to examine the mechanism. At his touch there was a sharp click, and the door opened with a slight creaking.

"Hmm," said Artus. "Didn't expect *that* to happen."

He pushed it open the rest of the way, and together, the companions entered the room at the top of the stairs.

"If you're here about the annotations, you're early."

Chapter Fifteen

The Cartographer of Lost Places

The room was expansive, but not overly so. The walls—what could be seen of them—were stone, but every available surface was covered with maps. Old ones, new ones, maps topographical, cultural, political, and agricultural. There were maps of the moon, as well as Antarctica, and even maps that were obviously of the Earth, but of a kind that seemed to have coalesced the continents into a single landmass.

There was a scattering of bookshelves, all laden with volumes of what they presumed were more maps. And save for the two pieces immediately in front of them, no other furniture. The rest of the room was filled with globes, surveying equipment, and rolls upon rolls of parchment, all of which served the purpose and namesake of the man they had come to find.

There, in the center of the room, sketching at a carved wooden desk, was the Cartographer of Lost Places. He was sitting on the edge of a high-backed chair with the emblem of a Sun King carved into the top, intensely focused on the task at hand. He would draw a few quick lines with a large quill, before dipping it into an inkwell on the desk while considering what to do next. He would then make a few more lines, and repeat the entire process.

The Cartographer, for all the legendary dross of rumor and mystique that surrounded him, was rather unremarkable in appearance. He was shortish and stocky, and he wore spectacles that were perched on a bulbous nose. His hair, which was dark save for two streaks of white that grew above his temples, was swept back and flowed to his shoulders.

He wore the scarlet robes that a knight who might have served during the Crusades, or possibly the Inquisition, would have worn. His belt was Roman or Greek, bound tightly over a skirt fashioned from strips of studded leather; and underneath all the rest, he was wrapped in strips of cloth that covered his legs and feet and extended to his wrists.

"Yes?" he said, finally taking notice of his visitors. "If you're here about the annotations, you're early. It's the wrong damned Friday."

With that he resumed his work as if they were not even there.

The clock in the corner ticked away for a few minutes before John finally cleared his throat, loudly. Twice.

The Cartographer rubbed his pen on the blotter and looked up. "Aren't you from the Merchants' Guild? You are Lorenzo de Medici, are you not?"

"Uh, no," said John. "I'm the Caretaker of the *Imaginarium Geographica*."

The Cartographer's eyes widened, and he dropped his pen. "The Caretaker? Really? How extraordinary."

He hopped out of his chair and gestured for them to enter. "Do come in, come in," the Cartographer said. "I hope you will understand and forgive. I've been under this terrible deadline to complete the maps of Florence Below for the Magnificent—"

"Excuse me," said Charles, "but Lorenzo de Medici died in 1492."

"Did he really?" said the Cartographer. "That would explain his failure to forward the additional reference material. I should have expected he would lose track of everything once he started getting distracted by this 'New World' nonsense."

"Do you mean the Americas?" Jack asked.

"It was called something like that, yes," the Cartographer said. "I'm not sure—I tend not to pay attention to these newish countries until they've had a chance to become better established."

"They've been settled for going on three centuries now," said John.

"Well then, they've got a decent start now, don't they?" said the Cartographer. "Another century or four and they might turn into a place worth taking note of."

"I beg your pardon," said Bert, "but we've come seeking your help."

The Cartographer lifted his spectacles and peered more closely at Bert. "I know you, don't I?" he said matter-of-factly. "You seem familiar to me. Not in a 'blood brothers' way, but more of a 'so-you've-come-to-date-my-daughter' sort of way."

"He was one of the most recent Caretakers," Charles said.

"That's not it," said the Cartographer. "I can't place the face, but the hat is memorable." He snapped his fingers. "That's it—we met in the future. I remember now. That nasty business with the Albinos. How is that dear girl Rose, anyway? Is she well?"

"How can you remember him from the future?" asked John.

"Because those who forget the past are doomed to repeat it," came the reply, "but those who remember the future can plan ahead for the weather."

"What good is it to know the future if you can't remember the past?" said Charles. "It seems impractical."

"You could stand with a little impracticality, I think. Your springs seem to be wound a little too tightly. Besides, the past is over, and if you think on it too closely, you either get lost in the misery of the things done poorly, or you get tangled up patting yourself on the back for the things you did well—which no longer matter, because they're in the past, anyway.

"The future, however, is still to come—and it's always fun to look forward to the good events, as well as have an opportunity to plan for the bad."

"If you know something bad is coming, can't you plan to avoid it or try to do something differently?" said Charles.

"Probably," said the Cartographer, "but then the good events would have no flavor. The joy you find in life is paid for by suffering that comes later, just as sometimes, the suffering is redeemed by a joy unexpected. That's the trade that makes a life worth living.

"Take this tower," he explained, gesturing at the room around them. "An extraordinary place to visit, but you wouldn't necessarily want to live here—especially if you could not leave."

"You're a prisoner here, you mean," said Charles.

"The circumstances that resulted in, shall we say, my compulsory residency here in the Keep of Time were of my own making. And while there are moments when I wish I could regain my freedom, given the opportunity, I would still make the same choices."

"How long have you been here?" asked Jack.

"What year did you say it was?"

"It's March of 1917," said Charles.

"About one thousand five hundred years, give or take," said the Cartographer. "But it's not as if I haven't had plenty to do. It is a large Archipelago, after all, and *someone* has to keep track of it."

"You haven't been outside of this room in over a millennium?" Charles said.

"Oh, it hasn't been easy," said the Cartographer. "It can be excruciating waiting for someone to come along with something interesting to do, or better yet, someone who brings gifts, like Paralon apples, or whiskey from Heather Blether. There are also times I think it would be interesting to have stayed in your world," he finished. "I would like to have seen what Hitler would make of someone like me."

"Who?" said Charles.

"Never mind," said the Cartographer. He turned to John. "As you were saying, you're the Caretaker—so you've either come to have me make additions to the *Geographica*, or you want me to destroy it, which I should state right now is just not an option. I'm not about to shred something I spent nearly two thousand years making. So, where is it?"

"I, ah, I seem to have lost it," John said.

The Cartographer rolled his eyes and sighed. "I should have guessed as much. The simple things can be done solo; catastrophes require an entourage."

He shook his head. "It's the Cervantes Dilemma all over again. But what's done is done, and it can't be helped."

The Cartographer walked briskly back to his desk, took a seat, and, whistling a little tune, began working on another map.

The companions looked at each other, bewildered. Finally, John cleared his throat again.

The Cartographer looked at them. "What, are you still here? Do you need validation?"

"Ah, no," John began, "that is, I mean—"

"Spit it out, boy. I'm a very busy man."

"Well, what are we supposed to do now?" said John.

The Cartographer turned to them and pushed his spectacles up onto his forehead. "I'm sorry if I was oblique. Let me try to summarize things in a more concise manner.

"You need the *Imaginarium Geographica* to avert whatever disaster is looming on the world at large. You are the Caretaker of the *Geographica*. You lost the *Geographica*. Ergo, you and everyone you know, love, care about, or exchange pleasantries with as you gather your mail are about to perish in darkness and misery. I hope that's cleared things up for you."

With that, the Cartographer turned back to his map and continued to draw.

John leaned close to Bert. "What do we do now?" he whispered.

"I haven't the faintest idea," Bert replied. "I've never been here. Maybe you should go back and ask Stellan."

John shook his head. "I don't think that's a good idea. The tower grew, remember? That door may not open into the same time or place."

"Drat," said Bert.

"Pardon me," said the Cartographer, "but just how did you people get in here, anyway?"

"You said to come in," said Jack.

"I said to knock down the door or go away," said the Cartographer, "and I expected you to go away, because that door is impossible to knock down. I know. I spent most of the seventh century trying to do it myself."

"Then how does anyone ever get in?" asked Charles.

"The Caretakers are always permitted to enter with the *Imaginarium Geographica*," said the Cartographer. "It's like a golden ticket that opens doors, or a magic word, like 'Open Sesame.'"

"Actually, that's two words," said Jack, "and the magic word was 'Alakazam.'"

"Don't correct your elders, boy," said the Cartographer. "So, out with it. How did you open the door? You said yourself that you'd lost the *Geographica*, and the only other way to get in is with the permission of the king—and pardon my assessment, but none of you look to be the kingly sort."

"You'd be wrong," said Aven, stepping forward and giving Artus a nudge. "*He* opened the door."

The Cartographer hopped off of his chair and shuffled over to Artus. "Ah," he muttered, looking at the young man, who was reddening under the scrutiny. "Ah, I see it now. That nose is unmistakable—a descendant of Arundel, of the House of Eligure, unless I miss my guess. What do they call you, boy?"

"Um, Bug—Artus, that is."

"Umbugartis—unusual name for a king, but there's no accounting for taste," said the Cartographer. "What may the Cartographer of Lost Places do for King Umbugartis?"

"*There* we go," whispered Charles. "We finally have his attention."

"It's just Artus," said Artus, "and it's my friend Sir John, the Caretaker, who needs your help."

The Cartographer looked warily at John over the top of his glasses. "You again. I thought we'd established that there was nothing to be done, since at the moment you don't seem to be the Caretaker of anything."

Charles and Bert started to come to John's defense, but he cut them off with a gesture and looked squarely at the Cartographer. "That's not true," John said. "I may have lost the Geographica, but that doesn't mean I'm not still the Caretaker."

The Cartographer held his gaze, then folded his arms and sighed. "Continue."

"When I was asked to be the Caretaker of the *Imaginarium Geographica*," said John, "I didn't *want* the job. I wasn't prepared. And I certainly didn't want the responsibility. But then I realized there was no one else who *could* do it—and that a lot of people were counting on me to see it through. And there is only one thing you can do in a situation like that—rise to the challenge and bear whatever must be borne to complete the task."

"Interesting," said the Cartographer, "but I'll point it out again: You don't *have* the *Geographica*. How can you fulfill any obligations as Caretaker?"

"It's about more than the book, isn't it?" said John. "It's about taking care of the lands within it too—and right now, that's all I'm trying to do. Having a book of maps won't do anyone any good if the Archipelago is consumed by war—but if we can find a way to prevent that happening, wouldn't that be more important than whether or not I've been able to safeguard the book?"

"That," said the Cartographer, as his eyes glittered and a smile began to spread across his face, "is the first time I've heard you speak like a *real* Caretaker."

He moved back to his chair and picked up his quill. "I'm sorry I don't have anything for you to sit on," said the Cartographer as he resumed working. "So you'll just have to make do with the seating apparatus the gods gave you. Pull up a piece of floor, and tell me what's been going on in the world."

It took the better part of three hours to recount all that had happened to the companions since they left London up to the point where they reached the tower. It was a silent consensus among them not to mention the incident with the sea monster; and the others left it to John to decide whether or not to mention his encounter with the professor, which he chose not to do.

"Ah, yes. Sigurdsson," said the Cartographer when they mentioned the murder. "Pleasant fellow. Came by to visit several times. Brought cookies. Do you have any cookies?"

"We did have a cookbook," said Charles. "But we gave it away."

"You lot seem to have an awful time holding on to books, don't you?" said the Cartographer. "How on earth did you get picked to be Caretakers?"

"It's a long story," said John. "So, can you help us?"

"I'm a little fuzzy on the details," said the Cartographer. "What exactly is it you think I can do?"

"To be honest, I'm a little unclear on that myself," said John. "We think that Magwich is taking the *Geographica* and the Ring of Power to the Winter King, so that he can summon the dragons—"

"Oh he *has* the Ring of Power, does he?" the Cartographer said, interrupting John. "Wears it around his neck, hey?"

"Uh, no—probably on his finger," said Jack.

"Oh ho—even better," said the Cartographer. "I'd like to see *that*. Hmf," he snorted. "That fellow is in for a surprise, I think.

"Well, if you're bound and determined to try to do something constructive, I suppose I should go ahead and help you. That way, if it all goes badly and the world starts to be consumed in death and fire, you can't go around saying, 'It's the Cartographer's fault. If only he'd helped us, we wouldn't be in this pickle.'"

"Fair enough," said John.

"You don't need the *Geographica*, because there is only one island in the Archipelago where he *might* summon the dragons," the Cartographer said. "That's where you'll find him with his 'ring,' trying to summon dragons, and stealing people's shadows, and whatever else it is evil conquerors do these days."

"We'll still need directions to the island," said John. "The *Geographica*—"

"Young man, I am the Cartographer. I *created* the *Geographica*. It is certainly within my powers to recreate a single, solitary map."

He drew a single tanned sheet of parchment from the stack next to his desk, dipped his pen in the crusted inkwell, and quickly began sketching in light, fluid strokes.

As his hand flew back and forth across the parchment, a picture of the island began to emerge.

"Amazing how he can keep his maps so clean when he makes such a mess of the work," Jack whispered to Charles. "He must have ink up to his elbows."

The Cartographer paused and looked up at John. "Navigational directions?"

John nodded. "Yes, please."

"No, no, no," said the Cartographer. "In what language would you like the navigational directions?"

John shrugged. "Whatever you like."

The Cartographer's head lifted almost imperceptibly. "Very good, young man."

He continued adding lines and notations to the sheet until it seemed complete enough to be fully useful. Finally, he set aside the pen and sat back in his chair, giving the freshly created map one last cursory glance and a nod of satisfaction.

The Cartographer sprinkled drying dust across the ink, rolled up the map, bound it with twine, and handed it to John.

"Remember," he said, taking them all in with his gaze, "there is a price to pay for the choices we make, and my permanent confinement in the Keep of Time is part of the price I've paid for choices of my own. Be wary that the choices you make in the coming days do not limit your own paths into the future. Remember it for what you want it to be, and then do that.

"You will find the one you call the Winter King on the Island at the Edge of the World."

. . . the Winter King had been searching for them after all.

Chapter Sixteen

Fire and Flight

As the companions descended the staircase, the tower grew three more times. "Walk faster," Bert admonished. "It's literally going to be a longer walk going down than it was coming up." Nevertheless, surprisingly, it took them a considerably shorter time going down.

"Just like sledding," Charles observed. "It's the long walk up that makes the slide down fun."

Unlike their ascent, which had been done in silence, the companions could not resist discussing the strangeness of the Cartographer as they descended.

"I think it was a great waste of time," said Aven, who had taken the lead along with Jack. "Even if we'd had the *Geographica*, it was clear he wouldn't have destroyed it."

"We might have just left it," John said thoughtfully. "For him to safeguard."

"Yes," added Bert. "I doubt the Winter King would have made the effort to go clear to the top."

"Not to mention that he wouldn't have gotten in," said Charles, giving a knowing smile at Artus. "Not without royal blood."

"Or the *Geographica*," Aven put in, "which he *does* have."

"At least we know he can't destroy it either," said John.

Aven stopped. "Isn't that what we wanted?"

"Not now," said John. "Not now that we know the real stakes."

"Meaning what?"

"Meaning that he intends to use both the Ring of Power and the summoning in the *Geographica* to try to call on the dragons," said John, "and I don't think that's all there is to it. Look at what happened above—Artus opened the locked door with a touch, because he is the true heir. Don't you think the same conditions might hold for summoning the dragons as well?"

"That's an excellent deduction, John," said Charles.

"Agreed," said Bert.

"No pressure," Jack said to Artus.

At the bottom of the staircase (where Artus surreptitiously closed a certain door), the companions laughed with relief and gratitude—happy sounds that ceased the moment they stepped free of the keep.

There, silhouetted by the rising sun, they saw a ship equally as large as their own moored next to the *White Dragon*. It was the *Black Dragon*—the Winter King had been searching for them after all.

Aven cursed and cast a venomous look at John. All of his notes in the *Geographica* had been in unaffected modern English—a child could have located the island.

Leading the Winter King and several dozen Shadow-Born–bearing longboats onto the shore was Magwich. The Steward was clutching the *Imaginarium Geographica* closely to his chest. And even at that distance, they could see that the Winter King was wearing the ring.

"He has what he wanted," said Jack. "There's no reason to come looking for us here."

"Unless he came to the same conclusion we did," said Charles. "Magwich heard the same story from Ordo Maas that we did, remember? The Winter King now knows exactly who Artus is."

"Do we run?" said John. "He's cut off any chance of retreat to the *White Dragon*."

"Quickly," Charles said to the others, "come back onto the stairs."

"Are you stupid?" said Aven. "We'll be trapped."

"No," said Charles. "I don't think we will." Without another word, he started racing back up the steps.

Jack and John exchanged looks of confusion.

"It took us half the night to reach the top," said Jack. "I'm already exhausted. We can't repeat that again, even if we're being chased."

Aven grabbed them both and propelled them toward the stairs, where Bert and Artus were already following closely behind Charles. "No time to argue," she said. "It's the only option we have."

Strangely, the Winter King's henchmen didn't seem to be pursuing them, instead remaining at the bottom.

They were several flights up when Jack stopped, sniffing at the air, then peering down the stairwell.

"Smoke," he cried. "They've set fire to the keep! We have to go back!"

Charles stopped and looked at Jack. The younger man was breathing hard, more from fear than exertion.

"Jack," Charles said, "throughout this entire adventure, you have jumped willingly into every fray. You have accepted every fantastic marvel and irregularity we have encountered as if nothing were amiss. And all the while, I've done very little but question the reality of what we have seen."

"That's why I don't understand what you're doing now," said Jack. "It doesn't make any sense. It's not logical to climb higher into a tower that's just been set on fire."

"Precisely my point," Charles said as he continued to climb. "It *isn't* logical. But then, nothing about this tower is. But I just saw my friend John go into a room and talk to someone we know to be dead, and emerge a changed man for having done it. And I believe that it happened. So if I'm going to take one thing on faith, I think I can take another—so shut up and follow me!"

"Are you going back to the Cartographer?" Jack said, panting. "He's more trapped here than we are, remember?"

"Not that high," Charles said over his shoulder. "Not quite."

Bert grinned. "I think I know what he has in mind. Quickly now—do as he says."

The companions continued their flight up the stairway as the minions of the Winter King began to fill the openings at the base of the tower, while the smoke rose up behind them, as if it were a predator in pursuit of its prey.

Charles's assessment that the tower did not play fairly with the laws of space and time appeared to be correct: In a fraction of the time taken for their original ascent, they had reached the upper levels of the keep. The smoke from the fire below, while still evident, was no longer the air-constricting cloud it had been earlier, and the sounds of their pursuit had faded.

"Why wouldn't they follow us?" Jack said.

"I think they are," said Bert. "The Shadow-Born wouldn't fear the fire—but perhaps the tower is growing for them while it's been shrinking for us."

"It's the same kettle," said Charles. "To them, it's not yet begun to boil—while to us, it's boiling already, even though it's been the same amount of time."

"We're nearly at the top," John said. "We've passed the door that led into London, so we won't be going to last week. And the Cartographer can't help us. So where *are* we going, Charles?"

"There was one more door before the Cartographer's, remember?" said Charles. "If the one below was the recent past, and the one above is the present, then the one in-between might be just what we need."

"And what if it opens onto Outer Mongolia?" said Jack.

"It won't," said Charles.

"How do you know?"

"I don't," Charles said, grinning. "But I believe."

"That's not very logical," said Bert, trying to suppress a grin.

"No, it isn't," said Charles as they reached the next-to-last landing, "but it wasn't logical for John's door to open into a study in London, either. It was just what he needed it to be."

"And what do you need it to be?" Bert asked as Charles extended his hand to touch the door.

"The base of the keep, right after we entered," said Charles.

The door swung open onto the grassy knoll that sloped down to where the *White Dragon* was anchored. The moon was still directly overhead; not morning, but midnight. And there was no sign of the *Black Dragon* or the Winter King.

"Hang on," said Jack. "If we just came out of the keep right after we entered it, then aren't we still inside somewhere? And won't we—they—still be trapped when the Winter King *does* arrive?"

"I don't think so," said Charles. "I think they'll do as we've just done, and escape unscathed as we're about to do."

"What if they choose a different course?" asked Jack. "What if the 'us' in the keep now don't listen to you?"

"It doesn't work that way," Bert assured them. "Trust me—I've done research.

"That's the thing about time travel—you're always moving forward, even when you go back."

Safely aboard the *White Dragon*, they cast off from the shore and circled around to the other side of the island before they unrolled the Cartographer's map.

"It's a simpler course than it would seem," said John. "We have to go a bit farther north, but then, it's all due west. West, to the very edge of the world."

"Best watch we don't sail right off, eh, Aven?" Charles joked.

"Agreed," she said, folding her arms. "Good thinking, Charles."

"Oh, ah, thanks," Charles stammered. "I wasn't serious, you know."

"You should be," said Aven. "I've heard of this place—Nemo said the other sailors all talk of it in hushed whispers when they've had too much ale. It really is the end of the world, and if we're not careful, it's entirely possible that we'll sail right over the edge. But don't worry," she added with mock sweetness. "I understand that there's no ending to the void beyond, so we'd never hit bottom."

"Well, that's good, isn't it?" said Artus.

"No," said Bert. "It means we'd just keep falling, and falling, and falling, for all eternity."

"Oh," said Artus.

"If we set out right away," said John, "we'll have the entire night to gain an advantage over the Winter King. Remember—he's going to be coming here, looking for us."

"I still don't understand why he won't find 'us,'" said Jack. "This time stuff makes my head hurt."

"Trust me," Bert said again. "We're ahead of him, in more ways than one."

"What happens when we do reach the island?" said Aven.

"We have the advantage of surprise," said John. "Whatever is to take place there, we'll be able to prepare for, long before he reaches us. We have the *White Dragon*—it should get us there with exceptional speed."

"She, not it," said Aven. "Let's do it."

Jack and Charles set about preparing the sails for travel northward—although the ship was already prodding itself in that direction. Not all of the motive power would come from the winds.

Aven took the wheel, and Artus, trying to make himself useful, climbed up to the crow's nest.

Bert and John stood at the prow, enjoying the respite they'd found, however limited it might be.

"Tell me, lad," said Bert. "What did the professor say to you in the tower?"

John smiled. "He said to listen to you, and that he had all the confidence in the world that we would defeat the Winter King."

Bert gave John an odd look. "Did he really say that?"

"Close enough," said John. "But then, the Cartographer said as much, didn't he? We went in with nothing, and came out with little more. What did he tell us that we didn't already know, except that our victory or defeat may come down to a matter of will?"

The old man nodded. "I'm glad you got that chance," he said, "to see him—Stellan—one more time. I would have liked to myself. Ah, well—plenty of time to do that in the future, eh, my boy?"

Bert walked away to speak to Aven before John had a chance to ask him what he meant.

The *White Dragon* left the islands of Chamenos Liber in relative silence, and calm seas. Only one pair of eyes watched it pass. High above them in the clear night sky, the great silver and crimson crane watched a few minutes longer, then wheeled about and began to fly south with increasing speed.

Part Five

The Island at the Edge of the World

"I greet you also, my friend the Far Traveler."

Chapter Seventeen

Hope and Despair

The journey from the Cartographer's island to the Island at the Edge of the World was the most peaceful and least eventful passage they had experienced since the original voyage from London into the Archipelago. The night air was clear, and the stars above stunning in their brilliance.

Artus was pointing out constellations to his companions; constellations, not all of which existed in the world beyond.

"Do you see that pattern of stars in the east?" he was saying to John. "The jagged grouping, there?"

"Yes, I see them."

"That's Athamas and Themisto. They're pursuing that cluster there, to the north—we call that one Salmoneus. He was a merchant who stole forty pieces of silver from Athamas, and they are chasing him across the sky, to make him give back the silver."

"What's that one, there?" asked Charles, pointing. "The line that looks like Orion's Belt?"

"It's Orion's Belt," said Artus.

"Ah," said Charles.

"What is that one?" asked John, pointing to the west. "The bright grouping, shaped rather like a tree?"

"Astraeus," Aven called out. "God of the four winds and friend to sailors. Say a little prayer when you look at him, so he will give us what we need to keep our course."

"A little prayer?" said Jack. "To a constellation?"

"To what it represents," said Aven.

"But I don't believe in what it represents," said Jack.

"Prayers aren't for the deity," said Aven. "They're for you, to recommit yourself to what you believe."

"Can't you do that without praying to a dead Greek god?"

"Sure," said Aven. "But how often would anyone do that, if not in prayer?"

The companions slept in shifts throughout the remainder of the night: John, Artus, and Bert first, then Aven, Jack, and Charles, with Bert assuming control of the wheel.

Aven awoke just as the sun was cresting into view, a wheel shooting great spokes of radiance across the sky. The light was brilliant, and the sky at the horizon a startling robin's egg blue, which paled farther up into the sky along the sun's eventual arc.

But to the west, directly in their path, was the darkness they'd earlier assumed to be a line of storms; a sister Frontier to the one that guarded the boundary at Avalon. But they weren't storms at all—it was simply, purely, darkness. Darkness . . .

. . . or Shadow.

They heard the sound first, before the island came into view, and John was very grateful for the Cartographer's precise navigational instructions, for if they had approached the island at an angle just a few degrees less or more, the *White Dragon* would not have been able to resist the pull.

The sound was a roar as big as the world; it was the sound of a waterfall as wide as an ocean, falling into an endless void as deep as Hades itself.

The Island at the Edge of the World was larger than Avalon and Byblos together. It was a flat, rocky plain, which rose to a scattering of hills in the center, then sloped up westward to a peak that extended beyond the edge, over the waterfall.

John shuddered with the realization of what must lay beyond. There were no stars, and the light from the rising sun seemed to be swallowed up by the darkness. The island truly was an Ending of Endings, and somehow he knew that the confrontation with the Winter King would end here.

One way or the other, it would end.

Aven guided the *White Dragon* through a wicked-looking reef to a spot on the southern shore where she could be safely anchored. They could see the entire shoreline in both directions—to the east, from which they'd just arrived, and west to the edge. There were no other vessels in sight, and most importantly, no sign of the *Black Dragon*.

The companions disembarked so they could begin to explore the island, and they quickly determined that it was a singularly unremarkable place.

"Well, except for that waterfall," said Charles. "It's sort of like that place in America, where that big canyon is—somewhere you wouldn't really go to, except to see a great big hole that will be your death if you fall in."

There were no structures of any kind, save for the occasional standing stones that were set pell-mell across the fields and at the top of the bluff on the western side.

"So what do we do now?" said Jack. "Do we just camp out and wait for the Winter King to arrive, or what?"

"We should finish scouting the rest of the island," said Aven. "We have a good lead on him—we should endeavor to make the most of it."

"Sensible," said Bert.

With Aven leading, they crossed the first low valley and headed for the hills in the center. It was, except for the bluff and peak itself, the highest point on the island, and would be an excellent vantage point from which to organize their efforts.

The darkness beyond gave the landscape an unearthly glow, with the sunlight highlighting the muted colors of the rocks and grasses. Everything stood out in high relief—which made the sight beyond the hills more unreal than they could have imagined.

They'd been correct about the view: From the center, they could see the entire expanse of the island, including the north side that had been hidden from sight on their seaward approach.

All along the northern edge of the island were encampments; glowing fires, and the bustle and clatter of warriors preparing for combat. They could see trolls by the thousand, and more Wendigo than they could have imagined existed. And all throughout the encampment rose the black banner of the Winter King.

Even John, who had seen combat, and the most terrible battlefields of war, was struck speechless by the implied violence and destructive force spread before them.

"No wonder we could never find him," Aven whispered. "In all these years, he always evaded his pursuers, and simply moved from land to land, conquering them, then returning to a place we could never discover. He found the best hiding place in existence—the actual ends of the Earth."

"He didn't need to beat us here," Bert said. "The Winter King's army has been here all along."

"I think we're in trouble," said Charles.

"That's the understatement of the year," said Jack. "We're in for a difficult battle, that's for certain."

Aven stared ahead at the hundreds of glowing fires. "There must be thousands of them," she said. "This is not going to be a battle—it's going to be a slaughter. *Our* slaughter."

"I don't think I want to be king anymore," said Artus. "I nominate Jack."

"Aw, don't give up hope," said Tummeler. "This is the part in stories where they gets real good—valiant friends in a struggle 'gainst impossible odds."

The companions heard what the badger said, but it took a few seconds to process that he was standing on the rise next to them, since they had left Tummeler on Paralon.

"Tummeler?" Charles said, incredulous. "Is it really you?"

"Su'prise," said Tummeler. "I brung . . . brang . . . bringed . . . I'm with th' cavalry. We've come t' save th' day."

After a round of excited hugs and greetings, Tummeler explained to the companions what else was transpiring in the Archipelago, and for the first time, they felt a glimmering of hope.

"It were ol' Ordo Maas," said Tummeler. "He said y' would be needin' some help, an' he sent out his sons to all the corners of the Archipelago. One of them watched the *White Dragon*, t' see where y' be going, and the others went t' alert all your friends—and you have more than y' be knowing y' do."

"His sons?" Jack said in surprise. "How could they go to find allies? We took the only ship on Byblos."

In answer, Tummeler pointed to the sky. Circling above the *White Dragon* was a scarlet and silver crane, which dipped its wings in greeting.

"I was with Mister Samaranth when the crane come in, an' I hitched a ride back on one o' th' ships. And I came ready to fight," said Tummeler, proudly showing off his battered knapsack and an equally battered shield that was larger than he was, and that he could lift only with considerable effort. "After all," he finished, "I don't want to be missin' any o' th' fun."

"Is Samaranth coming?" asked Bert. "Will he be joining the battle?"

Tummeler shrugged. "Can't say if he will. I know he left Paralon when we did, an' said he was going to find some others t' help, but what that means I can't say."

"How did you get here, then?" said Charles, "if not with Samaranth?"

"I brought him," said a voice of command, "and while he's skilled with maintenance of the ship, it's his culinary skills I find most valuable. We've never eaten better."

It was Nemo.

In the distance behind him, out in the shallows of the expansive inlet and to the rear of the *White Dragon*, lay the gleaming form of the *Nautilus*.

"Ho, Aven," Nemo said in greeting, laying his fist across his chest.

"Ho, Nemo," Aven responded, offering the gesture in return. "Well met."

Nemo turned to say hello to Bert, but before he could voice a greeting, the little man rushed over and embraced the surprised captain in a bear hug.

"Oh, my stars and garters!" Bert exclaimed. "I've never been so happy to see . . . well, almost anyone!"

"Is that so?" Nemo said with a wink at the others. "That's too bad," he finished, gesturing over his shoulder with his thumb, "because they'll be disappointed if they get less of a reception, just because I beat them here."

"What is it?" said Jack. "Who's coming?"

"It's the other ships," Bert said, eyes glittering with barely contained excitement. "The Dragonships have come together once more."

The companions, together with Nemo and Tummeler, raced back to the beach where the ships were anchored, as the first of the other Dragonships began to arrive.

"The *Orange Dragon*," said Bert. "The Dwarves, I think, run that one these days."

It was a Viking longship, broad and flat across the middle, from which extended three steeply pointed prows and a tall mast with the largest sail John, Jack, and Charles had ever seen. It was also, Bert explained, the only one of the Dragonships with three dragonheads, one on each prow.

"I suppose the Vikings thought that where one was good, three might be better. Although," he added, "given their successful track record for looting and pillaging, I can't say that they were incorrect."

The captain of the *Orange Dragon*, who Aven explained was also the king of the Dwarves, splashed through the shallows carrying a massive ax and a stern expression. He shook hands with Nemo and gave a curt nod to Bert and the others.

"A little grim, isn't he?" said Charles.

"Grim?" said Bert in surprise. "You don't know dwarves. For him, that greeting was positively giddy."

"That, I'm assuming," said Charles, pointing seaward, "is the *Blue Dragon*, unless I miss my guess."

It was. The Elves had arrived with the greatest of the Dragonships, an immense vessel that towered over the other ships as if they were toys. It was fully five stories tall, and almost three times as long and as broad as the *White Dragon*. The sails were barely visible, but it obviously had other means of propulsion, much like the *Nautilus*.

The Elders of the Elves disembarked through a hatch that appeared just above the waterline and came over to greet the companions. They were several of the same elves who'd been present at the Council on Paralon, and they greeted John, Jack, and Charles as if they were visiting dignitaries.

"Ho, Caretaker," the Elf King, Eledir, said in greeting to Bert. "The Ancient of Days told us that you could use our assistance."

Bert bowed his head. "And we are grateful for it," he said with sincerity. "How many have you brought?"

Eledir pointed at the *Blue Dragon* in answer, as dozens of elves, armored and equipped for battle, flowed out onto the beach.

"Six hundred," said the Elf King. "More ships will follow, but this number was the best we could arrange and still arrive in time."

"Every one is a help," said Bert. "We won't complain."

The next ship to arrive was the *Green Dragon*—which seemed to be under the stewardship of the mythological creatures of the Archipelago.

It was not unlike the *White Dragon* in appearance, except for the fact that it seemed the timbers from which it was made had never lost their ambition to be trees, and had kept on growing accordingly. There were branches and tufts of leaves everywhere. And the sails were so overgrown as to nearly collapse with the weight. The occupants were not merely on the deck, but also clambered up and around the branches and spars as easily as walking on the ground.

From their vantage point on the beach, the companions were able to make out fauns and satyrs ("Great," Aven grumbled. "As if they'll be a lot of help."), more than a few animals (including several badgers, wolverines, and at least one creature Jack identified as a Tasmanian devil), and the core of their force, a herd of centaurs.

The captain of the *Green Dragon* was a centaur whom Nemo greeted as Charys. He was massive, standing eight feet tall at the shoulder, and kicked up a curtain of sand as he trotted over to the companions.

"Greetings, Sons of Adam," said Charys. "Which one of you is the Caretaker Principia?"

"That would be me," John said.

"Nemo told me of you when he came to Praxis to enlist our aid," said Charys. "I like your style. 'Let's go thataway,'" he said with a deep horsey laugh. "Oh ho ho! Now that's the way we navigated in the olden days!" He laughed again and trotted off to greet the dwarves.

"I think he was poking fun at me," said John.

"He was," Charles agreed, "but I don't think it's advisable to make an issue of it."

Bert was pacing the shoreline, watching the water for more arrivals. By their count, there were two more Dragonships that might still come.

"One, actually," said Aven. "The *Violet Dragon*—the ship of the Goblin King."

"I don't know," said Bert. "I feel we may yet see the other as well."

"Is it possible?" said Aven.

Bert scanned the horizon, then shook his head. "No, I don't think so. It was too much to hope for, I know, but still . . ."

"What are you looking for?" John asked.

"The first Dragonship," said Aven. "The *Red Dragon*. It hasn't been seen since shortly after Ordo Maas created it.

"As Ordo Maas said, all of the ships—even our own *Indigo Dragon,* bless her spars—were made from existing hulls. They were not new-built, but created from ships that knew surf and storm and had proven themselves able to cross into waters of a new world. And the *Red Dragon* was the greatest of them all."

"What was the *Red Dragon?*" asked Charles. "Anything we might know?"

"Yes," said Bert. "In fact, it was the original ship that showed Ordo Maas the secret of passage between the worlds and led him to the idea of living mastheads—for it had one of its own.

"Before it was remade as the *Red Dragon,* it was a ship known as the *Argo.*"

• • •

The kings and captains of the ships sat together in a council of war, while the others helped to organize their troops and make themselves ready for whatever was to come.

Jack immediately positioned himself alongside Nemo and Eledir as a representative of Man, although Bert had already explained Artus's true identity and put him forth as the heir to the Silver Throne.

Nemo seemed to accept this news with aplomb, but Eledir and Falladay Finn, the Dwarf King, were more reserved.

"We've been through one round of false kings and queens, presented by the humans," Eledir said, referring to the Council. "The Archipelago cannot continue to be supportive of a race that is unable to even police its own."

Falladay Finn nodded in agreement. "If what you say is true, you will have the support of the dwarves. But," he added, looking at Artus, "the first duty of a king is to rule for the benefit of his subjects, and not for himself. Your grandfather forgot that. If you survive this day, see to it that you do not."

He placed his hand over Artus's own in a gesture of support, followed quickly by Charys and more grudgingly by Eledir. Despite the official endorsement, their faces still showed the doubt and fear they felt.

"Cheer up, boy," Charys said, bellowing with laughter at Artus's crestfallen expression. "The way things are looking, none of us is going to survive anyway, so you won't have to worry about it."

Farther south on the beach, Charles was struggling with a leather-and-mail vest that one of the dwarves had offered him—which was three sizes too small. As he tried unsuccessfully to fasten the buckles, his little friend from Paralon plopped down on the sand next to him.

"Ready when you are, Master Scowler," said Tummeler. He still had the heavy knapsack, which he was dragging around inside the old bronze shield he'd arrived with, and he had fashioned a helmet from an apple pail. It kept slipping down onto his nose.

"Tummeler!" Charles exclaimed. "No offense, but I don't think badgers are suited for battle!"

"Really, think as such, do ye, Master Scowler?" replied Tummeler. "We badgers be gentle creatures, true—but I be thinkin' ye've ne'er seed a badger with his fur all adander."

"Now, now," Charles began, keeping a nervous eye on the all-too-close soon-to-be battlefield over the rise.

"I know what ye be thinkin'," said Tummeler. "My smallish happearance an' happy-go-nancy nature bein' what they is, ol' Tummeler can't possibly be a warrior.

"Well," he continued, "I's hopin' that th' enemy thinks as such—then I c'n take 'em out with my secret weapons."

"Secret weapons?" said Charles.

"Yup," nodded Tummeler. "Gots 'em right here."

The small mammal opened his heavy carryall and showed its contents to Charles and John, who had been eavesdropping as he strapped on armor of his own.

"Muffins?" Charles and John exclaimed together. "Your secret weapons are muffins?"

"Not just any muffins," said Tummeler. "Blueberry."

"I'm sorry," Charles began.

Tummeler ignored him and instead removed a fist-size (badger-fist-size) muffin from the bag, took careful aim, and lobbed it considerably farther than either of the men expected was possible. It soared into the air and landed with a thunk onto the helmet of a satyr who had been slinking around the *Orange Dragon* at the landing fifty yards away. The satyr dropped to the ground, knocked out cold.

"Bloody hell," said John.

"Amazing," said Charles.

"Hard as rocks," said Tummeler. "Whipped them up after I saw y' off from Paralon, just in case."

"Amazing," Charles said again. "You made a blueberry muffin into a weapon."

"Atchly, any kind of muffin will do," said Tummeler, "but I found out that y' needs t' use blueberries if y' wants t' get it *just so*. It's my own secret contribution," he added.

"Won't breathe a word of it," said Charles.

Jack came running over to his friends, breathing hard.

"What is it?" said Charles. "What's happened?"

"It's the Goblins," Jack panted. "The *Violet Dragon* has arrived at last."

The last of the Dragonships resembled an elaborate Chinese junk, which was in line with the elegant mannerisms of the Goblin King and his entourage. It was smaller than the rest, more of a size with the *Indigo Dragon*, but tall, and it had a beautiful mainsail that shimmered in the light.

"I am very happy to see you," said Bert, offering his hand in greeting. "My friend, Uruk Ko."

The Goblin King hesitated, then took the old man's hand, giving it a single dignified shake. "I greet you also, my friend the Far Traveler."

"How many have you brought with you?" asked Nemo, looking with a barely disguised disdain at the *Violet Dragon*, which seemed manned by only a few officious types, none of whom were outfitted for war. "Are they coming by other means?"

"Yes," said Uruk Ko. "Other ships of the kingdom bore my warriors here—more than a thousand, to be exact."

Bert and Aven exchanged relieved glances. This battle would be more evenly matched than they'd first feared. "Do you realize," Bert said, "that your goblins represent more than half of our defensive force?"

"Yes, I do," Uruk Ko said. "I am pleased you also realize that. It will make what must happen easier to bear."

"Whatever do you mean?" said Bert, scanning the horizon for a sign of the Goblin army's ships. "When are they expected to arrive?"

"You misunderstand me," said Uruk Ko. "They are already here."

"Really?" Bert said, squinting. "How did I miss them?"

"Because," said the Goblin King, "you are looking in the wrong direction."

"What?" Bert breathed.

As one, the other captains and kings turned, then made their way up to the first of the hills, where they could look out over the enemy's encampments. There they saw the black standards of the Winter King, as well as the flags of Arawn—but also, to the north, they saw with rising dread the unmistakable silken banners of the Goblin King.

"It was because of our friendship that I felt honor-bound to tell you myself, and in person," said Uruk Ko, "and now I have done so. Please—as one who has stood with you as an ally, choose wisely, and leave the battlefield before we must come face-to-face as enemies."

The expressions of the other kings darkened, and a menacing growl came from deep inside Charys's massive chest, as he moved defensively in front of Artus.

Aven spit, cursed, and began to lunge forward, drawing her sword. "What kind of man . . . ," she began, just as Bert stopped her advance.

"Not a man," said Uruk Ko, as he turned to make his way back to the *Violet Dragon*. "A goblin, and a Child of the True Archipelago, who wishes only to drive out the usurpers that have ruled for far too long.

"Leave, my friends. A new age is dawning, and it will be birthed in fire. A new age; an age of Goblin, Troll, and Shadow.

"The age of Man is over."

"They will attack within the hour," Charys said . . .

Chapter Eighteen

The Final Battle

At noon the *Black Dragon* arrived.

It eased along the eastern edge of the island, safely in the lee of the pull of the falls, where the Winter King could take stock of the allies before making his way to where his army was massing.

"They will attack within the hour," Charys said to the assembled war council, which was still reeling from the defection of the Goblin King.

"How can you be sure?" said Bert.

The centaur indicated the motion of the sun across the sky, moving westward, and the council saw what Charys had surmised. The terminus of the void, the edge to the darkness beyond, was only a few degrees away from the sun's position and would soon engulf it.

"That's why they have the fires and torches lit in broad daylight," said Jack. "The Winter King is used to being here and knows it's going to be dark soon."

Charys nodded. "We will be in absolute darkness, and it will be difficult to separate friend from foe, much less counter the attacks of the Shadow-Born."

Aven volunteered to start gathering torches, or anything that could be assembled into torches, from the ships, taking with her a company of fauns.

"Despite the stated intentions of Uruk Ko," said Bert, "we must remember that the Winter King has another agenda. He plans to attempt to summon the dragons back to the Archipelago."

Eledir gave what amounted to a restrained snort of derision. "Impossible. Only the High King has ever known how to do this. Even my own ancestors, who were confidants of the great Samaranth, did not know the secret."

"Yes," said Falladay Finn. "When Archibald offended them, the dragons left the Archipelago forever. We need to deal with the army that has been assembled here and now, and not the imaginary one we worry may come."

"With respect, I disagree," said John. "The secret of the summoning is in the *Imaginarium Geographica,* which was stolen and is now in the possession of the Winter King. He also has Archibald's Ring of Power, which the *Geographica* says will allow the summoning to take place."

"Even I have a Ring of Power," snorted Falladay Finn, extending his hand, which bore a ring identical to the one Magwich had stolen.

"As do I," said Eledir, "as do my lieutenants. Rings of Power, as you call them, are symbols of office and fealty, nothing more. My ancestor Eledin received his at the same time as the High King Arthur, and he never saw a difference in the two."

"It doesn't matter if we believe it," said John. "The Winter King does. And if he's right, then we'll be lost. But if he's wrong, then maybe we can divert his attentions away from the battle long enough to gain an advantage."

The kings and captains exchanged knowing glances, and John realized that there would be no advantages to be gained by a distraction. Once joined in battle, the opposing force would be irresistible and would flow over the assembled forces of the allies like a wave.

"We still do not know the real scope of his army," said Falladay Finn. "As yet, we have not seen any of the Shadow-Born among the assembly."

"That's a concern," Eledir said. "Perhaps greater than the Trolls and Goblins, who can still be killed."

"May I say something?"

The council turned to look at the speaker—Artus, who had not ventured an opinion since they'd begun, instead allowing John, Jack, or Bert to speak for Men and Paralon.

Charys nodded. "You are the heir to the Silver Throne," he said. "Speak, and we will listen."

"Well," Artus began, "I've been thinking—Ordo Maas told us that the Shadow-Born were created by that magic kettle, right?"

"Pandora's Box," Eledir said. "A myth. Nothing more."

"Ordo Maas didn't think so," said Artus. "And besides, the Shadow-Born came from somewhere, didn't they? Do you have a better explanation?"

Eledir remained silent and indicated with a nod for Artus to continue.

"If my grandfather—King Archibald—started creating the Shadow-Born by opening the box, and the Winter King created more of them and began taking over the Archipelago by keeping it open, then why don't we just do what Aven suggested, and find it, and close it?"

This suggestion was met with a resounding silence, which was then shattered by Charys's booming laugh.

"By my body and bones, that's either the most kingly thing I've ever heard, or it's the single stupidest plan on Earth," he said, laughing and stomping his hind legs.

"If that is the source of his ability to create Shadow-Born," Artus continued, "then by closing it, we can prevent him from creating more."

"That's a good plan," said Nemo. "I wonder what effect closing the box would have on the existing Shadow-Born?"

"Also," said Artus, growing bolder with each comment of support, "it's probably here, on the island. The Winter King wouldn't have risked losing it to combat or weather by keeping it on board the *Black Dragon*, so if this is really his base, it's probably somewhere around here."

Bert, Nemo, Eledir, and Falladay Finn exchanged glances of unabashed admiration over the boy king's conclusions.

"If he does possess such a weapon," mused the Dwarf King, "he *would* keep it here. There may be something to this strategy after all."

"Right," said Artus. "So all we have to do now is go into his camp, sneak past all the goblins, trolls, Shadow-Born, and Wendigo, find Pandora's Box, and close it. It's simple, really."

Charys slapped his forehead. "Ah, boy," he said, resigned. "You had it going so well, up until the end."

"But he's right," said Charles, who'd been listening in from the perimeter of the council. "That's *exactly* what needs to be done.

"Look," he said, gesturing at the island beyond. "It's a natural battlefield—everyone is expecting that both sides will meet in the middle, and the Winter King's side is expecting the cover of darkness to be to their advantage. So no one would be looking if someone went behind their camp to snoop around while all their attention is focused on us in the center."

"That sounds like a plan," said Charys. "Good luck."

"What?" Charles said, his face suddenly gone pale. "I-I wasn't really volunteering. I'm not a soldier."

"Not many here are, lad," Nemo said. "But we're going to do what we can, all of us, nevertheless."

"We'll do it!" came an excited voice from somewhere nearer the ground. "Master Charles an' his faithful squire, Tummeler, vanquishing foes and, uh, closin' boxes!"

Charles blinked, then grinned. "I guess we're the stealth force," he said, looking down at the exuberant badger. "God help us all."

"The torches are ready," said Aven, approaching the council with several in hand.

"And just in time," said Nemo, shading his eyes and looking up at the sky. The sun was half-covered in Shadow. In minutes the island would be plunged into darkness.

It was determined that Eledir would command the primary force of the allies' army—appropriate, given that it was comprised mostly of elves from the *Blue Dragon*. The elves were primarily armed as archers, although they all bore wicked long swords for one-to-one battle.

Falladay Finn and his dwarves were the most heavily armed, as they'd been at the Council at Paralon, with each of them bearing heavy axes, braces of short knives, and archery equipment of their own. Finn, along with Nemo, served as Eledir's primary lieutenants, with Charys and the assembled creatures bringing up the rear.

Jack, despite cautions from both Charys and the Elf King, had chosen to join in the battle alongside Nemo. Aven and Bert tried to dissuade him, but Jack would brook none of their concerns. His eyes were shining from the fire that blazed in his belly to see real combat. He didn't understand that skirmishes aboard a ship, which were all he'd really experienced, were not the same as war, and further justified his choice by pointing out that he was at least as physically able as John, who'd been a soldier, and was more willing to boot.

"I'll be fine," said Jack. "No one's gotten killed so far, have they? And you know it yourself—I've proven myself to be braver and more resourceful than you thought I'd be. So don't worry. I'm going to do things on this battlefield you'll remember for the rest of your life."

Aven flashed a concerned look at Nemo, who indicated with a brief nod that he would try not to be separated from Jack during the battle.

As she walked back to the beach for more torches, Aven wondered if of the two, she was actually concerned for the right one. Like a drowning man can drag down his rescuer, she hoped that Jack's inexperience in combat would not similarly impair Nemo. She though of going back and saying something more, but she had other matters to attend to and soon forgot about her concerns.

"We're going to find the Winter King."

John said it matter-of-factly, but it sounded more ludicrous out loud than it had inside his head.

He and Bert had reasoned that the Winter King would not engage in the actual battle—not if his goal was still to summon the dragons. John surmised that to make the attempt, the Winter King would move as far away from the battlefield as he could get—and that meant the rocky bluff to the west, which sharpened to a peak high above the roaring falls.

"That's where he'll be, I'm sure of it," said John. "And Artus and I will have to be there too."

"Why me?" asked Artus. "Shouldn't I be on the field, with all the rest?"

Bert took the young man by the shoulders and peered at him over the top of his glasses. "You should not," he said with equal parts sternness and affection. "If John is right, then you may be the only one of us who is able to summon the dragons, and that means you are too valuable to risk putting in open combat. Go with John, and see what you discover. We'll buy you as much time as we can."

The old Caretaker embraced the boy king in a brief hug, then turned and walked to the top of the hill, where Aven was waving a torch.

The sun vanished, and a cry and hue rose up from the other side of the island.

The battle was beginning.

The enemy force was moving south with a slow, deliberate pace, but Eledir directed the elves to rush forward and establish a center line to hold as far into the shallow valley as possible. Against the greater force, they would eventually, inevitably lose ground and be driven back to their ships. Eledir wanted to make sure they had as much ground to lose as possible.

Falladay Finn and the dwarves could not quite keep pace with the elves, so he instructed them to sheath their axes and pull out their bows and arrows. They would fire behind the enemy lines, then pick up their axes again to push forward when the elves were pressed to their first retreat.

Charys and the centaurs had one mandate: to flank the rest, and make sure that none of their enemies were trying to outflank *them*. It was bound to happen at some point, as battles frequently spill past their prescribed boundaries, but with John and Artus heading to the west, and Charles and Tummeler heading east, it would be better to keep as much of the action corralled in the valley as possible.

Nemo, for his part, was firing a weapon of his own manufacture, an air-propelled gun of some kind, which had greater range than anything in use by the other races, and he was augmenting his assistance to Eledir by taking out the Troll and Goblin commanders long-distance.

From the hills behind, Bert watched and worried, too old to join in himself. It was not the battle ensuing that worried him, but the one still to come. The trolls and goblins had engaged them, but the hundreds of Wendigo, who were better fighters than the trolls, and more fearsome than the goblins, were still inexplicably clustered around the tents. He had also been scanning the encampment with Aven's spyglass since the battle began, but still . . .

. . . There was no sign of the Shadow-Born.

Charles's plan was for himself and Tummeler to skirt around the eastern shore of the island and come around behind the Winter King's encampment, there to look for the kettle. They were dressed in dark leathers and would carry no torches, planning on Tummeler's animal senses to guide them through the darkness.

They were preparing to move down to the beach, when something in the torchlight caught Charles's attention. He stopped and looked more closely, then his eyes widened in shock, and he dropped his supplies to go find Aven.

"Master scowler?" said Tummeler.

"Stay there," said Charles. "I'll be right back."

"Aven!" Charles said, finding her gathering more flammable materials from the *Green Dragon*. "Listen to me. Something is wrong! Something is wrong with Jack!"

Aven started a curt retort, but bit it back. Something in Charles's tone told her that this was not an unconsidered assessment. "What is it? What's wrong with him?"

Charles took her arm and pulled her closer. "I couldn't put my finger on it until just now. For the last few days, he's grown more and more brash, reckless even. I thought . . ."

He blushed. "I thought he was just trying overhard to impress you."

"Since the moment we met," said Aven. "What of it? He's grown confident. He's become a man—maybe even a warrior, although I'd cut out my own tongue before I let him hear me say that."

"I thought the same, but—"

"But what, Charles?"

Charles pointed to the rise twenty yards off where Jack was organizing several of the fauns and satyrs into a staggered line of archers. Aven was right: He *was* more confident. He *did* direct them with an authority that belied his youth, and he had proven himself in every battle they had joined. But Charles's suspicions had manifested themselves in a form visible yet subtle, and Aven's breath caught in her throat when she saw it.

Jack had no shadow.

The first engagement had gone badly.

The elves, impressive as they were in battle, were not a match for the trolls, the smallest of which outweighed the largest, stockiest elf. It was only the quality of their elf-forged armor that saved them from being completely overrun, and they retreated to switch to bows and arrows.

Unexpectedly, the dwarves fared better at hand-to-hand combat against the trolls, and they added to the attack a benefit for the Elven archers to the rear. The dwarves' short stature meant that the huge trolls had to stoop to strike a blow, exposing the backs of their heads and shoulders to the arrows, while the dwarves whaled away at their legs and midriffs with the massive battle-axes. Still, the overwhelming might of the trolls was something to be held, and held only, not beaten back.

As they'd feared, the goblins had attempted a flanking action, only to be forced back into line with the others by the centaurs. The goblin archers' aim was deadly, but the centaurs shrugged off the arrows as if they were wasps.

The other archers and pikemen gleaned from the mythbeasts and animals, led by Jack, came in behind the centaurs, and in moments the goblins were in full retreat. The trolls made another great push forward, then, amazingly, began to pull back as well.

"They're retreating," Charys said in amazement, blood streaming from his wounds, running freely down his flanks. "The goblins, and the trolls—they're retreating!"

As unlikely as it seemed, the centaur was right.

With a cheer, the elves drew their swords and pressed ahead—then, suddenly, Eledir gave the command to stop, and the dwarves and centaurs also wheeled about.

Nemo signaled desperately to Bert, then gestured to the Winter King's encampment, calling out something Bert couldn't discern over the din of battle and roar of the falls.

He put the spyglass to his eye and looked in the direction Nemo had indicated. As if on cue, the Wendigo opened the tents all along the shore, which they'd assumed to belong to trolls and goblins who'd come from their homelands to fight.

They were mistaken. The Shadow-Born had been there all along—they had merely waited until the light and heat of the noonday sun had been enveloped in Shadow, when their power would be at its strongest, and they would be able to move almost invisibly in the dark.

"Dear God in Heaven," said Bert. "This may truly be the end for us all."

Aven spun around and suppressed a shudder, then, worse, began to silently weep.

John and Artus, who had not yet gone west, exchanged worried looks, then clambered up the rise to see what had shaken Bert and Aven so badly. A moment's glance and an instant of comprehension was all that they needed.

They had expected, even planned for, the army of Wendigo; the trolls, guided by the traitorous Prince Arawn, had also come as no great surprise. Even a few of the lesser races from the edges of the Archipelago could have added to the bulk of the opposing army without rattling a veteran such as Aven. But what they saw not a mile away chilled the marrow in their bones and clenched their spirits in fear and growing horror.

At the edge of the vast plain of the battlefield, the great host of the Winter King had begun its approach. Marching toward them, from horizon to horizon, were the howling, snarling forms of Wendigo, and with them, mute and relentless, came the hooded specters of thousands and thousands of Shadow-Born.

Chapter Nineteen

The Circle of Stones

There was an unusual kind of quietude on the stony peak that rose above the waterfall at the edge of the world. An almost white noise, created by the commingling of the sounds of battle from the valley to the east and the never-ending combustion engine of the falls to the remaining west.

The Winter King made his way along the bluff line, taking care not to slip on the rocks that were dampened and slick from the eternal spray. It was slow going, for he had only the hook to reach out with to steady himself. In his good hand he was clutching the *Imaginarium Geographica*. He didn't trust his translator to carry it—if Magwich were to drop it over the edge, accidentally or otherwise, he'd have to kill him, and as it was, he was merely planning on forcing the hapless Steward to look into Pandora's Box and become a Shadow-Born.

He'd have done it long before, were it not for the fact that Shadow-Born were mute—and annoying as it was, he still needed Magwich to retain the ability to speak.

For a little longer, anyway.

"How much farther?" whined Magwich, who trailed his master by several yards.

"That's the place," said John . . . "I'm certain of it."

The Winter King spun about. "What? You're the one who said this was where we had to be to speak the summoning!"

"Well," said Magwich, "I told you it said in the *Geographica* that you could use the Ring of Power only at the place in the Archipelago farthest to the west, which, technically, is here on the bluff. I don't really know if the exact spot where you do it is important."

The Winter King glowered. "Don't waste my time, Steward. Are we there or not?"

In reply, Magwich motioned for the *Geographica*. The Winter King passed it over, then watched impatiently as the Steward thumbed through several pages, leafing back and forth between them, making little humming noises as he did so.

"Well?"

The Steward shook his head. "I don't think it matters. I'm pretty sure we have all you need, and we're in the best place to do it."

"Pretty sure?" said the Winter King. "I thought you had been trained to read that atlas."

Magwich shrugged. "I never actually finished training, remember? A few of the languages here are just beyond me—but I can still get the gist of it, so what does it matter if we miss a few details?"

"Never mind," the Winter King snapped, snatching the book back. "Let's just get this done, and then after I've assumed control of the entire Archipelago, I'll make sure you get the reward you've earned."

Magwich licked his lips and bowed deeply. "Thank you, my Lord."

"Idiot," said the Winter King.

"Whatever you say, my Lord."

"Just shut up, will you?"

"As you command, my Lord."

The Winter King clenched his jaw. "If you say one more word, I'm going to put my hook through both of your eyes and pull your brain out through the sockets."

"Sorry, my Lord."

The Winter King sighed heavily and opened the *Geographica*. "Just show me where the summoning is, and tell me what to say."

A hundred yards into their mission, Charles already regretted having agreed to it. He was soaked from head to toe in seawater, and he smelled faintly of brine. Worse, Tummeler was also soaked, and the odor of wet badger fur emanated from him in waves.

They had decided to keep to the edge of the shoreline, the better to steer clear of any stragglers from the Troll or Goblin armies. But unlike the beaches on the south, which were smooth and sand-covered, the eastern side had been subject to the unending tidal forces created by the pull of the falls—and as a result, the beach was rocky and uneven. Every few steps, one or the other of them had taken a tumble into the surf, only to reemerge splashing and sputtering.

They were noisy, dragging a trail throughout the visible sand, and were projecting a smell that could be followed by a blind Wendigo with a head cold.

They were, Charles decided, the worst stealth force ever to be sent on a mission during wartime.

"Don't mind my sayin' so," said Tummeler, "but you're starting t' smell funny."

"I was about to say the same thing," said Charles.

Tummeler stopped, and looked visibly hurt by the remark. "What d' you mean?"

"Nothing—forget it," said Charles, realizing the badger had meant *his* remark as a compliment.

He was outfitted in light armor the elves had given him to replace the ill-fitting Dwarven tunic, but otherwise carried only a short sword and small hatchet, as he thought appropriate for a stealth mission. Tummeler, however, not only had a large knife, but also was still dragging his supply of rock-hard muffins inside the battered bronze shield.

"Listen, Tummeler," Charles began, "do you really think it's justified to take along all this, this, *stuff*? After all, we're supposed to be sneaking in to search for Pandora's Box—not engaging in a conflict."

Tummeler puffed up his chest in a gesture of badgerly defiance. "Better t' make th' effort t' bring it, then t' find ourselves in a situation where we wants t' have it, and finds it's not there."

Charles thought about that a moment. "Now that you've put it that way," he said, "it is a bit comforting to have more weapons along. But do you really need the shield? It's leaving quite a track."

"Mister Samaranth gave it t' me," said Tummeler, "and told me t' bring it here. He said we'd need it, sooner or later, so bring it I done."

"Fair enough," said Charles, "but what say I carry it, so we make better time?"

"Okee-dokee," said Tummeler, hefting the knapsack over his shoulders and passing the shield to Charles.

"Heavy," Charles muttered as he slipped the shield over his back.

"Y'r not kidding," said Tummeler. "Onward."

With the retreat of the trolls and goblins, the strategy of the Winter King was now obvious. The first onslaught by the denizens of the Archipelago was meant merely to test the resistance of the allies at best, and to cut down as many of the opposing forces as they could at worst. For their part, the trolls and goblins were merely cannon fodder—if they survived the initial attack, and damaged the allies in the process, then all was good. But if they faltered, and many lost their lives—just as good. Because the main force of the Winter King's army were the Wendigo and the Shadow-Born, and there would be no testing or trials, no retreat and withdrawal—just brutal, bloody combat to the end.

The nearest wave of Shadow-Born had reached the advance line of elves and dwarves, and the method of battle they intended to use to defeat the allies became blindingly clear.

The Shadow-Born brushed off arrows like toothpicks, and while a direct blow from an ax or a pike might slow them it wouldn't stop or damage them. And then they were close enough to grasp the shadows of the warriors and rip them free.

The dwarves and elves who lost their shadows screamed, then dropped to the ground, drained of their will and resistance. Then, as the Shadow-Born moved on to other victims, the Wendigo fell on the helpless soldiers to slaughter them in a rending of claws and teeth.

"Douse your torches!" Charys called out. "Put them out!"

Eledir and Falladay Finn exchanged startled glances. It would reduce the threat of the Shadow-Born, true—but then they would be facing the Wendigo in the dark.

"There's no choice!" Charys yelled again. "Douse your torches and pull back, or we are already lost!"

At the rear of the field, Aven and Bert rushed forward to confer with Jack and Nemo.

"What are they doing?" Aven cried. "How can we fight in the dark?"

"Charys is right," said Nemo. "But it won't be completely dark. The Wendigo carry their own torches—but the light from those will cast our shadows backward, not ahead. That will give us a chance to fight, at least, before—"

He stopped and looked down at the ground where they were standing, where his own shadow overlapped with Bert's and Aven's—but not Jack's.

Bert saw it too, and looked at Jack with an expression both sorrowful and fearful.

Jack looked at the ground, then back at the others with a defiant set to his jaw. "I know. I saw it vanish some time ago. But I don't think it means anything—I'm on your side, remember?"

"Doesn't mean anything!" Bert exclaimed. "Jack—you've become a Shadowless! That's worse than a Shadow-Born!"

"How?" Jack said stubbornly.

"It means you have the capacity for darkness," said Nemo. "You may be choosing to stand with us in the light, but your heart is choosing to be in Shadow."

Jack made a cutting motion with his hand. "I don't believe you. Judge me on what I'm actually doing, not on what you think I believe."

"Remember what the Cartographer said about choices and consequences, Jack," said Bert. "Think about what happened to him, over choices he made!"

"The Winter King said the same thing on the *Black Dragon*, remember?" said Jack. "Which one do I believe? The one who's imprisoned and couldn't help us, or the one who's able to conquer?"

"The one who's trying to kill us, you mean," said Nemo.

"Can't I have both?" said Jack. "The conviction of the Cartographer and the strength of the Winter King?"

"You can't have one foot in and the other out," said Bert. "It doesn't work that way."

Nemo looked grimly at Aven. "We don't have time for this. If he's going to become one of the Lost Boys, it'll be his own cross to bear—but I have a battle to fight."

"Wait," Aven said, grabbing Nemo by the arm. "He is good, I know it. Take him, fight with him! If you can't trust him, then trust me!"

Nemo looked at Aven for a long second, then motioned to Jack. "Come on, then," he said. "If nothing else, you'll be the one fighter we have that the Shadow-Born can't touch."

The Steward of Paralon, previously a Caretaker-in-training, went over the summoning of the dragons for the third time before he was certain (to a degree) of the exact wording. It had been sandwiched in with the notations on the map for the Island at the Edge of the World and the actual location where the ritual was to be performed.

He was a bit relieved that the Winter King didn't question him (too) extensively as to the accuracy of the translation—if his master really knew how much supposition and guesswork was involved, he'd have already cut the Steward's throat.

But then, Magwich justified, if the Caretakers of the *Geographica* weren't meant to exercise a little creative license, then why were they given credit for having a good imagination?

"Well?" said the Winter King.

"I have it," replied Magwich. "Stand here, at the edge of the peak, hold forth the Ring of Power, and repeat what I say."

As Magwich began to read, the Winter King smiled and felt a shiver of anticipation run through him. Repeating the phrases given to him by the Steward, the Winter King raised his hand. The ring shimmered in the cloying air above the falls, at the edge of the void. And, suddenly . . .

Nothing happened.

Standing, hand upraised, the Winter King's eyes narrowed, and he looked sideways at Magwich.

"Perhaps you have to read it more than once," the Steward said.

The Winter King dropped his hand and looked closely at the ring. It was not a question of whether he'd been given a fake—the ring was embossed with the seal of the king: a scarlet letter *A*. It was the High King's ring.

Still, nothing. It wasn't working.

"So be it," the Winter King hissed. "If I must take the Archipelago with sharpened steel and smoke and blood and death, so be it."

He tossed the *Imaginarium Geographica* to Magwich and drew his sword. "Let us finish this."

With that, the Winter King turned and began to stalk back down the embankment.

"Wh-where are you going?" sputtered Magwich.

"I'm going to go to the battlefield and oversee my victory," the Winter King said without bothering to stop or turn around. "I could care less what you do."

"B-but what do you want me to do with the *Geographica*?"

The Winter King stopped and stiffened, then turned and spoke, his voice icy with hatred.

"Burn it."

It had taken very little time for John and Artus to make their way around the southern tip of the island, then scale the sloping rise of rock that led to the flat bluff and the peak beyond. They actually wasted more time than they'd spent climbing arguing about whether or not their place was alongside their friends on the battlefield.

John's logic won out over a still-reluctant Artus; a choice proven wise when they saw, off in the distance, the shapes of the Winter King and the Steward, arguing.

"Let's go!" whispered Artus. "He has the *Geographica*, and I'll bet my ring, too! Come on—we can take them!"

John knew Artus was more than a match for the Steward, but he was less confident about his ability to take on the Winter King mano a mano. But more than that, he was held back by a nagging in his subconscious; a sixth sense that was saying things to him in a still, small voice: *Wait. Wait. They do not have the power they believe they have. Wait.*

He shook his head and pulled Artus behind one of the scattered standing stones. "Not yet."

Artus arched an eyebrow. "But why? What if he's able to summon the dragons?"

"I've been thinking about that," said John. "Summoning and commanding are two different things."

"What do you mean?"

"Remember what Samaranth was like?"

"Sure."

"He said he took the ring from your grandfather when he proved himself no longer worthy to use it. Does it seem to you like the Winter King is any more worthy?"

"Not bloody likely," said Artus.

"Right. Now, if the Winter King *could* summon the dragons, can you imagine Samaranth doing anything he ordered him to do?"

"No."

"Exactly. So we wait. And watch."

Magwich cursed and stomped his foot on the ground in frustration. He'd used up all the matches he'd had in his wallet, and tried using his sleeves (which burned quite nicely) as tinder, but he couldn't so much as singe the cover of the *Imaginarium Geographica*.

He'd tried tearing out pages, to use them as starters, but they were tougher than leather and wouldn't even wrinkle. He had just about decided to chuck the thing over the edge and report in that he'd burned it to ashes, when he heard the footfalls behind him.

"Master, I was just about to . . ." he said, turning. He didn't finish. John smashed him across the face with a left cross, and the Steward of Paralon dropped to the earth like a puppet whose strings had been cut.

"Excellent!" Artus exclaimed. "Charles will be so disappointed that he didn't get to do it."

In the distance they could see the descending form of the Winter King, who was moving to join the fray. Suddenly, as they watched, all the torches on the allies' side of the battle went out, as if they'd been snuffed.

Artus and John looked at each other and swallowed hard.

John picked up the *Geographica* and turned to the pages with the summoning. "All of the information is here," he said. "Either they got it right, and the ring didn't work, or the ring could work, and they got the summoning wrong."

"Or," Artus said as John read, "the ring doesn't work and the summoning doesn't work. In any regard, we don't have the ring."

"I don't think we need it," said John, an undisguised excitement rising in his voice.

"Why not?"

John read, then reread, then re-reread the passages. "It's not a piece of jewelry," he said, astonished at the realization. "It's a *place*. The Ring of Power is a *place*."

He started pacing around in a broad circle, looking for all the world to Artus as if he'd gone insane.

"There," said John, pointing eastward, nearer the base of the peak. "Farther back, on the ridge."

Artus looked to where John was pointing, but there was nothing there except for more of the queer standing stones, which they'd seen a dozen of on their hike.

"That's the place," said John, his confidence rising with a flush in his cheeks and a quickening of his pulse. "I'm certain of it."

"How can you be sure?"

"We have a circle of standing stones just like it back home," said John. "We call it Stonehenge."

Chapter Twenty

The Return of the Dragons

The Winter King stepped onto the battlefield just as all of the torches began to go out, and he smiled broadly in response. His enemies would be doubly handicapped now. Fighting in the dark, against warriors who could not be killed. If they were wise, they'd drop their weapons and run for their ships, which would give them a temporary respite at best. As long as he had the ability to create more Shadow-Born, it would only be a matter of time before he eventually got around to conquering all the lands in the Archipelago.

Both the battle and the conquest, not to mention his inevitable expansion into the larger world beyond, would have been faster had he been able to summon the dragons. But there was no use complaining about what might have been when all he needed now was patience.

He'd waited for things before. He could wait again. Raising his sword, he shouted a battle cry and ran to join the Shadow-Born.

In minutes the elves had lost almost a quarter of their soldiers, and the dwarves, scarcely less.

Dousing the torches had helped, but it was only a remedy, not a cure. The Shadow-Born could push through archers like

"John," said Artus breathlessly, "those aren't stars . . ."

stones through water, and only heavy weapons gave them any pause at all.

Eledir ordered his troops to pull back, but Falladay Finn had fallen, his shadow torn away by a Shadow-Born. Only the swift actions of the dwarves, and the self-sacrifice of several of them, allowed his limp, pallid form to be taken to safety.

Charys, leading the centaurs, took over the front lines. They had the greatest reach, and using pikes and long bardiches, could hold the line of Shadow-Born from advancing too quickly. Under their flanks, the Dwarven, faun, and animal archers held back the Wendigo in a similar fashion with a never-ending hail of arrows.

They were defending with darkness; Jack decided they needed to create an offense of light.

Jack had taken a few moments to examine Nemo's weaponry aboard the *Nautilus*, and he'd found among the various hydraulic and steam-powered weaponry a few devices of a more conventional nature, which he could adapt to better use. Including, namely, the ingredients for gunpowder.

Nemo had been running back and forth, guiding the efforts of the mythbeasts and animals, taking shots at the Wendigo when he could. Jack yelled at him and they dropped behind a hillock to examine Jack's contraption.

"It's called a grenade," Jack said.

Nemo was incredulous. "There are reasons I don't use explosives in warfare, young Jack," he said. "They're too unpredictable."

"In your world, maybe," said Jack, "but not in mine. This is my kind of weapon, from the real world. If Shadow-Born can be pushed back, they can be blown up."

Nemo looked unconvinced. "Do you have any experience making this sort of device?"

"I've read a lot about them," said Jack, "and I used the cannon on the *Indigo Dragon* pretty effectively."

Nemo started to rise in protest, but Jack cut him off.

"This is the place where imagination counts for as much as everything else, right?" said Jack. "So I improvised a little. It'll still work. I've been improvising since I came here—and I always seem to come through."

Nemo bowed his head, considering, then met Jack's eyes. "All right. What do we need to do?"

"Sound a retreat from the valley," said Jack. "Get our troops coming up the hill, then light the fuse and fling it into the center of the enemy force, at the lowest point. If it works, I can fashion several more from what you have aboard the *Nautilus*."

Nemo seemed impressed, then took a closer look.

"I don't think there's a long enough fuse," he said, examining Jack's handiwork. "What if—"

"Are you questioning me?" Jack shot back. "Just do as I tell you, and everything will be fine."

Nemo gave him a long, considered look, then nodded. "Aven trusts you, and so I cannot do less. Get more of them ready. We're going to need them."

Nemo conferred with Charys and Eledir, and the retreat was sounded. The allies turned and ran up and out of the small valley, away from the carnage that was taking place among their fallen comrades.

The enemy wasted no time in surging forward, only now they were under the direct command of the Winter King, who led the charge.

Jack was running down the hill past the retreating centaurs with the second grenade as Nemo lit the first device and threw it directly at the Winter King.

The charge exploded prematurely, almost as soon as it was thrown, showering the phalanx of Wendigo and Shadow-Born in dirt, but nothing more. The effect on the captain of the *Nautilus* was a different matter.

The right half of Nemo's torso, including his arm and shoulder, was completely gone, blown away by the charge. His face was burned and blistered, and the corneas of his eyes had been utterly scorched. He was blind, and dying in agony.

All because he had trusted Jack.

Jack ran to his fallen comrade and dropped to his knees. With the retreat, he and Nemo were alone on the battlefield with several thousand of the enemy approaching fast. Jack fumbled with the second grenade, but before he could light it, the Shadow-Born were on him.

Without a pause, the Shadow-Born rushed past and continued up the hillside.

Jack looked around wildly, confused, as thousands of the cold, black forms flowed around him. Even the Wendigo did little more than pause to sniff at Nemo before moving on. Then the Winter King was there, looking down at him.

In answer to Jack's silent plea, the Winter King spoke, a cruel light glittering in his eyes.

"They left you, Jack, because Shadow-Born do not consume their own."

With a cold smile and a wink, the Winter King ran past.

As he stared on in horror, Jack's shadow flickered back into view, then solidified. But it was too late—the damage had been done. Nemo was dead.

Jack knelt in the blood-soaked earth and began to scream.

Charles and Tummeler had to twice submerge themselves in the surf to avoid random groups of Wendigo that had caught their scent and come looking. Being completely under water hid their smell, but did little for their spirits.

Nevertheless, they had managed to make their way around the entirety of the east side and had drawn up alongside the *Black Dragon* itself. Charles's biggest concern had been identifying the tent of the Winter King, but that proved not to be a problem. It was not only the largest tent in the encampment, but also the only one with posted guards—two nasty-looking Wendigo.

"That'll be what we're looking for, no doubt about it," Charles whispered. "I'm sure Pandora's Box is inside. Why else bother posting guards on a tent behind an army the size of the one he's got?"

"Agreed, Master Scowler," said Tummeler. "So—when we gets inside, what's y'r plan? Do we try t' steal th' kettle, or just cap it here?"

"Steal it, if we can," said Charles. "I haven't the faintest idea how we'd go about closing it. There's bound to be some sort of magic involved, so I doubt it'll be as simple as nailing a board to the top and adding a 'Do Not Touch' sign."

"Okay," said Tummeler. "I know you'll do for th' best."

"We should have brought Jack," Charles lamented. "He's got a knack for improvising in difficult situations."

As they whispered back and forth, they moved stealthily out

of the water, using the bulk of the *Black Dragon* as a blind. On the sand, Tummeler shook the water out of his fur and plopped down on his haunches, and Charles squatted down next to him, dropping the heavy shield to rest.

"There be just somethin' I been wond'ring," said Tummeler. "If it's a big ol' cooking pot, why does everyone call it 'Aunt Dora's Box'?"

"Pandora's Box," Charles corrected, "and it's just the nature of things to change. That's the nature of storytelling—a kettle becomes a cauldron becomes a crochan becomes a box, all depending on who's telling the story. And since Pandora had it last, that's the story—and name—everyone knows.

"Take your shield, for example," he continued, turning over the shield and dusting off the sand. "It was probably used by a Roman soldier, or a legionnaire, or someone like that, and it was called 'Polemicus's Shield,' or something like that—but I'll always know it as 'Mr. Tummeler's . . ."

He stopped, mouth gaping.

"Master Charles?" said Tummeler. "What is it?"

Charles was looking at the surface of the shield. The pattern forged on it was a bit tarnished, but still gleamed with visible detail. It was a stylized depiction of the Medusa, from Greek myth.

"Tell me again what Samaranth said when he gave this to you, Tummeler."

"Samaranth said it belonged to a famous hero in your world," said Tummeler. "Pericles, or Theseus, or . . . or . . ."

"Perseus," said Charles, as a connection clicked in his mind. "The shield belonged to Perseus."

"That's it!" Tummeler said excitedly. "Samaranth said that

even th' smallest o' us c'n be a hero, if they have th' chance—and he said this shield would give me th' chance."

"Did he now?" said Charles as a smile began to cheshire over his face. "I think he's right—and I think we're about to deal a nasty blow to the Winter King."

"It only makes sense," John said as he and Artus climbed the low rise of the ridge. "Arthur created the Silver Throne to rule in both worlds—our world *and* the Archipelago. If part of his power was the ability to summon the dragons, he would want to be able to do it no matter which realm he was in."

Artus nodded, mute. It was beginning to be evident to him that John really believed he could make something useful happen—and Artus didn't believe that himself. In the last few days, he'd seen a sharp line drawn between his boyhood fantasies about being a knight and the realities of living in a world where actions had real consequences.

It took only a minute for them to ascend to the rough circle of stones. As they stepped inside, a chill wind began to rise, concentrated within the circle itself.

"I think this was maybe a bad idea . . . ," Artus began.

John gripped him by the shoulders and spun him around. Artus expected a lecture, but John just smiled at him, as the wind grew in speed and intensity. "Think of it this way—if it works, it works. If it doesn't, we tried. If knights only went on quests they were sure of, they'd never go at all."

"Good point."

The wind swirled about them as if it intended to rip them from the very Earth and fling them into the abyss. The roar of the falls echoed against the stone of the bluff, and the spray plastered their hair to their faces. The elements seemed to be conspiring to drive them back as John opened the *Geographica* and turned it to the page Artus needed.

"John," Artus called out, "are you certain of this?"

"As certain as I can be of anything," John called back over the violent storm.

"How can I do this, John?" Artus yelled. "I can't! I'm not ready for this!"

John thrust the *Geographica* into Artus's hands.

"You wished all your life to be a knight," he said, his voice firm and his eyes clear. "Now claim your destiny, and become a king."

Artus drew a deep breath and began to calm down. His eyes darted back and forth from the desperately earnest face of his friend to the near-holy book in his hands—a book that could create a king, that *would* create a king, if only he so chose.

Reading a few lines from a book to claim his heritage, his throne, and his destiny. As simple an action as drawing a sword from an anvil.

Artus looked over the lines a final time, then closed the book and began to recite:

By right and rule
For need of might
I call on thee
I call on thee

By blood bound
By honor given

I call on thee
I call on thee

For life and light your protection given
From within this ring by the power of Heaven
I call on thee
I call on thee

With the last word, the tempest around them suddenly began to fade.

Finished, Artus looked at the darkness, then at the book, then again out into the void. "Did I do it right?"

"You did just fine," said John. "You certainly did *something*."

"How long is it supposed to take?"

"It doesn't say."

They waited for five heartbeats, then ten.

Then twenty. Then twenty more.

Nothing happened.

Too much ground had been given in the effort to use Jack's offensive. Charys and Eledir had trusted Nemo and Nemo had trusted Jack, and the line had been irrevocably moved. The allies had lost more than half of their soldiers to the Shadow-Born, and although the Wendigo had at worst killed only a small number of the fallen, it was going to happen to the rest sooner or later.

What remained of the elves, dwarves, animals, and myth-beasts had come together in a hollow just opposite the beach, where they were ringed in by Charys and the centaurs, who stood as the last line of defense.

The Shadow-Born had swarmed past, and for a few moments Aven and Bert thought that some miracle had occurred—but it was no miracle, just more strategy. The dark specters had cut off the path of retreat to the ships. There would be no escape.

At the command of the Winter King, a Wendigo sounded a hunting horn and summoned the Troll and Goblin armies back to the field.

The battle was over.

Artus and John had not seen the events of the battlefield. They had fixed their attention outward, toward the void.

Artus drew in a sharp breath, then glanced quickly at John, who held his gaze steady.

"Something's wrong, John."

"Have patience, Artus. I believe in you."

Artus seemed to shrink inward. "I don't know if I do."

"That's all right," John said, gripping the younger man's shoulder. "I believe enough for both of us."

Then the world shifted. Something changed. The air was stilled, and even the eternal roar of the falls became muted, as if the world had begun to hold its breath.

The eye of the storm had opened up around the small, noble ring of standing stones, and it extended its pull into the distant reaches of eternity—and there, something entered the open doorway of the eye.

"Look!" said John. "Look to the void—there, in the darkness! Do you see it?"

Far above their heads, deep to the west, a single point of light had appeared, small, but sharp and bright.

A star.

"I see it," said Artus. "But what does it—"

"Another one!" said John, pointing. "And there! Another!"

As they watched, the sky beyond began to fill with stars that flickered and flared into bright life. Then, unexpectedly, some of the stars grew brighter. And brighter. And then they began to move.

"John," said Artus breathlessly, "those aren't stars . . .

". . . those are *dragons*."

At last—at long last, the dragons had returned to the Archipelago.

Part Six

The Summer Country

"I still intend to have my victory here and now."

Chapter Twenty-one

The High King

The air above the Island at the Edge of the World echoed with the sound of a hundred thunderclaps as the great beasts dropped out of the sky.

Three dragons, elders by appearance and manner, came swiftly to rest in front of the stone circle, where they bowed in deference before Artus.

"I think they want instructions," John whispered.

Artus looked at the magnificent creatures before him, then turned and pointed at the battlefield.

"Help them. Help my friends."

It was apparently instruction enough. The dragons bowed their heads a second time, then stroked their wings and rose into the air.

Directly to the east, the Troll and Goblin armies had just marched back onto the battlefield at the center of the small valley and were expecting to participate in the wholesale slaughter accorded to overwhelmingly victorious armies. Thus, they were surprised to suddenly be themselves overwhelmed by a larger, stronger army of dragons.

Uruk Ko, whether through wisdom or cowardice, immediately signaled for his troops to lower their weapons and their banners. As many kings retained their thrones through diplomacy as through conquest, and it made more sense to acquiesce than to go through what would be a pointless loss of soldiers in the name of pride.

The commanders of the trolls did not engage in a similar burst of reasoning, and instead opted to fight the incoming dragons.

The conflict lasted all of three minutes, and that was only because the dragons kept having to move out of one another's way as they proceeded to incinerate, chew up, or step on the soldiers of the Troll army.

The Shadow-Born would not fall so quickly, or easily.

Tummeler was very disappointed.

"Cheer up, old sock," Charles said as they entered the tent of the Winter King. "I couldn't have done it with a dozen cannonballs, let alone three blueberry muffins."

"It would've been just th' two," Tummeler complained, "if that first Wendigo hadn't turned 'is head just as I conked 'im."

"Still," said Charles, "when you got him with the third muffin, he was at a dead run—and that made for a much more impressive display of sportsmanship."

"Really?" Tummeler said, brightening. "Thanks, Master Charles."

Inside the tent, Charles lit the torchieres on either side of the door, and what their light revealed was unmistakable.

It was in the center of the tent, on a simple wooden platform that had leather handles for easier transport. As they'd expected, it was an iron kettle about three feet high and slightly less in circumference, giving it a somewhat elongated appearance. The exterior was decorated with bronze platings of cuneiform writings and stylized images of ravens.

They had found Pandora's Box.

There was no cover or lid, just the remnants of wax around the edges.

"So," said Tummeler, "what's y'r grand idea?"

"We can't look into it," said Charles, "so transport is going to be a problem. So we have to go with our original plan and close it—and I think that Samaranth knew more than he was telling us. That's why he gave you the shield."

"Let me do it," said Tummeler. "I can't see into it at all—it's an insufficiency of height, as my friend Falladay Finn would say."

"Go ahead," said Charles, handing him the shield.

With considerable effort, Tummeler hefted the heavy piece of bronze above his head and approached the open kettle. In one fluid motion, he slid the shield off his head and onto the top of the iron container—where it clicked into the raised lip, fitting perfectly.

Before Tummeler could move or speak, the kettle they called Pandora's Box began to glow with an unearthly light.

"That's either really good, or really bad," said Charles. "But I expect we're going to be finding out which sooner than we realize."

When the dragons arrived, the Winter King had been facing the leaders of the bruised and battered allies, appraising them. Charys and Eledir were prepared to fight to the death—but Aven and Bert had all but given up hope. The death of Nemo had been a great blow, and the apparent loss of Jack an even greater one. Thus, the

Winter King was expecting a complete submission when, in a few moments, his world turned upside down.

At first he attributed the dragons' sudden appearance to his summoning, figuring the delay was due to the rotation of the Earth, or dragon inefficiency, or something he could get angry about, being that he now commanded them. It wasn't until they started squashing trolls that he realized they weren't there in service to *him*.

A shout of triumph rose from the ragged allies, which brought a snarl to his lips.

The Winter King spun about. "Cheer all you like," he said bitterly. "You won't be alive long enough to savor your victory—not while I still command the Shadow-Born!"

The timing could not have been better to render the Winter King utterly speechless—for as he spoke, the thousand-strong Shadow-Born wavered, and vanished.

"Well," said Charys, stamping his hind legs and shifting his grip on the massive pike he held, "I would like to announce that the school of 'Beating the Tar out of Wendigo' is once more in session."

Once more, the battlefield was a frenzy of activity, lit brightly by the flames of the dragons. The elves, dwarves, and centaurs formed a blockade around the Dragonships and their injured comrades and kept the Wendigo in a thick cluster with a flurry of arrows.

Staying together in a pack made sense when in combat against fauns; against dragons, not so much.

In the chaos of the fighting, the Winter King slipped away. Aven was making her way back into the valley to look for Jack, when she saw the Winter King scaling the embankment to the west. She paused for a second, uncertain of what to do, then turned and began to follow him.

The rest of the fray lasted only minutes, as the dragons were pretty much impossible to defend against, much less attack with any success. With the battlefield clear of combatants, the allies were free to return and tend to their fallen comrades, where they made a startling discovery.

All the soldiers who'd been struck down were still *alive*.

The opposing army had lost many of their soldiers. But it was the plan of the Winter King to harvest the stolen shadows of the fallen warriors to create still more Shadow-Born. So while there was damage, and blood loss, and the occasional missing limb, the bodies of the elves, dwarves, and mythbeasts were otherwise unharmed.

It was not a total victory: Most of the fallen had lost their shadows to the now-vanished Shadow-Born and were little more than rag dolls. But they still lived. And where there was life, there was hope.

"Extraordinary," said Eledir. "The Winter King's own greed gave us more than a victory—we'd have lost more if he'd simply planned for slaughter, rather than angling to use our fallen as his servants." He shook his head in wonder. "When I saw the dragons arrive, I was hopeful of a victory, but to have *no casualties . . .*"

"You're wrong," Bert said sadly. "There *were* casualties—one dead, and one that may wish he had died."

Charys had returned to the campfires with two bodies slung across his massive back. One, the fallen captain of the former *Yellow*

Dragon, who had been the most valiant of them all; the other, the young man who wanted more than anything to go to war, to be in battle, and show the world his worth and mettle. The eyes of both were closed—but only one would ever open them again.

In the circle of stones, John and Artus watched with amazement as the dragons utterly transformed the shape, scope, and outcome of the battle that had been raging below.

"It's no wonder that everyone swore oaths of fealty to Arthur," said Artus, "if this was what happened when someone ticked him off."

"I doubt he called on the dragons for every little dispute," said John, "but the possibility would certainly have been an effective deterrent."

"It was," said a cold voice, approaching from below. "Why else would the other races have been held in check on merely the possibility of a human king who could summon them?"

It was the Winter King. He stepped inside the circle of stones, sword drawn and at the ready.

"That was very impressive, the way you switched the books," he said. "I'd been torturing my chief navigator for nearly an hour before I realized why all of his incomprehensible coordinates involved mentions of blueberries."

"Thanks," said John. "I didn't expect it to work myself."

"Of course, you should have kept a better eye on it later," said the Winter King, noticing the just-stirring Steward of Paralon lying some distance away, "or else that imbecile wouldn't have been able to take it away from you."

"True," John admitted. "Still it seems to have worked out for the best—for everyone but you, anyway."

The Winter King's eyes blazed. "You think so? You've lost more than you know, boy—and I still intend to have my victory here and now."

"Artus summoned the dragons when you could not," said John. "If you'd had a better translator than that fool Steward, you might have too. But what victory can you have now? The ring you wear is meaningless, and even the *Geographica* won't do you any good now."

Hearing them talking about him, Magwich came fully awake. "Master!" he screamed. "Master, help me! That one, there—he hit me! On the head!"

The Winter King barely bothered to glance back at his hapless servant. "I told Magwich to burn it," he said, giving the Steward a withering glare, "but it seems he's unable to do even the simplest of tasks. But I don't need the book or the ring to become the High King."

"They will fight you," said John. "All the races of the Archipelago will fight you. They'll never let you take the Silver Throne—not while a true heir still lives."

A wicked smile spread across the Winter King's face, and John realized with horror that that was precisely what he had in mind.

Protectively, he moved in front of Artus, placing himself between the two kings.

"You can try to kill him," John said, "but that still will not make you king—not of a throne that has been passed along the only bloodline to have the mandate of the Parliament."

"But I *do* have the mandate," said the Winter King. "The blood that flows through his veins flows though my own."

"You're a member of the royal line?" John said in astonishment. "I don't believe you! It's a lie!"

The Winter King chuckled. "No, it isn't." He paced slowly in front of John and Artus, taking great pleasure in the effects of his revelations. "Do you think the Parliament would spend decades locked in debate, or even entertain the notion of a usurper taking the throne, if I didn't have a legitimate claim?

"No," he continued, "they have been unable to choose a new High King precisely *because* there was one of royal blood who could block all comers—myself—but whom they in their foolishness could not bear to appoint."

"How could you be an heir?" asked Artus. "All of the king's family—my family—were killed."

The Winter King laughed. "Boy, I am much older than you give me credit for—in fact, I am almost as old as that fool shipbuilder Thoth, or Deucalion, or whatever it is he calls himself now.

"I am even older than the Silver Throne itself," he continued, "and I swore to your grandfather's grandfather's grandfather's grandfather that his heirs would one day kneel before me. And here you are."

Suddenly, the Winter King struck out with his sword, creating a deep, brutal gash across John's chest. The Caretaker screamed and dropped to his knees, trying futilely to draw his own sword. The Winter King kicked it away, then gestured for the approaching Magwich to take it up and hold the sword over John.

Artus managed to get his own short sword free of the sheath, but he was no match for the Winter King's prowess. In seconds the heir to the Silver Throne was weaponless and helpless before his attacker.

"It's ironic," said the Winter King, "that I should be holding a blade to your throat twenty years after I held it at the throat of your grandfather, and your father before him."

Artus looked up. "*You* killed my family?"

The Winter King nodded. "That's what I find ironic—the entire Archipelago believed your grandfather to be an evil man, when he was actually one of the greatest kings ever to rule here. His only mistake was in placing too high a value on protecting his family."

"What do you mean?" said John, who was still breathing hard, although the bleeding from his wound had slowed. "Archibald killed his family."

"So the story goes," said the Winter King. "But in truth, all he ever did wrong was overstep his bounds, when he asked that idiot to steal Pandora's Box. That was a forbidden magic—and its use brought with it a mandatory expulsion from the Archipelago."

"Then why did he risk using it?" said Artus. "What was so terrible that he would risk losing even the support of the dragons?"

The Winter King grinned. "That would be me. I had been in exile myself for many years in his world," he said, flicking his hook at John, "and had only recently returned after discovering the secret of passage to the Archipelago. I built the *Black Dragon* and went to Paralon to demand that Archibald relinquish the throne.

"He equivocated and stalled long enough to find a greater magic with which he could defeat me—Pandora's Box. And when he opened it, he lost the mandate of the dragons, and that fool Samaranth took his ring, when he should have taken the box instead."

"Why didn't Samaranth just let him use the box?" said Artus.

"Because," John cut in, spitting flecks of blood as he spoke, "even the king has to abide by the rules—and using evil to fight evil was not the way of the Silver Throne."

"Well put, if misguided," said the Winter King. "Archibald had lost the ability to summon the dragons—but would not name me his successor. So I killed his family, one by one, and then the king himself. I thought I'd gotten them all," he said to Artus, "but it seems I was mistaken.

"And now I will offer you one small, final mercy. The same one I offered your grandfather, which he refused."

He sheathed his sword and stepped closer to Artus, extending his hand, palm down. "Kneel before me, boy. Swear fealty to me. Make me the rightful heir. And I will give you a quick and painless death. Refuse, and your agonies shall be unending.

"Kneel and swear fealty to your ancestor. . . .

"Kneel, and swear by my true name—Mordred."

"Mordred!" John said, eyes blazing. "I don't believe it!"

"It doesn't matter what you believe," said Mordred. "All I need is his oath—and then I shall be king of *your* world, too."

"I don't think that's going to happen."

Aven stood just outside the circle of stones. She was holding two swords—one pointed at Magwich, and one pointed at Mordred.

"Ah—the Pirate Queen," Mordred said, redrawing his sword. "If you don't mind, we're dealing with men's business here, and we'd like our privacy."

"Not going to happen," Aven said again. "Everyone in the Archipelago will know what you've done, and there's no way in hell you'll ever sit on the Silver Throne."

"There are two of us, and one of you," Mordred said.

"Two of us, and one of you," Magwich repeated with shaky bravado.

"How can you get to me before I cut the young king's throat?"

"You won't cut his throat," said Aven, "because you need him to swear the oath to you—and he won't."

"He will," said Mordred, "if I order Magwich to kill his friend the Caretaker."

Aven looked at Magwich. "Listen to me, Steward. Whatever else happens here, I will kill you. Whether or not John dies, or Artus dies, or I die—I will kill you with the last of my strength, no matter what."

Magwich screamed and dropped John's sword, then ran down the hill, shrieking and madly waving his arms.

"Well?" said Aven, turning back to Mordred, as John scrambled to his feet and retrieved his sword. "Two against one, in our favor this time."

"But my sword is at the boy king's throat," said Mordred, "so it seems we have a stalemate."

"Actually," a deep voice rumbled from above, "this is what's called a 'checkmate.'"

Samaranth dropped out of the sky, and with one swift motion disarmed Mordred and carried him back into the air, clutching the Winter King in a great gnarled claw. He stroked the air with ancient wings, and they hovered almost motionless high over the edge of the waterfall.

"You were a terrible student," said Samaranth, shaking his head. "I understand your ambition, and your desire for greatness, but you've handled things so poorly these last twenty years since your return, that I think it's time for you to step offstage, so to speak, and let others direct the course of affairs in the Archipelago."

"You don't have the right to command who rules in the Archipelago," said Mordred.

"Neither do you—but Archibald deserved better than to die. And you'll die yourself long before you ever have a chance to sit on the Silver Throne."

"I'll live to suck the marrow from your bones, you old fool," Mordred spat. With a sudden motion, he drew a wicked-looking dagger from one of his boots and stabbed it into the great dragon's claw. The dagger broke off at the hilt.

Samaranth sighed.

"It's not that I dislike you, Mordred," the dragon said, "because I do like you, a great deal. But at heart, you really are a stupid little man."

Samaranth opened his claw.

Mordred—the Winter King—fell soundlessly into the void and disappeared into the darkness.

Chapter Twenty-two

All Their Roads Before Them

The remainder of the night was spent in caring for the wounded and obtaining oaths of fealty from the Goblin King and Troll commanders, and all of the things that must be attended to at the conclusion of a war—which, all things considered, was far preferable to going through the same motions from the losing side. However, despite the return of the dragons and the victory over the Winter King, the struggle for control of the Archipelago was not yet over.

Arawn, the Troll Prince, had claimed the Silver Throne for himself and had overrun Paralon with his own armies, while sending the rest to fight with the Winter King. It would take planning and the support of the other races to regain command of Paralon—but given the ease with which the dragons had dispatched the trolls the night before, it was less a matter of "if" than "when."

The Wendigo, the worst and most fearsome of the enemy force, had been cornered against the base of the western bluff by Charys and his centaurs—and thus had an unobstructed view of the fate of the Winter King. Their response was unexpected. They turned from the centaurs, howling, teeth gnashing, and began to flee in the only direction available to them.

"The dragons have returned . . . whether or not we stay is up to you."

As they went over the edge, they continued to howl and screech in rage, but the roaring of the waterfall quickly overwhelmed the sound, and no one heard them as they fell.

That left only one question to be resolved: What exactly had happened to the Shadow-Born?

"I think they may be able to tell us," said Bert, pointing down the shoreline.

Approaching along the sand from the east was a very unusual sight: Charles, walking slowly, was pulling on straps of leather attached to a makeshift wooden sled. In the center of the sled was the unmistakable shape of Pandora's Box—a great black kettle, lidded with a gleaming bronze shield. Tummeler was perched on top, munching away on a stale muffin.

"Hello, Master Scowlers!" Tummeler said. "We brung . . . brang . . . bringed . . . We got Aunt Dora's Box!"

Bert, Aven, Artus, and John ran over and joyfully embraced their two friends. "You did it!" Artus exclaimed. "You closed the box!"

"Well, that was the plan, wasn't it?" said Charles. "It would have looked bad for us if you'd asked us to do this one thing and we let you down."

"Right," said Tummeler. "Not that there was ever a question—after all, Master Charles be an Oxford scowler, an' he has a reputation t' maintain."

"Indeed," said Charles. "And I have to say, it's been a very difficult night, all told. So," he added, stretching his back and looking around. "How did everything go on this end?"

All the allies wanted to know what had happened in the enemy camp, and Charles and Tummeler told the story in a rush, there on the beach, pausing now and then to compliment one another on their stealth and prowess.

The elves removed Pandora's Box from the sled and, after some debate, secured it in the hold of the *White Dragon*. It wasn't until Charles and Tummeler had changed into fresh clothes and had something to eat, that their companions recounted all the events of the night—with one exception.

"Mordred, you say?" said Charles. "Astonishing. Absolutely astonishing. But tell me, where's Jack? I expected he'd have dispatched them all single-handedly, and you'd all have been carrying him around on a platform by now, giving him medals and whatnot."

No one answered, but the expressions on their faces said that something was terribly wrong.

"John?" Charles began. "He's not . . . Jack isn't dead, is he?"

"No," said John. "Not him—someone else."

"John wasn't there," said Bert. "Let me tell you what else has happened."

They talked for a long while, and wept, and mourned—not just for the loss of one friend, but for the burden the other would carry, which none of them knew how to lift.

Late in the morning, the landscape of the island had changed yet again. When they first arrived, it had been an unblemished plain, motionless in the serene anticipation of what was to come. Then, an overrun battlefield of warriors and churning movement, and later, a charnel field of suffering and loss. Now it was much as it had begun. The enemies had either become uneasy friends or been dispatched entirely. And those who'd come to their aid had been taken onto the ships to mend or were surveying the land, watchful, not quite certain that it was indeed over.

The dragons, having done what they were summoned to do, had largely left the island, appearing only in brief glimpses in the clouds above.

Only Samaranth remained, and he and the companions gathered together near the circle of stones to say their farewells.

"We have but a few moments to talk, here, in this sacred place," Samaranth said to them. "So speak. Ask of me what you will, and I shall do my best to answer."

Artus, John, Aven, Bert, and Charles were sitting on a flat patch of grass a short distance away from the standing stones, where Samaranth landed and sat, folding his wings deferentially.

"What do I do now?" said Artus.

Samaranth laughed, with a great huffing noise. "Do? Whatever you choose to. You are the High King now."

"That's what makes me nervous," said Artus. "I don't know anything about being a king."

"Your friends did not know anything about being Caretakers, and yet somehow they managed," said Samaranth. "Although they seem to be missing one of their number."

"Jack," said Aven. "He hasn't spoken to anyone all morning. He's locked himself in the cabin of the *White Dragon* and refuses to come out."

"Yes," said Samaranth, nodding. "Tummeler has explained to me what happened. Regrettable."

"Regrettable?" said John. "Captain Nemo is dead! And it was Jack's fault!"

"Perhaps," said Samaranth, "but Nemo was not a child. He

was not coerced. And he knew the stakes and the risks. Jack should learn from this and become stronger for the experience."

"Become stronger?" said John. "How?"

"An interesting question coming from you, little Caretaker," said the dragon, "for as I recall, much of this journey was set in motion because of another death."

John hesitated. "You mean the professor."

"Indeed."

"But that wasn't my fault," said John. "Not directly. There was no way I could have prevented it."

"Perhaps," said Samaranth. "But when he was offered the chance, did he not say that he was willing to die, because his work was done?"

"How could you know that?" said John.

Samaranth shrugged. "Ask yourself this, young Caretaker—do you feel you have achieved your purpose?"

John thought a moment. "Yes."

"Would the professor?"

"Yes."

"Then your redemption did not come through his resurrection, but through your belief in a greater purpose. Something Jack would benefit to remember."

"You know," said Charles. "I think you knew all along that you had the means to close Pandora's Box, and you could have given it to us on Paralon."

"Yes," said Samaranth. "I had Perseus's shield. When Archibald opened the box, Mordred stole it, but left behind the shield, never having foreseen needing it. I kept it, and Archibald's ring, for a time when both would be needed."

"But why didn't you just tell us that was how we could overcome the Shadow-Born?" said Charles.

"You didn't ask me that," said Samaranth. "You asked me how to deal with the pursuit of the *Geographica*."

"Couldn't you have just told us?" asked John. "It might have saved us a lot of time and trouble."

"The dragons do not exist to solve your problems for you," said Samaranth, "but to help you learn to help yourselves, and you have.

"You and your friends," he said to John, "needed to solve the riddles of the *Imaginarium Geographica* and the mysteries of the Archipelago, and you did. There was a price to pay, and each of you has paid it in your own way.

"You have managed to establish a new rule in the Archipelago, and that can only reflect well in your own world. And those who have paid a dearer price know this, and would not see you suffer for doing what you had to. Tell that to Jack, when you see him. And that should he ever need them, he has many, many friends in the Archipelago to call upon."

"I have one question," said Charles. "In all the hullabaloo, I lost track of that snake Magwich. What will we do with *him*?"

"Already dispatched," said the dragon. "He was taken up by one of my kin, who asked the same question, and after conferring with the king"—he finished, winking at Artus—"we realized that the Archipelago already had a means in place for dealing with his kind. We can only hope he redeems himself as well as did the last Guardian of Avalon."

Charles looked at his friends and shrugged. "Fair enough. I just wished I'd gotten to smack him across the head one more time."

Samaranth stood and stretched his wings to take flight.

"Wait!" said Artus. "Have the dragons really returned? They're back for good?"

Samaranth looked at the young king and smiled. "Yes," he said at last. "The dragons have returned, true—but whether or not we stay is up to you. Rule wisely. Rule well. And should the need arise, call on us."

He leaned over, covering the young man in shadow, and offered his claw. Artus held out his hand, and into it dropped the ring of the High King of Paralon.

"I took it from one king who was not worthy to wear it," the dragon said, "and did so again last night. I hope that you will never give me cause to do the same.

"Fare thee well, King Artus of the Silver Throne."

The companions gathered for one final council with the kings of the races and captains of the Dragonships to confer before going on to Paralon, and then their own homes. Command of the *Yellow Dragon* was given to Aven, until such time as the *Indigo Dragon* could be salvaged and repaired. Then she could choose which of the ships to command. In consultation with the cranes, which had remained at the island throughout the night, Bert had agreed to continue using the *White Dragon*, so that he could return Pandora's Box to Avalon, and John, Jack, and Charles to London.

Artus had decided that for the time being, the island would serve as an auxiliary to the Silver Throne on Paralon, reasoning that the seat of power was wherever the king wished it to be. "I've given the island a name," said Artus. "Not that what it was called before wasn't a name, but it's rather unwieldy to keep calling it 'The Island at the Edge of the World,' don't you think?"

"Probably," said John. Tell me what you call it, and I'll make the appropriate changes in the *Geographica.*"

"Terminus," said Artus. "The name of the island is Terminus."

Aside from continuing to care for those affected by the Shadow-Born, the effort of which was being guided by Charys and the centaurs, preparing the ships for departure from Terminus was the last item on the allies' agenda.

"I think the High King may be angling for a queen," John murmured to Bert, tipping his head in the direction of Artus and Aven, who were examining the repairs to the hull of the *White Dragon*.

Aven was as sharp-tongued as ever, but when Artus spoke, she now looked at him differently, considering his words with gravity and respect—and something more. Not quite affection, but the whisper of it. And there was no mistaking the way that he looked at her, nor the familiar way he placed—and she allowed him to place—his hand around her waist as he guided her around the ship.

"Yes," Bert sighed. "I could see it coming several days ago. Still," he said, "there are worse fellows she could have chosen, you know?"

A bag dropped behind them, and they turned to see Jack striding away.

"Oh, dear," said Bert. "Do you think he overheard me? I certainly didn't mean . . ."

"I know you didn't," said John. "But I think of all of us, he's had the worst of it."

Aven also noticed Jack's abrupt departure. She gave Artus an affectionate squeeze on the shoulder and walked across the sand to find Jack.

Among the supplies being loaded onto each of the ships were multiple copies of Tummeler's cookbook, which he had managed to convince Nemo to bring from Paralon "just in case."

"Tummeler!" said Charles. "I'm quite impressed with your fortitude. I have no doubt your book will eventually become very successful."

"I've got a plan," said Tummeler, proudly showing some designs he'd been scribbling on a sheet of parchment. "Th' next one will be even better. Take a look."

"I don't understand," said Charles, peering closely at the parchment. "You're going to publish the *Imaginarium Geographica?*"

"Yup," Tummeler nodded. "I discussed it with th' High King. We decided that part o' the problems caused by th' Winter King were because of all th' secrets. Secret lands, secret places, secret secrets. But if all the captains have their own *Geographica,* then no more secrets. And maybe, we can all just start getting' along."

"Sensible thinking," said Charles. "It certainly would have helped us out every time we lost ours if we could have popped around to the local shop for a replacement."

"It'll look good next to the cookbook, too," said Tummeler.

"I still don't understand the significance of the blueberries," said Charles.

"Simple," Tummeler replied. "Blueberries is one of the great forces o' good in the world."

"How do you figure that?" said Charles.

"Well," said Tummeler, "have you ever seen a troll, or a Wendigo, or," he shuddered, "a Shadow-Borned ever eating a blueberry pie?"

"No," Charles admitted.

"There y' go," said Tummeler. "It's cause they can't stand the *goodness* in it."

"Can't argue with you there," said Charles.

"Foods is good and evil, just like people, or badgers, or even scowlers."

"Evil food?" said Charles.

"Parsnips," said Tummeler. "Them's as evil as they come."

"Hang on a minute," Charles said, thumbing through Tummeler's recipe book, "you've got a recipe for Parsnip Pudding right here on page forty-three. If parsnips are evil, how do you explain that?"

Tummeler looked at him thoughtfully for a moment. "Two reasons. One, because th' Harpy sisters invented it, and they always come t' market days in Paralon, and they found out about my book, and one thing led t' another, and before I knew it, they wuz insistin' that I put their recipe in my book. And believe you me, y' don't ever want t' upset th' Harpy sisters.

"And second, just because parsnips is evil doesn't mean that they won't someday become good—or at th' least, be part of a good recipe.

"Mind you, I don't think ol' Tummeler will be th' one t' do it, but somehow it didn't seem fair to pretend there's nothin' but good foods in th' world. There has to be balance, y' know? Do y' understand, scowler Charles?"

"Yes," said Charles, "I do."

Aven found Jack at a window high in the cabin of the *White Dragon,* where he could watch the loading of the other ships.

He didn't acknowledge her as she entered, but the pattern of his breathing changed, and she knew he was aware of her presence.

"Jack," said Aven. "Will you be all right?"

"I don't know," he replied at length. "Truthfully, I feel like I may never be all right, not truly, ever again."

"There was much at risk," Aven said. "No one who fought in that battle was there without knowing the risks involved, or the stakes."

"Not true," said Jack. "I didn't know the stakes—or at least, chose not to believe them. And Nemo died because of me. Because he trusted that I knew what I was doing, and I didn't, and I failed him, and he died."

"Jack," Aven began again, "you hadn't been in a situation like that before. Everyone knows you were doing you best."

"Don't treat me like a child," Jack shot back. "Don't you think I knew what was happening? Don't you think a man notices when he begins to lose his own shadow? And it didn't happen last night—it wasn't even because of the Winter King. I started giving it up on my own."

Aven was taken aback. "You mean on the Indigo Dragon?"

"Of course," said Jack. "And he saw it there, too. Th-the Winter King. Mor-Mordred. He knew."

"He knew you had the potential, Jack. That's all he saw in you. And when it came time to make a choice, you chose to be with us, and that was what mattered."

"My choices killed Nemo," said Jack. "You say what was in my heart was different than what I chose to do, but I think you're wrong. I think what is within affects what we do. Sooner or later, we have to face that."

"And you did," said Aven, looking at his shadow on the floor.

"Yes," he replied, looking at the shadow. "I just did it too late."

Aven's face showed the conflict she felt in deciding what to say next. Finally, one side of the struggle bested the other.

"Jack," she said. "You . . . you could stay here, in the Archipelago."

He shot her a glance, and briefly, there was a light in his eyes and countenance that said he'd considered doing just that. But the light sparked and died, and he slowly shook his head.

"I can't. I—I don't think it would help. I let my emotions, my passions, get the better of me," he said, again looking fleetingly at her, "and that's exactly what he knew would happen. And someone suffered and died."

He shook his head again and chuckled, a bitter, mirthless sound. "I won't make that mistake again."

Jack turned back to the window and watched as Bert continued to guide the loading of supplies onto the *White Dragon*. Aven remained standing behind him, silent.

After a time, she extended her hand to touch him, to say something to change his mind, to reassure him that what he was going through, while bitter, and a harsh lesson to learn, was nevertheless just a part of growing up. But somehow, none of the words seemed adequate to express what she felt, and they died in her throat.

Aven held her hand near his shoulder a moment more, then dropped her hand and walked out of the room.

Aboard the *Blue Dragon*, which had been converted into a makeshift hospital, Charys shook his head in defeat. "I don't think there's anything I can do."

The centaur was tending to the pallid forms of those who had fallen to the Shadow-Born, including Falladay Finn. The centaurs had long been valued for their knowledge of medicine and the healing arts, but what had been done to his friends and comrades was beyond his ken.

"I don't know," he said again, with uncharacteristic reserve. "They live, but have no will, no fire. Their spirits are gone, and I have no idea how to restore them."

"It stands to reason," Charles suggested, "that they are trapped inside Pandora's Box, doesn't it? If the Shadow-Born are created by forcing someone to look inside, and they are capable of ripping away and . . . and . . . *absorbing* the shadows of others, then where else could they have gone?"

"That's true," said Aven. "They all disappeared at the moment you and Tummeler closed the box."

"I think the best thing we can do is to take it back to the Morgaine on Avalon," said Bert. "They've had it longer than anyone. They might be able to help us."

"Or Ordo Maas," said Charles. "He has experience with it as well, although considering that it involved his wife, and her expulsion from the Archipelago, I can imagine that he won't be too happy to see it again."

"There must be some way to do it," said John. "I can't believe that the process is irreversible. The problem is, the only way to let anything out is to open it," he continued, "and then you're back to the problem of not being able to look inside without being trapped yourself."

"There's obviously some trick to it," said Charles, "or else Mordred wouldn't have been able to use it either."

"I know how the Winter King did it," said a voice from the doorway.

It was Jack.

"I know how the Winter King did it," Jack said again. "And I can do it too.

"I can free the Shadow-Born."

. . . a throng of people—hooded, gray as death . . .

Chapter Twenty-three

Into the Shadowed Lands

Jack came into the room and stood facing his friends, arms folded in a gesture that, John thought, seemed very much like one the old Jack would have made: defiant, confident, sure.

"Now, Jack," Bert began, "I know you want to help, but . . ."

Jack ignored him. "I've been thinking about this a lot," he said, pacing across the room, "and there is only one reason that the Winter King could use the box without being trapped in it himself—he had no shadow."

John and Charles looked at each other, startled. That was one point they hadn't considered.

"So," Jack continued, "it stands to reason that only someone with a similar condition could reopen, and use, Pandora's Box to free the shadows trapped within."

"That's a huge leap of logic," said Bert. "None of us knows enough about it, or even the process he used to steal shadows, to risk using the box."

"I can," Jack said for the third time. "Do you remember, on the *Indigo Dragon*, when the Winter King asked me to join him, and I refused?"

"Yes," said John. "He whispered something to you—something you claimed you couldn't even understand."

"I didn't understand it until now," said Jack. "It didn't make any sense to me then, but after Aven and I talked a little while ago, I remembered something similar the Cartographer said. And that's when I realized what I could do."

"What did Mordred say to you, Jack?"

"He said, 'Shadows cannot exist without the light. But without the shadows, the light has no meaning.'"

"A wise statement," said Charys, "even considering the source. But why would that make you think you could look into the vessel without losing your shadow?"

"Because," said Jack, "I'm the only one here who knows what it is to give up one's shadow—and then to choose to take it back."

"There remains one problem," said Eledir. "The box is known to be a forbidden magic. Samaranth has made this clear. It was not to be used by Archibald, and we know what happened when Mordred used it. If you were to try, would that not incur the wrath of the dragons yet again?"

"Not to make it worse," Charles put in, "but we also need to consider something else. When Tummeler and I closed the Box, the Shadow-Born disappeared. What if we open it again, and they all reappear? We could suddenly find ourselves up to our necks in Shadow-Born."

"No, I don't think they would, and I don't think we will," said Artus.

"Archibald and Mordred both used it to subvert another's will," he continued, "to control. Jack would not be using it to conquer, but to restore. And I don't think even the dragons would have an argument with that. And I think bringing forth Shadow-Born is a matter of intent. Sometimes Mordred needed a dozen, and sometimes a thousand. He just withdrew the number he needed. But it was always an act of will, not just happenstance. The same rules apply."

"The High King has spoken," said Charys. "I will not oppose it if Jack wishes to try."

"Agreed," said Eledir.

"All right," Artus said to Jack. "Do what you will."

The rest of the group moved to the far side of the room, so as not to inadvertantly look into the cauldron. Jack sat in a wooden chair between it and the bed where they'd lain Falladay Finn, facing away from the others. He looked back at his friends and gave a little smile. Then, with no preamble, he reached up and removed the shield from the top of Pandora's Box and looked directly inside the opening.

He sat motionless for a few seconds, and then his shoulders started to shake.

The companions exchanged worried glances, unsure if he was in trouble, or if they should risk stepping forward to help him. They could not see his face, so they were not sure if what was happening was affecting him for better or worse. Then Jack turned and looked at them, and they realized he'd been weeping.

"It's beautiful," he said. "It's full of light."

Whatever he was seeing was for his eyes alone; from their vantage point, nothing exceptional was happening.

Jack turned back and reached one hand into Pandora's Box, and it was quickly absorbed into the darkness visible. Without hesitating, he reached out with the other hand and placed it on Falladay Finn's chest.

As they watched, a tendril of darkness wound its way out of the cauldron and along Jack's arm, then across his chest, and down his other arm, finally bleeding out across Falladay Finn's limp body until it formed a complete, whole, natural shadow on the far side of the light.

Jack withdrew his arm from the cauldron and placed his hand on Finn's forehead, bowing his head as he did so—whether in prayer or concentration, they couldn't tell.

A minute passed, then another. Then Finn's eyelids fluttered, and opened.

He looked around at the group clustered around him. "Drat and damnation," he growled. "Is it over? Did I miss the entire fight? Will someone please tell me what's going on?"

The king of the Dwarves had his shadow back, and with it, his spirit, and his life.

And Jack still retained his own.

"All right," Jack said, rolling up his sleeves, the old fire shining in his eyes once more, "who's next?"

It took the rest of the day and well into the night for Jack to restore the shadows to the warriors who had had them torn away during the battle. It was a great relief to the kings and captains to see their warriors, who had become soulless, half-living shades, restored once more to their old selves. And it was a greater relief to the companions to see how the praise for the task only he could do was restoring Jack's own spirit.

As Jack worked with Charys and the centaurs on the restorations, John pulled Bert aside to talk.

"Those who fell on the battlefield are not really Shadow-Born, are they?" he asked. "Not like the ones who were forced into service by Mordred."

"Not exactly," said Bert, "although I don't really know all the specifics myself. I know that a Shadow-Born can tear away and then absorb a shadow, and we know that Mordred was keeping the victims here alive because he planned to make Shadow-Born out of the captured shadows and increase his army.

"Shadow-Born become more substantial with age. As they steal the shadows of others, they gain in substance themselves. That's why we could recognize the features of the kings of Parliament—they must have been among the first taken.

"Shadows just taken, but not yet pressed into service—I suppose these are like Shadow-Born-in-waiting. Why do you ask?"

"I've been looking through the *Geographica*," said John. "And while the Shadow-Born disappeared when the box was closed, the maps of the Shadowed Lands are still in shadow. Why would that be?"

"No one knows," said Bert. "Any expeditions to the Shadowed Lands never returned. Even Nemo could only get so close before turning back. He said they were guarded by Shadow-Born."

"That's what I thought," said John. "What were the Shadow-Born guarding?"

"I don't see what you're getting at."

"It's simple," said John. "If the bodies that provided the shadows for Mordred's invincible army had to be kept alive, then it stands to reason that all of the people in the lands he conquered are still there, with no Shadow-Born to keep us out."

Bert's eyes widened. "Oh, my dear boy . . ."

"Exactly," John said. "Jack may be able to free everyone conquered by the Winter King.

"He can free the entire Archipelago."

When Jack had finished his labors with the restorations, and was able to rest and have some tea, John and Bert explained their theory to him. He accepted without pause. "I think you're right," said Jack. "I can feel all of them in there, and I know that there has to be a way to free them all."

"You realize, Jack," said Charles, "that those you've freed here numbered in the hundreds—but the Winter King had been claiming shadows for two decades. There could be thousands upon thousands of spirits in there to be restored."

"I know," Jack said, eyes shining. "I think I'm the luckiest man in the world."

The companions went to say their good-byes to all of their newfound friends as, one by one, the Dragonships began to leave Terminus. Tummeler had elected to go with Aven and Artus aboard the *Yellow Dragon*, and he embraced them all with tears and promises to visit.

To his surprise, Charles was reluctant to part with the small mammal.

"Chin up, Tummeler," said Charles. "I'll be back—and I'm sure you'll have an occasion or two to visit Oxford, eh?"

Tummeler's whiskers twitched. "Oxford? Really? Oh, Master Charles, that would be the greatest day, just th' greatest day!"

He gave Charles one more hug, then scampered aboard the *Yellow Dragon*.

"That's it, then," said Bert. "I think we must be on our way—

there's no telling how long our expedition's going to take, so we'd best get started right away."

"Wait," said Jack. "There's one more thing that needs to be done, and with everyone's permission, I'd like to do it here."

"What's that, my boy?"

In answer, he turned to Aven. "Where . . . where is he?"

She started, then answered. "In his cabin, wrapped in one of the High King's banners. We thought to bury him on Paralon."

Jack turned to Artus. "You declared Terminus to be an extension of your throne, so this would be as good. And besides," he added, "no one paid a higher price for the victory won here. I think he'd like it."

"I agree," said Artus.

"Do you need a hand, Jack?" said John.

"No," said Jack. "I think I'd rather do this on my own, if you don't mind."

"Of course, old boy," said Charles, "of course."

"Jack," Aven began.

"You can come too," said Jack. "I know you were close to him. It's only right."

The two of them had started to walk up the hillside, when Jack stopped and walked back.

"Artus," said Jack, extending his hand. "Will you help us?"

"Of course, my friend," said Artus, taking Jack's hand. "You didn't even have to ask."

They buried Nemo just west of the circle of stones. Samaranth had called it a sacred place, and they reasoned that there could not be a better resting place for the captain of the *Nautilus* than at the far reaches of the world, where his spirit could look out over the limits of existence.

"Technically speaking," said Charles when they'd returned, "that's the same place Samaranth left the Winter King."

"One difference," said Bert. "Nemo is at rest—but Mordred will never stop falling. He's going to spend the rest of eternity dreading the inevitable impact that will never come."

It took less than a day to reach the first of the Shadowed Lands, and according to Bert, it was the greatest loss of the Archipelago.

"It's called Prydain," Bert said, showing them the blank parchment in the *Geographica* where the map had been. "A number of the kings and queens of Parliament were from this place, and most of the great warlords who served directly under Arthur himself.

"It was also the source of much of the music and literature of the entire Archipelago," he said, "with libraries second only to those at Paralon. Its loss was profoundly felt."

The shadows that obscured the islands were in fact clouds, thick and black, that had settled down onto the land itself. The clouds not only cut off the land from view, but also the light of the sun. A dead gray light was all that penetrated through the clotted air, leaving a soft, chalky, shadowless light that resembled nothing so much as the mythical land of the dead.

The *White Dragon* approached slowly and cautiously, but no signal heralded their arrival. It was as if no one noticed they were there.

A small harbor was found, where they could moor the ship and get a closer look at the shore. And what they saw was both horrifying and heartbreaking in its enormity.

The island was thickly wooded, with trees similar to those on both Byblos and Paralon. All along the shore were willow trees that had wildly overgrown, as if they'd not been tended to in many years. Among the trees was a throng of people—hooded, gray as death, and all but motionless.

As they looked, they could see thousands upon thousands more silhouetted in the dim light. This was indeed the source of Mordred's army, for these half-living beings looked just like the fallen warriors on Terminus.

"Oh my," Bert said softly. "This may take a very long time."

"No," said Jack. "Maybe not. It's not just the people—the spirit of the land is sick too. Can't you feel it?"

"What do you want to do, Jack?" said John.

"Help me carry the cauldron to the shore," said Jack. "Then I'll do what I've always done, and make it up as I go along."

On a rocky outcropping of the shoreline of Prydain, Jack once again opened Pandora's Box—but instead of placing his hand over the heart of one of Mordred's human victims, he placed one hand inside the box and put the other deep into the loamy soil of the land.

In moments there was a flash from the cauldron. Then a river of shadow and light twined together and ran across Jack's shoulders and into the earth.

As they watched, the light and shadow streaked across the landscape, touching every tree, rock, house, and hovel as it raced along unopposed by anything in its path.

All of the people touched by shadow wavered and fell, then began to stir, and finally rose to their feet, shaking their heads as if waking from a bad dream.

And, in a manner, they were.

"How is this possible?" John said to Bert. "How can he be doing this, all from a talisman that caused so much evil and misery?

"He can do this," said Bert, "because he reached into it more deeply than the Winter King wanted to, or ever would.

"Remember the legend of Pandora's Box? When it was opened for the first time, and all the evils of man escaped out into the world, there was still one thing left inside, which was the redemption of all the rest.

"Hope."

In minutes the entire land had been completely transformed. Every person in sight bore a shadow, now clearly visible as the clouds burned away and let the unaffected sunlight stream through.

Jack turned to his friends, panting from exertion but smiling broadly. "How's that?"

John and Bert cheered, and Charles pumped his fist in the air. "That's the way, Jack! That's how an Oxford man gets things done!"

All the lands that had been shadowed were along the southern edge of the Archipelago. So the *White Dragon* simply traveled in a slow curve along the lands, guided to where they needed to be by the telltale smudge of darkness the shadow created on the horizon.

As Jack transformed each land, the map would reappear in the *Imaginarium Geographica*, as if it had always been there and always would.

"We'll have to let Tummeler know," said Charles. "Or he'll be stuck publishing an abridged edition."

They visited land after land; lands they had never heard of, and others they knew well from story and myth. Hy-Breasil. Lilliput. Charos and Styx. Hel. Asmund. And on and on and on. And finally, at the end of more days than they would have liked, but far, far fewer than they had first expected, they realized that there were no more blank pages in the *Geographica*, and no more dark clouds below the horizon.

They could, at last, go home.

Bert turned the great wheel and pointed the *White Dragon* in the direction of the Frontier.

"Bert," John began, as he, Jack, and Charles approached the little man one evening. "We've been looking through the *Imaginarium Geographica*, and we think there's a land missing."

"Really?" said Bert. "But I thought we'd taken care of all the shadowed lands. How could we have overlooked one?"

"Not one of the vanished maps," said Charles. "A map that's never been in it to begin with."

"Ah, I see," said Bert. "Which land were you thinking we've misplaced?"

"We've only heard about it here and there," said Jack. "But Ordo Maas mentioned it first. He called it the Summer Country."

"Ah," said Bert, smiling. "The Summer Country. One of the greatest of the lands, and spoken about with reverence for many, many years. It's interesting that you should mention it, for the Summer Country was one of the lands that Mordred—the Winter King—wished to find more than anywhere else."

"The way Ordo Maas spoke of it," said Jack, "made it seem as if it might be another place altogether—as if that's where he would go when he died."

"Heaven?" said Bert. "It's entirely possible. It all depends on your point of view."

"How can the existence of a place depend on one's point of view?" asked Charles.

"Very easily," said Bert, "or have you already forgotten the Keep of Time? There were real, physical places behind those doors—but you can argue that they didn't exist until the door was opened. When John opened a door and found the professor, that place existed for him, based on his belief that it was there. As did the door that provided our escape. It was what Charles needed it to be. In a manner of speaking, he believed it into existence. So is it with the Summer Country."

"So the Summer Country is whatever people want it to be?" said Jack.

"It is the way most people speak of it," said Bert, "but you are correct—the legend is based on a place that actually exists.

"The Summer Country is a land greater than any in the Archipelago of Dreams, because it has within it everything to be found in the Archipelago, and more. But where someone like Ordo Maas could find it anywhere, the Winter King would never find it at all. Because to him, it is always just out of his reach—when, in truth, he had it in reach all along."

"It sounds," John said, "as if you're talking about *our* world."

"Yes," said Bert. "Your world *is* the Summer Country."

Chapter Twenty-four

The Return to London

Much of the remaining voyage back was spent reexamining the *Geographica* and making notations on the maps that had reappeared since the defeat of the Winter King and the reawakening of the Shadowed Lands. Until just a few days before, the companions would have given—would have done—anything, for immediate passage home. Now it seemed as if England were in the dream world to which they might travel, if only they believed in it enough. And while they still believed in England, and London, and Oxford, and all the rest in the world of men, they had come to know that there was another world that was just as real. And they were no longer certain they wanted to leave.

"We've got a limited crew this time through," said Charles. "Namely, us. Will the *White Dragon* have any trouble navigating the storm line?"

"It's meant to keep people out, not in," said Bert. "You'll find it's a much easier passage going east than west."

John didn't say what he was thinking—that he was already anticipating having to push through the storms again, going in the opposite direction. That he wanted to return to the Archipelago, and soon.

. . . twinkling in friendly greeting, the lights of London began to appear.

"Here's something I never expected I'd be saying out loud," said Jack, "but does anyone else find it comforting that there are at least three dragons shadowing us from above?"

High in the atmosphere, a greenish dragon and two smaller amber ones were diving and soaring in and among the clouds of the storm line, dipping their wings in greeting as they noticed that the companions were watching.

"The mariners had it wrong," said Charles. "'Here, There Be Dragons' wasn't a caution. It was a reassurance."

"I think that would depend on your relationship with the dragons," said John. "Remember—when we met, Samaranth's other option was to eat us."

As the *White Dragon* passed through the storm line and into more traditional waters, the dragons wheeled away and vanished into the ether.

In the distance, they could just make out the silhouette of Avalon, soft and verdant in the light of dusk.

"What do you say, lads?" asked Bert. "Want to stop off and pay your respects to the Morgaine?"

"Depends on the day, doesn't it?" said Jack. "Tuesday we can manage, but I'd rather not catch Cul in a fouler mood."

"Good call, Jack," said Bert. "Next time, then."

The sunlight faded quickly with the sudden smothering of clouds that marked the crossing of the last boundary. Soon, the familiar English fog had begun to coalesce around the ship, and then, twinkling in friendly greeting, the lights of London began to appear.

"Now I know we're home!" exclaimed Charles. "Look at that water! It's absolutely filthy! God bless the Thames!"

The companions' happy laughter was cut short when the shrillness of an air-raid siren split the night air, shattering the stillness into pieces that fell with John's smile. He looked to each of his friends, and then to Bert.

"We're still at war," John said, crestfallen. "We defeated the Winter King, but our world is still at war."

"Well, of course it is," Bert said, chiding. "The conflict in the Archipelago is not over either, for that matter."

John furrowed his brow. "But we won. Artus is the new High King. We restored order in the Archipelago, and Jack freed the Shadow-Born."

"Did we now?" said Bert. "Yes, we found the heir and reestablished the continuity of rule in the Archipelago. But just because a man sits on a throne doesn't mean automatic fealty."

"He has a point," Charles put in. "There's still the Troll Prince, Arawn, to deal with—and the Four Kingdoms have to come to grips with having a new king on the Silver Throne. Artus has quite a row to hoe."

"Does that mean we're going to remain at war until Artus has things in hand in the Archipelago?" said John.

"You misunderstand," said Bert. "It isn't like pulling a lever—as the conflict in one world is mirrored in the other, so is the peace and harmony we helped to set in motion in the Archipelago going to be reflected in this world. But the events that have occurred here must still take their course. There is the matter of free will to consider. We have removed the catalyst, true—but the world of men must still work to repair the damage that has been done, and then, ultimately, must choose peace."

"I think I understand," said John. "I suppose that somehow I was hoping for a more magical instant solution. Like 'drink me' and 'eat me' in *Alice's Adventures in Wonderland*."

"Now, John," Bert chided. "That's just a story. We should stay focused on the real world, don't you think?"

The journey ended exactly where it began, at the dock in London where they had fled from the pursuing Wendigo. It had only been days, but it already seemed a lifetime ago—and in a sense, it had been.

"I have to let my wife know I'm all right, then I'm back to Staffordshire, I expect," said John. "And then probably back to France, as I'm still enlisted for the duration. I just hope my absence hasn't been long enough for them to notice and declare me missing—I'll never be able to explain where I've been!"

"I'm overdue myself," said Charles, "although I expect that the Oxford dons might be more forgiving than the military."

"I still think I'll be joining up before I start my term at Oxford," said Jack. "After all, the war should be over soon anyway, right?"

"We can hope, young Jack," said Bert. He turned to John. "I'll check in now and again, to see how you're coming along. I must admit, it's a nice thought to realize that I can actually retire, knowing that the *Geographica* will be in good hands. Now I must go—I have to return the *White Dragon* to Ordo Maas, and then attend to the repair of the *Indigo Dragon*, bless her timbers."

He bowed his head, chewing his lower lip, before continuing to speak. "There is one last detail to which we must attend," Bert said, his voice trembling with emotion. "It has been tradition, these many centuries, for the Caretakers to add their names to those who came before. I would be honored if the three of you would do so now."

"The three of us?" said Jack. "But John is the Caretaker."

"The Caretaker Principia," Bert corrected, "but there have always been three. The purpose of the other two Caretakers is to help the Caretaker Principia fulfill his responsibilities—and I daresay that's what the both of you have been doing these long days."

"Not to seem ungrateful," said Charles, "but with Tummeler about to start a publishing empire based on the twin pillars of cookbooks and atlases—namely, the *Geographica*—what is the point of having Caretakers? Why take care of a book that everyone in the Archipelago will now have access to?"

"Remember what John told the Cartographer?" said Bert. "It's about more than safeguarding a mere book—it's a far greater responsibility than that. You are the Caretakers of the lands within it. The Caretakers of the Imagination of the World. And you've proven yourselves more than worthy, and more than able."

Jack and Charles looked at each other, then at John, who tilted his head and smiled. "Why not? Who else can we tell about all these adventures we've had, if not each other?"

"Sounds good to me," said Jack. "I for one intend to write it all down before I forget what happened. Not that there's much chance of that," he added quickly.

"I don't suppose it's coincidence that we're all Oxford men, is it?" Charles joked.

"No, it's not," said Bert. "It isn't a rule that the Caretakers be from Oxford, or even English; but for some reason it seems to better the odds. Both times we had a Cambridge man—John Dee, and then Lord Byron—it was an absolute disaster. I even heard rumors that Dee had something to do with Atlantis sinking, although how that might have occurred I have no clue."

"Sorry I asked," said Charles.

"Where do you want us to sign?" said John. "Do we choose a favorite map, or what?"

"Do you mean to tell me that in all this time, you never took a look at the endpapers inside the cover?" Bert said with astonishment. "Blow me down and call me Shirley."

"It wasn't a map," said John. "Forgive me for being goal-oriented. I was under a lot of stress, you know."

Bert smiled and shook his head in mock dismay as he opened the front cover of the *Geographica* and turned it around for them to read.

"Amazing," said Charles. "If we hadn't just been through what we have, I don't quite think I'd believe this was real."

"Amen," said Jack.

John said nothing, but began tracing his finger underneath the names inscribed on the two pages; names that contained within them much of the cultural and scientific history of the entire human race.

Edmund Spenser. Johannes Kepler. William Shakespeare. Chaucer was there, as were Roger Bacon, Alexandre Dumas, Cervantes, Nathaniel Hawthorne, and Jonathan Swift. Tycho Brahe. Jacob (but not Wilhelm) Grimm. Hans Christian Andersen, and Washington Irving.

Coleridge was there, and both Shelleys: Percy Bysshe and Mary Wollstonecraft. Arthur Conan Doyle, whom they expected, and Harry Houdini, whom they did not. Goethe. Dante. Edgar Allan Poe. And on and on and on.

"Poe?" Jack said in surprise. "And Mark Twain?"

"Jules Verne, as well," said Bert. "He's the one who passed it on to me."

"Extraordinary," said Charles.

"The earliest of the Mapmakers' names are not there, of course," said Bert. "It was almost a thousand years after the Cartographer began to compile it that the first Caretaker took over."

"Who was that?" said John.

"Geoffrey of Monmouth," said Bert.

"These aren't copies," said John, touching the pages with reverence. "These signatures are all originals."

"Here," said Bert. "You can sign underneath our names."

There at the lower part of the right-hand page was the elegant script of Professor Sigurdsson's name, followed by a signature that had been crossed out.

"That's the rebel Caretaker's name, isn't it?" asked Charles.

"Yes," nodded Bert. "Stellan never forgave Jamie for turning his back on us."

"What was his full name?" asked John, peering at the list.

"You may have heard of him," said Bert. "He's just been knighted recently—Sir James Barrie."

John stood up abruptly and looked at Charles and Jack in astonishment. Jack leaned forward and furrowed his brow. "Where's your name, Bert?" he asked. "Shouldn't it be under the other two?"

"Not under," said Bert, "above. I was given it first, remember? I then recruited Stellan, who in turn recruited Jamie."

As one, the three men looked to the name above the professor's—and as one, all three jaws dropped open in surprise.

The signature read "Herbert George Wells."

"I never really liked Herbert," said Bert, "and couldn't see myself as a George either, for that matter."

"It's an honor to . . . ah . . . ," John began, raising his hand for a shake. He looked at his proffered hand, then sheepishly withdrew it. After all they had been through together, Bert was no longer a stranger to them, but family—whatever his true name.

"Hang on a minute," said Charles. "There's a problem with that. You see, I've actually met H. G. Wells, and—no offense, Bert—but he's a lot younger than you are."

"Oh, you've misunderstood me," said Bert. "I'm not that H. G. Wells. I mean, I am him, but not the him from now—I'm the him from then, in the future."

"The future?" said John.

"Eight hundred thousand years," Bert said, checking his watch, "next Thursday."

"That's fantastic," said John. "You *are* the Time Traveler you wrote about in your book."

"Guilty, I'm afraid," said Bert. "Nemo and I built the device based on designs conceived by Leonardo Da Vinci, and my first journey 'out' was when I met Aven's mother, Weena. I wrote down an account of the whole adventure and wished desperately to share it with the world at large—but I realized that it would never be taken seriously as a nonfictional, biographical accounting. So I revised it—considerably, I might add—and published it in the version you all know."

"That's not a bad idea," said Jack. "To disguise the true story as fiction or allegory. I might take a stab at that myself."

"It seems a shame, though," said John, "not to be able to tell anyone what really happened. But then again," he added, "I don't think I could talk about what's gone on in the Archipelago with anyone but you three. No one else would believe it."

"So, Bert, when I met him, uh, you . . . ," Charles began.

"You met a much younger version of me," said Bert, "and I remember the meeting well. That's when I first pegged you as a potential Caretaker."

"You were scouting me?" said Charles.

"Sure," said Bert. "Who do you think it was who recommended you for the editorial position at the Oxford University Press?"

"Were you watching me, too?" said Jack.

"No," said Bert. "You hadn't written enough yet to draw my attention."

"Oh," said Jack, a bit crestfallen.

"Awfully glad you came along, though, Jack," said John. "Couldn't imagine having gotten through it all without you."

"Thanks," said Jack.

"When you came to the club," Charles said, "you didn't act as if you knew me."

"Because I didn't," said Bert. "I knew your work, and that's it, and that's all. There were about a dozen of you whose writing bore the marks of a potential Caretaker—imagination, innovation, conviction, and clarity—and I left it to Stellan to choose who to train further. He chose John."

"But if there were potential Caretakers available to be trained," said Charles, "couldn't we have been recruited sooner, after the other Caretaker left his post, so that the crisis with the Winter King could have been averted?"

"Mordred's plot was already well under way before Jamie came along," said Bert, "or even myself and Stellan, for that matter. Nothing could have been done to prevent the events from proceeding as they did up until the point where he came out in the open. And by then it was too late."

"You don't think James Barrie could have prevented the war if he'd stayed on with the professor?" said John.

Bert shook his head and walked past them, clasping his hands behind his back. "I've wondered that myself," he admitted, "but I doubt it. Jamie just wasn't suited to it, and it all but broke Stellan's heart when he walked away. I do know this," he added. "Whatever the difficulty was in seeing through your obligations, I know that Stellan saw your acceptance as a redemption of sorts."

"A redemption of himself? Or of me?" said John.

"Does it matter?"

"Maybe. Maybe it does."

"Then take this as your answer: When the time came, you did all that the professor and I hoped you would be able to do. And while the struggle was not pleasant to endure, I think it made your victory all the sweeter. And wherever he is now, I think the professor is glad of the faith he placed in you, and I know he's proud of you, John."

"I have a pen," said Charles. "Who's to go first?"

"Go ahead," said John.

Smiling, and with a trembling hand, Charles inscribed his name in long, looping letters:

Charles Williams

He handed the book and pen to Jack. "Thanks," said Jack. "Can you steady the book for me?"

"Certainly."

Jack thought a moment, then signed, and passed the book over to John, who looked quizzically at the signature:

C. S. Lewis

"I always hated the name Clive," said Jack. "My brother Warnie called me Jack, and it stuck."

"Fair enough," said Bert. "And now you, John."

John took the pen in hand and paused to look at his friends, who had become his allies, and confidants, and his family in the short time they had known each other. He considered how they had come together, and the price each of them had paid to do what needed to be done—but even then, it had been a grand adventure, and, he suspected, only the first they would have together. It was, after all, a very big world.

"Here's to remembering the future," said John.

"To the future," said Jack and Charles.

"Well said, my boy," said Bert.

John signed his name with clear, tight strokes:

J. R. R. Tolkien

And closed the book.

Epilogue

High on a bluff on the Island at the Edge of the World, the High King sat, idly chewing on one of the long grasses that had begun to grow again on the fields decimated by the battle.

Nearby was a ring of standing stones that brought him comfort by their very presence, and the newly blessed grave of a dear friend, which, strangely, had the same comforting effect.

He sat, chewing, and looking into the darkness beyond the great waterfall, and wondered.

In just a few short days, the world—two worlds, in fact—had been irrevocably altered, and as High King of the Silver Throne of Paralon, it was now his duty to see that the changes benefitted the peoples of a hundred lands, even those peoples who did not claim him as king, or support his rule. Such was the burden of a kingdom.

He wondered about the woman with whom he'd been traveling, and working beside, and sharing his dreams with, and whether she would stay with him, and help him rule his kingdom, if he asked.

Artus wondered if it had really been his summoning that drew the dragons, or if it had been the intervention and call of Samaranth.

He wondered what might have happened had the dragons not

come at that precise moment he appeared to summon them, or worse, not come at all.

He wondered what might happen if he should ever need to call on them again. In the days since the conflict, dragons soaring high in the skies above were not an uncommon sight—but neither were they seen in the numbers that had appeared at that crucial moment during the battle.

He wondered what was really out in the void; and what lay below. He wondered if, when someone went over the waterfall, if there was eventually an ending to it, or if you would just keep on falling for eternity.

And sometimes . . .

Sometimes, he just wondered.

Author's Note

History is comprised less of certainty than of supposition. Go back far enough, and fact begins to merge with fiction—or at least with traditional tales, which bear a truth all their own.

To me, the most interesting stories are those that have one foot firmly planted in fantasy, and the other in the real world; and the best way to create a marriage of the two is to find those gaps in history where there is no certainty, and create a supposition.

Suppose the worlds of make-believe had a basis in reality. Suppose that we could, in the right circumstances, visit them. And suppose that the proof of their substance was strewn throughout both history and fiction, if only we knew where to look. . . .

At first glance, it seems that Ordo Maas's story is that of Noah; but in fact, the origin is deeper and older. Ordo Maas says he has many names; and later on, Mordred refers to him as "Deucalion." In Greek myth, Deucalion was the son of Prometheus (who gave him the fire at the end of his staff) and was married to Pyrrha—who was Pandora's daughter. When the gods punished mankind by flooding the Earth, they were saved when Prometheus gave them fire, and told them to build an ark. After the flood, they repopulated the Earth. As Deucalion's father gave *him* a gift, so did Pyrrha's mother give *her* one: Pandora's Box. My supposition here was that Pyrrha, not her mother, was the one who opened the box, after the flood.

The Egyptian equivalent of Deucalion was Thoth—whose daughter, Bast, was the goddess of Cats.

Tying the Pandora myth to the Fates (The Three Who Are One) and calling them the Morgaine ties together Greek myth with Welsh and Celtic lore—as does Ordo Maas's claim that the first Dragonship was the rebuilt *Argo,* which the Greek hero Jason used to find the Golden Fleece.

The Green Knight ties the Arthurian myth to contemporary fiction via Dickens's *Tale of Two Cities,* as, of course, does Magwich.

The Cartographer of Lost Places is entirely my own invention—but as with the rest, his origins lie in a supposition, and the clues to his true identity are there for careful enough readers.

And finally, I wanted to start off the adventure in a place that had a mysterious resonance of its own. The address of the club Charles leads John and Jack to—221B Baker Street—is well known to any Sherlock Holmes reader as the detective's home. A perfect place to begin a "dark and stormy night" story.

James A. Owen
Silvertown, USA

Check out a sneak peek
of the next book in
The Chronicles of the
Imaginarium Geographica

THE SEARCH FOR THE RED DRAGON

The small cottage where Jack was staying was near a cozy little village at the edge of Oxford city. They parked the car on a patch of gravel just off the road, and after checking on the *Geographica,* went to the front door and knocked.

The door was opened immediately by a thickset, tanned fellow in military dress, who bore more than a passing resemblance to the young man they both remembered. John and Charles both hesitated, before remembering that it was Jack's brother who had summoned them there in the first place.

John immediately stiffened into the formal posture he affected when addressing a fellow officer. "You are a captain, I believe?" he asked before the other waved off the question.

"Please, we're all informal here," the man said, shaking John's proffered hand. "I'm heading swiftly for retirement in a few more years and plan to soon be devoting my time to assembling the family papers and as much reading as I can manage."

"I'm John, and this is Charles. We came as quickly as we could."

"A pleasure," said Charles, stepping forward to shake the man's hand. "You're Warren?"

"Call me Warnie—Jack does. I'm very grateful to both of you for coming. Although I must admit, it is a bit odd that he should ask for you."

"Why is that?" said Charles.

"As I understand it," Warnie explained, "you've not actually become officially acquainted since he began teaching at Magdalen. In fact, before yesterday, Jack never so much as mentioned either of you at all."

It was a testament to the swiftness of their self-control that neither John nor Charles exchanged a glance at this.

"It's just that Jack is an intensely private person," Warnie continued, "and while he's an excellent tutor, and is very affable with our circle of friends, it's unlike him to be so open about personal matters with, er, ah, strangers, so to speak. And especially so to invite them here to his private study. No offense."

"None taken," said Charles, trying to keep the mood light. "If I'd come here for a bit of solitude, I wouldn't want to be disturbed either. This is a lovely accommodation. It's called the Kilns, isn't it?"

"Yes, it is," said Warnie, nodding, "after the brick buildings down the way.

"We've taken it for a few months so that Jack could get some work done," he went on. "It's a very pleasant place, actually, and very convenient to Oxford, as you've seen. The gardens are quite large—almost a park—and extremely overgrown. But I wouldn't mind settling here for good, if we had the coin to afford the price."

He regarded Charles appraisingly. "You called it the Kilns—you know Headington Quarry, then?"

"I've had my opportunities for walking expeditions from the city," replied Charles. "Not so much now that I'm based in London, but I do like returning here to Oxford now and again."

"I haven't been out this direction yet," John said, "but now that I've been given the new position at the university, I expect I'll have plenty of opportunities."

"New professor of Anglo-Saxon, Jack said?" asked Warnie.

John nodded. "Yes. The professors and college tutors don't have too many occasions to socialize, but I imagine we'll be coming together sooner or later."

"How is it that you know Jack, if you don't mind my asking?"

"We, ah, we met during the war," said John. "The three of us, that is. It was a very unusual circumstance...."

Warnie made a dismissive gesture but smiled knowingly. "Say no more. It's all clear to me now. The war created brothers in an instant, and made allies of enemies and vice versa. I was wary that he's asked me to summon colleagues he's never mentioned to me—but if you served together in the war... I didn't mean to pry, but brothers should look out for one another, you understand?"

"We do," said Charles. "That's why we didn't hesitate to answer your summons."

Warnie smiled again. "Good show, good show. Let me take you back to Jack's study—he's waiting for you there."

"You said it was personal matters he wanted to discuss," John said. "But it wasn't clear in the telegram you sent what exactly Jack wanted to see us about."

"He's stopped writing in his journal—stopped writing altogether, now I think on it," said Warnie. "Then he stopped reading. That's when I really began to worry."

"Why?" asked John.

"He lost a very close friend in the war. And although he was nowhere near at the time, Jack feels he is somehow responsible for the fellow's death."

Charles and John each drew a sharp breath. That had to be a factor in why Jack had asked for them. In the battle with the Winter King, he had been responsible for the death of an ally, and it had affected him greatly. But Jack seemed to have reconciled himself to it well before their return to London—or so they had assumed. Apparently they were mistaken.

"How is he sleeping?" John asked.

"He isn't. Night terrors, I'm afraid," Warnie said somberly. "They've been going on for several days now, and there's been little I could do to help. The worst was two nights ago. Lots of screaming and thrashing about, and calling out a word over and over—'Aven.' I have no idea what it means, and Jack wouldn't speak of it. It was that next morning he told me to seek out the two of you and ask you to come here."

He paused at a sturdy door and hesitated before knocking. "I'll leave the three of you to catch up. I'll be puttering about in the garden if you need anything."

As Warnie moved back down the hall, John and Charles opened the door and entered the book-crammed study. Jack—taller, broader, more manlike than the boy they'd known—stood at the window with his back to the door.

"Jack?" Charles ventured. "Jack, we've come. It's Charles and John."

Jack tilted his head slightly, acknowledging their presence, but he did not turn around. Instead he asked a question.

"Was it real? Did it all really happen, after all?"

It took a moment for them to realize what he was asking.

"Yes," said John. "If you're asking what I think you are."

"So...the Archipelago of Dreams...the *Imaginarium Geographica*...."

"Yes," John repeated. "It's all real."

Jack turned to look at them, his face inscrutable. "Do you have the atlas with you? Can—can I see it?"

"It's, ah, it's in the backseat of the car," John admitted sheepishly.

"In a lockbox, or a leather bag, I'd assume?"

"No," said Charles. "It's protected by a thick layer of lectures on Ancient Icelandic."

Jack blinked and then snorted. "And they call you the Caretaker Principia. Did you at least mix in a few papers on old Anglo-Saxon? Or are you giving your professorship short shrift too?"

John and Charles stared at their friend for a moment before the somber expressions on their faces were broken by broad, transcendent smiles.

"Of course it happened, my good fellow," said Charles, clasping Jack by the shoulders. "Our adventure in the Archipelago of Dreams has become the stuff of legend. And you are one of the heroes."

Jack embraced each of his friends, then stepped back to look at them. "Charles," he said with a hint of teasing, "you've gotten *old*."

"Editors don't grow *old*," Charles retorted. "They just become more *distinguished*."

"And you," he said to John, "how are you finding teaching at your old stomping grounds?"

"I like it as much as I expected," said John. "Although I think I'd prefer to be left alone to write if I have another crop of students like the current bunch. Hardly an inquisitive or creative mind among them."

"It could be worse," said Charles. "You could be teaching at Cambridge."

At the mention of their old joke, the three friends doubled over in laughter. But soon enough a more serious mood settled upon them again, and the haunted look

Jack had worn when they entered returned to his face.

"Why have you called us, Jack?" John asked. "What's happened?"

"It's hard to say," Jack replied. "I came up here with Warnie to work on some of my poems—and perhaps a book or three—but several weeks ago I began to have nightmares, and in the last few days, they've gotten worse."

"Warnie said you called out Aven's name," said Charles.

"Yes," admitted Jack, wincing visibly. "I've tried not to think much about her since our return to England—but I've been dreaming about her. I—I think she's in terrible trouble of some kind. But I can't say what."

"Hmm," John mused. "What else has been in these dreams?"

"Well, dreamstuff, naturally," said Jack. "Things that come bubbling up from one's subconscious. Indians, and crows, and strangely...children."

"Do tell," John said, considering his own recent dreams. "If there were children, I'm assuming there were also...."

"...Giants," finished Charles. "If there were children, then there were also Giants. I've been having the same dream."

"As have I," said John. *About the Giants, but not about Aven,* he said silently to himself.

Before any of them could elaborate further, they were interrupted by a knock at the study door.

"I'm dreadfully sorry to interrupt," said Warnie, "but it seems we've, ah..." He paused and bit his lip, as a curious and puzzled expression came over his face.

"Warn?" said Jack. "What is it? What's happened?"

"Oh, nothing bad—I think," Warnie replied. "But it appears we have an angel in the garden."

There was indeed, as Warnie had surmised, an angel in the cottage's garden; or at least, something that was as close to a description of an angel as one might give if one was unaccustomed to finding such things in one's garden.

Sitting in a disarray of just-blooming bluebells, mud, and free-floating feathers was a small girl. A small girl with *wings*.

Her face was smudged with dirt, and her clothing, a simple brown tunic, belted at the waist and across the shoulders, was tattered and torn. Her wings were spread out behind her in a manner that was more awkward than graceful, and they were bare in patches where the feathers had detached themselves in an apparently difficult landing.

"More of a cherub, really, don't you think, John?" said Charles.

"And you would know this how?" asked John. "When have you ever seen a cherub?"

"Look," said Charles, "when he said 'angel,' I was expecting something a little more grown-up. This cherub can't be more than five years old."

"I'm eight, I'll have you know," the girl piped up. "Next Thursday, anyway. And I'm not a cherub or an angel, whatever those are. I'm Laura Glue, and Laura Glue is me."

"Your name is Glue?" asked Charles.

"Laura Glue," the girl protested. "There is a difference, you know."

She stood up and dusted off her clothes, all the while keeping a wary eye on her accidental hosts.

"How did you get here?" Warnie asked, looking around. "Are you with your parents, or on a school outing, perhaps? This is a private garden, not a picnic spot."

Laura Glue looked at him like he was speaking Swahili. "I flew here, I'll have you know. What d'you think the wings are for, anyways?"

Jack began examining Laura Glue's wings, and quickly discovered they were not naturally hers, but were in fact artificial. Delicately made, of extraordinarily inventive design, but constructs nevertheless.

"Hey!" Laura Glue cried, stepping back defensively. "You should ask permission b'fore poking someone's wings, y'know."

"My apologies," said Jack with a deferential bow.

"'S okay," Laura Glue said. "Longbeards *never* ask."

"I would not have been able to tell," said Charles. "From a distance they looked like they were quite real."

"Uncle Daedalus makes 'em for all the Lost Boys," the

girl said proudly, "but ol' Laura Glue's the only one what can fly with 'em. This far, anyways."

"Uncle Daedalus?" John exclaimed. "You don't mean to tell me these wings were made by the Greek Daedalus of myth? The one who lost his son Icarus when the boy flew too close to the sun?"

"What, are you daft?" said Laura Glue. "He'd have to be a thousand years old."

"Exactly," Charles agreed.

"You're thinkin' of Daedalus the Elder," explained Laura Glue. "The one what built my wings is Daedalus the Younger."

"A descendant?" John asked, teasing. "Or Icarus's brother, perhaps?"

"Pr'cisely," said Laura Glue. "An' the reason he don't use wax anymore when he makes the wings."

"All right," stated John. "So where were you flying to? Or do you mean to tell us that you planned to crash in Jack's garden?"

"Planned to crash, no," said the girl, "but this is where I'm supposed to be. I'm looking for the Caretaker. I got an important message from th' Archipelago."

John, Jack, and Charles exchanged terse looks with one another at the mention of the title. It could apply to any or all of them, but it most likely meant John. Warnie, of course, had no idea what she meant.

"I told you," he repeated, "this is a private garden. There is no caretaker."

"I'm not looking for a *gardener,*" the girl retorted. "I'm looking for the Caretaker of the *Imaginarium Geographica.*"

She rummaged around in her tunic and drew out a delicate flower that seemed to be made of parchment, on which three symbols had been carefully rendered. The flower also seemed to be glowing faintly.

John recognized the first symbol as the seal of the Cartographer of Lost Places—the man who had created the *Imaginarium Geographica.* The second was the seal of the High King of the Archipelago. "What's this third mark?" he asked.

"That's what makes it work," replied Laura Glue. "This is a Compass Rose. The seal of the king gets it through the frontier, the seal of the Cartographer tells it where everything is, and the third mark is what lets you find what you're looking for. In this case, the Caretaker. The closer I gets, the more it glows. And when I flew over your cottage, it went so bright it blinded me, and I crashed in your bluebells.

"So," she continued, marching around them with a determined look on her face, "where are you hiding him, anyway?"

"Look here, Jack," Warnie began.

"Perhaps you should go in and put a pot on to boil," Jack suggested. "She's obviously a troubled young girl, but I think we can sort it out."

Warnie nodded and headed for the cottage at a trot without looking back.

John knelt before the girl and noticed that the Rose was still glowing but got no brighter because of his proximity.

"I'm the Caretaker Principia, Laura Glue," he said gently. "Now can you tell us what this is all about?"

Her reaction wasn't what John expected. The girl's eyes grew wide with surprise, then narrowed in suspicion.

"You're not the Caretaker!" she exclaimed. "Where is he and what have you done with him? Tell me now, or I shall be very, very cross."

"But your Compass Rose is glowing," said John. "And I have the *Geographica* nearby. I *am* the Caretaker. Why would you think I'm not?"

"Because," answered Laura Glue, who had taken a defensive, defiant stance, "he called you John, and I know the *real* Caretaker's name is Jamie."

"Jamie?" Charles exclaimed, turning to the others. "It's no wonder she doesn't know any of us. She's looking for the *last* Caretaker—the one John replaced.

"She's looking for Sir James Barrie."